# 8 BLACK HORSES

## AN 87TH PRECINCT NOVEL

# ED McBAIN

AVON BOOKS  NEW YORK

AVON BOOKS
A division of
The Hearst Corporation
105 Madison Avenue
New York, New York 10016

Copyright © 1985 by HUI Corporation
Published by arrangement with Arbor House Publishing Company
Library of Congress Catalog Card Number: 85-7348
ISBN: 0-380-70029-8

First Avon Books Printing: June 1986

AVON TRADEMARK REG. U.S. PAT. OFF. AND IN OTHER COUNTRIES, MARCA
REGISTRADA, HECHO EN U.S.A.

Printed in the U.S.A.

K-R   10   9   8   7   6   5

# ED McBAIN

# 8 BLACK HORSES

"Nobody writes better detective fiction than Ed McBain. Nobody."
*West Coast Review Of Books*

"The writing is, as always, utterly convincing... McBain is *sui generis*, without fictional fore-bears... Combines mystery with suspense, shifting from procedural inquiry to pure tension."
*Boston Globe*

"Ingenious... The author keeps the tension at white heat from the first word to the shattering conclusion"
*Publishers Weekly*

"Suspenseful... McBain's people have enough substance to make you genuinely care when the author places them in jeopardy."
*Cosmopolitan*

"McBain has a great approach, great attitude, terrific style, strong plots, excellent dialogue, sense of place and sense of reality."
Elmore Leonard

"It's hard to think of anyone better at what he does. In fact, it's impossible."
Robert B. Parker

*This is for*
**VANESSA HOLT**

The city in these pages is imaginary.
The people, the places are all fictitious.
Only the police routine is based on established
investigatory technique.

# EIGHT
# BLACK
# HORSES

# 1

THE LADY WAS EXTRAORDINARILY NAKED.

That is to say, she *looked* extraordinarily naked because she was so very white. There are, after all, no degrees of nakedness. You are either clothed or you are unclothed. The lady was very definitely unclothed, but all the detectives gathered around her agreed that she looked more naked than any naked person they had ever seen in their collective lives.

"It's because she's so white," Monoghan said.

"Looks like an albino," Monroe said.

Monoghan and Monroe were Homicide detectives. They had been called in the moment it was ascertained that the lady lying on the withering leaves off the park path was indeed dead. It did not require much detection to determine that she was dead. The foot patrolman had known she was dead the moment he saw the bullet hole at the base of her skull. When he'd got on the walkie-talkie to the desk sergeant at the Eight-Seven, he had, in fact, said, "Sarge, I got a female stiff here in the park." Carella and Brown knew the lady was dead, too. That was why they'd called back to the station house to ask Sergeant Murchison to inform Homicide.

None of the men were wearing overcoats.

After the recent rain the October weather had turned mild enough to permit shorts and sandals, which many of the curious onlookers behind the Crime Scene signs and barricades were, in fact, wearing. In contrast, Monoghan and Monroe were both wearing black suits, white shirts, blue ties, and gray fedoras. They looked like

1

chunky undertakers waiting outside a funeral home to greet mourners.

Arthur Brown was wearing a tan tropical-weight suit. Steve Carella was wearing blue slacks and a darker blue sports shirt rolled up at the cuffs. They could have been two ordinary citizens, a pair of married men—which they were—who had strolled into the park on a lovely Tuesday morning to get away from the wife and kids and discuss football scores.

The gathering crowd knew Brown was a cop, though, because he looked mean. Scowling, he stared down at the body on the leaves. The temperature when he'd awakened this morning was sixty-eight degrees Fahrenheit—or twenty degrees Celsius, as the damn forecasters insisted on translating—and so he'd put on the lightweight tan suit. The suit made him look very brown, which in fact he was. He did not like to think of himself as a black man, which—in today's nomenclature—he also was. He did not know any black men who were really black. Black was an *absence* of color, wasn't it? He had always thought of himself as "colored," in fact, until it became almost mandatory for a black man to start thinking of himself as black. If you didn't think of yourself as black, you were betraying the race. Black power. Bullshit. What Brown had was *brown* power, all six feet four inches and two hundred and twenty pounds of him. The crowd figured he was a cop because anybody so mean-looking, if he was standing with a bunch of cops and he wasn't wearing handcuffs, had to be a cop himself. Also there was a little plastic ID card clipped to the pocket of his suit.

The crowd, what with the World Series still fresh in their minds, thought Carella looked like a baseball player. They deduced this because of his athletic stance and his long slender body. They also thought he looked a little Chinese; that was because his brown eyes slanted slightly downward—or was that Japanese? They doubted there were very many Caucasian Chinese baseball players in America, though, so they figured he had to be a cop, too.

A clue to this was the plastic ID card pinned to his shirt pocket, just like the one the mean-looking black guy was wearing. Both men were wearing holstered pistols on their hips, another clue to their identity, though in this city—like in the olden days of the Wild West—you sometimes got cheap street thieves running around with guns right in the open.

Carella and Brown liked being partnered together.

They felt it was effective against the bad guys.

The bad guys took one look at Carella, and they figured *this* one is the pushover, it's the bad-ass nigger you gotta watch out for. Whenever they were partnered together, Carella and Brown played Mutt and Jeff to the hilt. Carella played Mr. Clean—"Golly, Artie, it don't look to me like this nice young man here even knows what marijuana *is!*" Brown played Big Bad Leroy, born in a ghetto garbage can, shooting dope since he was six years old, done time at Castleview upstate, seen the light afterward and became a cop by way of penance for his formerly evil life. Mean, though, still as mean as a hooker's snatch. "You lyin' little punk, I'm gonna kill you right here on the spot, save the state a 'lectric bill. Get your hands off me, Steve, I'm gonna throw this man off the roof!" Mean, oh man, *real* bad-ass. Big Bad Leroy. It worked nicely.

The sky overhead was as blue as a newborn baby's eyes.

The leaves in the trees lining the path were yellow and brown and red and orange.

The leaves under the dead lady were yellow and red. The red was caused by the wound at the base of her skull.

"This city," Monroe said, "you can carry a dead person in a park, she's got a bullet hole in her head and she's starkers, nobody bats an eyelash."

Carella was looking down at the lifeless white body on the blood-stained leaves. They always look all angles, he thought. The thought was short-lived, accompanied by a brief flicker of pain in his eyes. In solitude, on too many occasions, he had sat and wondered why the geometry of death left only angles.

"Let's roll her over," Monoghan said. "See she's wearing some ID pinned to her chest."

He knew they could not roll her over until the medical examiner got there. He just enjoyed hassling the detectives from the Eight-Seven. That was one of life's little joys. The bulls on this squad up here, they took things too serious. In Monoghan's universe a stiff was a stiff, period. Dressed, naked, stabbed, shot, strangled, incinerated, poleaxed, whatever, it was still only a corpse, and a corpse meant paperwork. In this city, though, the appearance of Homicide cops at the scene of a crime was mandatory. The case officially belonged to the detectives who caught the squeal, but the Homicide Division—like a nagging backseat driver—constantly watched over their shoulders, demanding progress reports at every turn in the road.

"What do you say?" Monoghan asked, not sure Carella had heard him. "We roll her over, see what she looks like from the front."

Carella didn't bother answering him. His eyes were scanning the leaves for any sign of a bullet or a spent cartridge case.

"How old you think she is?" Monroe asked. "Judging from her ass."

"That's a twenty-seven-year-old ass," Monoghan said.

"She's got a beauty mark on her right cheek," Monroe said.

"Good firm ass, she's got there," Monoghan said.

"I had a case once," Monroe said, "this guy died from a broken bottle shoved up his ass."

"Yeah, I remember that one," Monoghan said.

"Hemorrhaged to death," Monroe said.

"His boyfriend done it, right?"

"Yeah, his boyfriend."

Both men looked at the woman's buttocks.

"Twenty-seven years old, I'll give you two to one," Monoghan said.

"The legs look twenty-seven, too," Monroe said.

Brown looked up at the sky.

Not a cloud in it.

He took in a deep breath of fresh air.

"Morning gentlemen," a voice said, and they turned to look up the path where a man in his late fifties, wearing dark blue slacks, a seersucker jacket, a pink shirt, and a blue polka dot tie, was approaching. He was carrying a black satchel in his right hand. "Beautiful day, isn't it?" he said. "This the body?"

"No, the body's up in the trees there," Monroe said.

"It's an Indian body," Monoghan said. "They put them up in the trees."

The assistant medical examiner looked up into the treetops. Leaves fell everywhere around them, twisting on the air.

"We've had three naked bodies this week," the M.E. said to no one and then knelt over the dead woman.

"Where'd you hear that?" Monroe asked Monoghan.

"Where'd I hear what?"

"That Indians put dead bodies up in the trees."

"It's a fact," Monoghan said.

"Does Muhammad Ghandi know that?"

"I'm talkin' about *American* Indians," Monoghan said. "Somebody dies, they put the body up in the trees."

"What for?"

"Who the hell knows?"

The M.E. had rolled the body over. He was holding a stethoscope to the dead woman's chest.

"Whattya think, Doc?" Monroe asked. "She dead enough for you?"

"Quiet, please," the M.E. said.

"He thinks he's gonna get a heartbeat," Monoghan said.

The men fell silent. There was only the sound of the flutter of leaves on the sunlit air. The dead woman's eyes were opened wide. They were as blue as the sky above.

Her hair was as golden as the leaves beneath her. She appeared to be in her mid-thirties, a not unattractive woman except for the gaping exit wound in the hollow of her throat. Carella wondered if she'd ever been out in the sun, she was so white.

"She's dead, all right," the M.E. said, rising and putting his stethoscope back into his satchel. "You can put it down as a gunshot wound."

"While you're here," Monroe said, "I been having trouble with my throat. You wanna take a look at it?"

The next letter—well, it wasn't really a letter.

The next message—it wasn't *that*, either, not unless it *meant* something.

The next piece of folded paper with, well, *pictures* on it was waiting for them when they got back to the station house. It had arrived, Sergeant Murchison told them, in a plain white envelope with no return address on it. The postmark over the stamp indicated that the letter had been mailed here in the city on the twenty-fourth, yesterday. That spoke well for the Post Office Department; in this city it sometimes took four days for a letter to travel three blocks crosstown.

They did not know if this one was also from the Deaf Man.

That's because there was no ear on it.

They'd been fairly certain that the first letter—message, piece of folded paper, what*ever* the hell—had come from the Deaf Man. That was because they were all expert sleuths, and when their eyes fell upon a deaf ear, they recognized it at once.

The first—communication, they guessed it was—had arrived on Saturday, October 22. It had been addressed to Detective Stephen Louis Carella at the 87th Precinct, and it looked like this:

Well, everybody on the squad knew that those things prancing across the top of the page were horses. They also knew that there were eight of them, and they were black, and if you put all of that together, you got eight black horses. Which meant nothing, of course. Which, of course, if the Deaf Man had sent this thing to them, meant *something*. Because the Deaf Man often sent communications that looked as if they meant nothing until you figured them out and then they meant something. One thing they had learned about the Deaf Man over the years was that he always played the game fair. They didn't know *why* he played the game fair, but then again they rarely understood the workings of the criminal mind, especially the *master* criminal mind. In *their* minds the Deaf Man was a master criminal. That was why he played the game fair and sent communications that looked as if they meant nothing when actually they meant something.

They figured it was the Deaf Man because of the ear with the bar across it.

Most people do not have bars across their ears.

In international sign language, if you saw a cigarette with a bar across it, it meant NO SMOKING. If you saw the capital letter P with a bar across it, it meant NO PARKING. An ear with a bar across it could have meant NO EAR, but they suspected instead that it meant NO HEARING, which further meant DEAF, and since the ear wasn't a delicately shaped shell-like thing but instead a very masculine-looking ear (unless it was the ear of a female wrestler), they concluded that the picture of the ear with the bar across it meant DEAF MAN.

This conclusion was unsettling.

They did not want to believe that the Deaf Man was back in their midst.

They had posted the Deaf Man's message on the bulletin board and hoped it would go away. But this was Tuesday morning, October 25, and it had not gone away. Instead, there was a second envelope addressed personally to Carella. When he opened it, there was another single white sheet of folded paper in it. He unfolded the paper. He looked at it. This time there was no ear with a bar across it. Instead, there was—or were, as the case actually was:

Meyer Meyer was looking over Carella's shoulder.

He was wearing lightweight slacks and a short-sleeved polo shirt with a crocodile over where the pocket would have been if there'd been a pocket on the shirt. Most polo shirts did not have pockets these days. Meyer didn't mind that, now that he'd given up smoking. The shirt was a shade darker than his blue eyes. The trousers were a sort of cream-colored polyester, as pale as his bald pate. His wife, Sarah, had told him this morning that he looked tacky wearing summer clothes to work when it was already the end of October. He'd commented, wittily he thought, that maybe in his head it was October, but in the *rest* of him it was still June. Sarah suspected he was making a sexual remark.

"Is it him again?" he asked.

"I don't know," Carella said.

"So what are those supposed to be, anyway?" Meyer said.

"Radios, I guess," Carella said.

"Walkie-talkies, looks more like," Brown said.

"Five walkie-talkies," Carella said.

"No ear, though."

"No ear."

"Maybe it isn't him," Carella said.

"From your lips to God's ear," Meyer said.

"Five walkie-talkies," Brown said, and shook his head.

"He's giving us arithmetic lessons," Meyer said. "Eight, five . . ."

"He's jerkin' us off," Brown said. "Eight black horses, five walkie-talkies, those things don't have anything at all to do with each other."

The trouble with naked dead bodies is that they are not wearing clothes.

Clothing is an aid to identification.

Clothing is also helpful in determining who the perpetrator or perpetrators may have been. Hair clings to clothing. Stains cling to clothing. Bread crumbs, iron filings, sawdust, face powder, flea powder, gunpowder, all *sorts*

of juicy informational tidbits cling to clothing, making a
laboratory technician's life a bit easier. Nothing much
clings to a dead body. Unless it was raped, in which case
there are often wild pubic hairs tangled in the victim's
crotch or traces of semen to be found in the vagina.

According to the preliminary report of the medical
examiner's office, the lady in the park had not been raped—
either before her death or *after* it, a not uncommon occur-
rence in this civilized city.

She had been shot in the back of the head, gangland
style.

A single bullet had done the job, but there were no spent
cartridge cases or bullets at the scene. An automatic weapon
ejects cartridge cases when it is fired. A revolver retains
the spent cartridge cases in its cylinder. But *whatever* type
of pistol had been used, if the lady had been shot and killed
in Grover Park, there would have been a spent bullet somewhere in the vicinity. The exit wound in her throat told
them that. They could find no bullet. Which indicated to
them that the lady had been shot elsewhere and only later
transported to the park.

It is a myth that the Identification Section of any cosmopolitan police department can immediately identify anyone merely by checking his or her fingerprints against what
is known as the base file. The base file in this city was
divided into two sections, the largest of which—occupying
an entire floor of the Headquarters Building downtown on
High Street—was itself subdivided into two sections, one
devoted exclusively to maintaining an up-to-date fingerprint record of anyone charged with or convicted of a felony or a misdemeanor, the other composed of latent
fingerprints taken at the scene of a crime. The overall section was called the Criminal Section of the Identification
Section, or the CSIS, bastardized in police jargon to just
plain "Sissies." The Sissies file devoted to known criminals was called the A-file, and the file holding latents was
called the B-file.

A check of the A-file revealed no criminal record for the lady found dead in the park.

A check of the B-file came up negative against any latent prints on record.

This meant only that she had never committed a crime for which she'd been caught, and had never left her fingerprints at the scene of a crime.

The second file in the I.S. maintained fingerprint records of anyone involved in the city's vast law enforcement organization, anyone working as a security officer in a municipal jail or prison and anyone who had been granted a carry or premises permit for a pistol.

That was it.

On the municipal level.

But the United States is a big, big country, and it is also a *free* country, which means that *anyone*—even if he is intent on doing criminal mischief—can travel from city to city and state to state without an identity card or a by-your-leave from the local commissar. This is one of the nice things about living in a democracy. It is also a headache for law enforcement officers. The city for which Carella worked was the largest city in the state, but the fingerprint files in its police department's Identification Section were minuscule compared to those in the state depository, some hundred and fifty miles to the north. When Isola's I.S. section came up blank on Jane Doe, a search-and-return request was automatically sent upstate. The prints taken from the corpse were checked against the *state's* base file, and the results were identical: no record.

The buck could have stopped there, but it didn't.

A check with the FBI's *national* files came back with a negative response: no criminal record for Jane Doe. Neither had she ever been fingerprinted for service in the armed forces or for any job considered security-sensitive by the Nuclear Regulatory Commission.

Carella knew that the I.S. routinely ran courtesy checks for any institution whose employees handled large sums of money. Had any *bank* in the city sent Jane Doe's fingerprints to the I.S. for a verification check against Sissies? The I.S. replied that such courtesy checks were made on a search-and-return basis, as opposed to a search-and-*retain* basis. In other words, after either a full or limited search-and-return was made, the I.S. automatically sent the fingerprints back to the financial institution or other commercial entity making the request. They did *not* retain the fingerprints in their files. Even if someone in Jane Doe's immediate or distant past had requested a search against the Sissies file, there would be no record of it.

Period.

End of story.

All of this took the better part of a week.

By that time, though, the police department had circulated to the Missing Persons Section and to every precinct in the city a photograph and description of Jane Doe, together with a copy of the Detective Division report Carella himself had typed up on the morning the body was discovered.

On Wednesday morning, November 2, Carella got a call from a Detective Lipman at Missing Persons.

Lipman told him he had a positive ID on the dead woman.

# 2

THE WOMAN WHO HAD IDENTIFIED JANE DOE was staying at a once-elegant midtown hotel that now emanated an air of shabby dignity, like an exiled dowager empress praying for return to the throne. Huge marble columns dominated the lobby, where sagging sofas rested on frayed Persian rugs. The ornately carved and gilded mahogany registration desk was cigarette-scarred. Even the clerk who told them what room Miss Turner was in looked faded, his gray hair a shade lighter than his gray suit, his black tie as funereal as his dark somber eyes. The elaborate brass fretwork on the elevator doors reminded Carella of something he had seen in a spy movie.

Inge Turner was a slender blonde in her late thirties, they guessed, her complexion as fair as her sister's had been, her eyes the same shade of blue. She was wearing a simple blue suit over a white blouse with a stock tie. Medium-heeled blue pumps on good legs. A gold pin in the shape of a bird pinned to the lapel of the suit jacket. Blue eyeliner. Lipstick that was more pink than red.

"Gentlemen," she said. "Please come in."

The room was small, dominated by a king-size bed. Inge sat on the edge of the bed, crossing her legs. The detectives sat in upholstered chairs near musty drapes hanging over a window that was open to the sounds of traffic on the avenue six stories below. Already the second of November, and Indian summer was still with them. It would come with a vengeance, winter. It would come suddenly and unexpectedly, hurling false expectations back into their teeth.

13

"Miss Turner," Carella said, "Detective Lipman at Missing Persons tells us . . ."

"Yes," she said.

". . . that you've identified a photograph in his files as . . ."

"Yes," she said again.

". . . your sister, Elizabeth Turner."

"That's correct."

"Miss Turner, I wonder if you could look at that picture again . . . I have a print here . . ."

"Must I?" she said.

"I know it's difficult," Carella said, "but we want to make sure . . ."

"Yes, let me see it," she said.

Carella took the photograph from the manila file envelope. As photographs of corpses went, it was not too grisly—except for the exit wound in the hollow of the throat. Inge looked at it briefly, said, "Yes, that's my sister," and then reached for her handbag, took a cigarette from it, said, "Do you mind if I smoke?" and lighted it without waiting for an answer.

"And her full name is Elizabeth Turner?" Carella said.

"Yes. Well, Elizabeth *Anne* Turner."

"Can you tell us how old she was?" Brown asked.

"Twenty-seven," Inge said.

Both detectives thought, at precisely the same moment, that for once in his lifetime Monoghan had been right.

"And her address?"

"Here or in California?" Inge said.

"I'm sorry, what . . . ?"

"She used to live with me in California."

"But she'd been living *here,* hadn't . . . ?"

"Yes. For the past three years now."

"What was her address *here,* Miss Turner?"

"Eight-oh-four South Ambrose."

"Any apartment number?"

"Forty-seven."

"Do you still live in California?"

"Yes."

"You're just visiting here, is that it?"

"Yes. Well, I came specifically to see my sister. We—do I have to go into this?" She looked at the detectives, sighed, and said, "I suppose we do." She uncrossed her legs, leaned over to an ashtray on the night table beside the bed, and stubbed out her cigarette. "We had a falling-out," she said. "Lizzie moved east. I hadn't seen her in three years. I felt it was time to . . . she was my sister. I loved her. I wanted to . . . set things straight again, on the right course again."

"You came here seeking a reconciliation?" Brown asked.

"Yes. Exactly."

"From where in California?" Carella asked.

"Los Angeles."

"And when did you arrive?"

"Last Thursday."

"That would have been . . ."

"The twenty-seventh. I was hoping . . . we hadn't seen each other for such a long time . . . I was hoping I could convince her to come home for Christmas."

"So you came here to . . ."

"To talk to her. To convince her that bygones should be bygones. I think I had in mind . . . I guess I thought if I could get her to come home for Christmas, then maybe she'd stay. In California, I mean. We'd . . . you know . . . pick up where we left off. We were sisters. A silly argument shouldn't . . ."

"What did you argue about?" Brown asked. "If you'd like to tell us," he added quickly.

"Well . . ."

The detectives waited.

"I guess she didn't approve of my life-style."

Still they waited.

"We led very different kinds of lives, you see. Lizzie worked at a bank, I was . . ."

"A bank?" Carella said at once.

"Yes. She was a cashier at Suncoast Federal. Not a *teller*, you understand, but a *cashier*. There's a big difference."

"And what sort of work do you do?" Brown asked.

"I'm a model," she said.

She must have caught the glance that passed between the detectives.

"A *real* model," she said at once. "There are plenty of the *other* kind out there."

"What sort of modeling do you do?" Carella asked.

"Lingerie," she said. "Mostly stockings and panty hose." She reached into her bag, took out another cigarette, lighted it, and said, "I have good legs," and crossed them again.

"And you say your sister disapproved of this?"

"Well, not the modeling as such . . . though I don't suppose she was too happy about my being photographed in my underwear."

"Then what *was* it about your life-style . . . ?"

"I'm a lesbian," Inge said.

Carella nodded.

"Does that shock you?"

"No," he said.

"You're supposed to say something like, 'What a waste,' " Inge said, and smiled.

"Am I?" Carella said, and returned the smile.

"That's what most men say."

"Well," Carella said, "actually we're only interested in finding whoever killed your sister. You don't believe your life-style—quote, unquote—had anything to do with her murder, do you?"

"Hardly."

"But you did argue about it."

"Yes."

"In what way?"

"She disapproved of the friends I invited to the house."

"So she came all the way east . . ."

"Not immediately. She moved into an apartment on La Cienega, a temporary arrangement until she could find work here."

"*Did* she find work here?" Brown asked.

"Yes," Inge said.

"Where?"

"A bank someplace."

"Here in the city?"

"Yes."

"Which bank?"

"I have no idea. This was all hearsay. A friend of mine used to live here in the city, and occasionally she'd run into my sister . . ."

"Does that mean you'd had no word from her . . . directly, I mean . . . in the past three years?" Carella said.

"That's right. Not since she left California."

"But you came here to see her . . ."

"Yes."

"Did you know where she lived?"

"Her address is in the phone book."

"Did you write to her first?"

"No, I was afraid to do that. Afraid she wouldn't want to see me."

"So you just came east."

"Yes."

Carella looked at his notes.

"Would you know your sister's social security number?" he asked.

"I'm sorry, I don't."

"The bank she worked for was Suncoast Federal, did you say? In California, I mean."

"Yes."

"And the bank she worked for here in the . . ."

"I told you. I don't know which . . ."

"Yes, but *when* was this, would you know? When you heard from your friend that she was working for a bank here."

"Oh. Two years ago? Perhaps a year and a half. I couldn't say with any accuracy."

"Would you know if she was *still* working at this bank? Immediately before her death, I mean."

"I have no idea."

"You haven't stayed in touch with your friend?"

"I have. But she's living in Chicago now."

"Then for the past two years—a year and a half, whatever it was—you really didn't know *what* your sister was doing."

"That's right. We lost touch completely. That's why I came here."

"And you arrived on October twenty-seventh, is that right?" Carella said.

"Yes. Last Thursday."

"Checked into this hotel, did you?"

"Yes."

"Planning to stay how long?"

"As long as was necessary. To see my sister, to . . . make amends . . . to ask her to come home."

"For Christmas."

"Forever." Inge sighed heavily and leaned over to the ashtray again, crushing out her cigarette. "I missed her. I loved her."

"When you arrived, Miss Turner, did you try to contact your sister?"

"Yes, of course. I phoned her at once."

"This was on the twenty-seventh of October?"

"Yes. My plane got in at six, a little after six, and it took a half hour to get into the city from the airport. I phoned her the moment I was in the room."

"And?"

"There was no answer."

"Was she living alone, would you know?"

"Yes. Well, I didn't learn that until later. When I went to her apartment."

"When did you do that?"

"Two days later. I'd been calling her repeatedly and . . . well . . . there was no answer, you see."

"So you suspected something was wrong, did you?"

"Well, I didn't know *what* to think. I mean, I'd been calling her day and night. I set my alarm one night . . . this was the night after I arrived . . . for three A.M., and I called her then and still got no answer. I went to her apartment the very next day."

"That would have been . . ."

"Well, the twenty-ninth, I suppose. A Saturday, I guess I was hoping she'd be home on a Saturday."

"But she wasn't, of course."

"No. She . . . was dead by then. But I . . . I didn't know that at the time. I went up to her apartment and rang the doorbell and got no answer. I found the superintendent of the building, told him who I was, and asked if he had any idea where my sister might be. He . . . he said he hadn't seen her in . . . in . . . three or four weeks."

"What did he say exactly, Miss Turner? Three weeks, or four?"

"I think that's exactly what he said. Three or four weeks."

"And he told you that she was living there alone?"

"Yes."

"What did you do then?"

"Well, I . . . I suppose I should have gone directly to the police, but I . . . you see, I was somewhat confused. The possibility existed that she'd met someone, some man, and had moved in with him. That was a possibility." She paused. "My sister wasn't gay," she said, and reached for her package of cigarettes again, and then changed her mind about lighting one.

"When *did* you contact the police?" Brown asked.

"On Monday morning."

Carella looked at his pocket calendar.

"October thirty-first," he said.

"Yes. Halloween," Inge said. "They told me they'd

turn it over to Missing Persons and let me know if anything resulted. I gave them an old photo I had . . . I still carried it in my wallet . . . and apparently Detective Lipman was able to match that against the . . . the picture you just showed me. He called me yesterday. I went down there and . . . and made the identification.''

The room was silent.

"Miss Turner," Carella said, "we realize you hadn't seen your sister in a long time . . .''

"Yes," she said.

". . . and Los Angeles is a long way from here. But . . . would you have heard anything over the years . . . anything at *all* . . . from your friend or anyone else . . . about any enemies your sister may have made in this city . . .''

"No."

". . . any threatening telephone calls or letters she may have . . .''

"No."

". . . any involvement with criminals or . . .''

"No."

". . . people engaged, even tangentially, in criminal activities?''

"No."

"Would you know if she owed money to anyone?''

"I don't know.''

"She wasn't doing drugs, was she?'' Brown asked.

The question nowadays was almost mandatory.

"Not that I know of,'' Inge said. "In fact . . .''

She stopped herself mid-sentence.

"Yes?'' Carella said.

"Well, I was only going to say . . . well, in fact, that was one of the things she objected to.''

"What was that, Miss Turner?''

"My friends and I did a few lines every now and then.'' She shrugged. "It's common in Los Angeles.''

"But your sister never, to your knowledge . . .''

"Not in L.A., no. I don't know what she might have

got into once she came here." She paused, and then said, "L.A. is civilized."

Neither of the detectives said anything.

"You see," Inge said, "this whole thing is so unbelievable. I mean, you'd have to have known Lizzie to realize that . . . that *dying* this way, dying a violent death, someone *shooting* her . . . well, it's unimaginable. She was a very quiet, private sort of person. My friends used to speculate on whether she'd ever even been *kissed*, do you know what I'm saying? So when you . . . when you . . . when the mind tries to associate Lizzie, sweet goddamn innocent *Lizzie* with a . . . with a *gun*, with someone holding a *gun* to the back of her head and shooting her . . . it's . . . I mean, the mind can't possibly make that connection, it can't make that quantum leap."

She looked at her hands. She had very beautiful hands, Carella noticed.

"Detective Lipman said . . . he'd read some sort of report that was sent to him . . . he said she had to have been on her knees when she was shot. The angle, the trajectory, whatever the hell, indicated she'd been on her knees, with . . . with . . . with the . . . person who . . . who shot her standing behind her. Lizzie on her knees."

She shook her head.

"I can't believe this has happened," she said, and reached into her handbag for another cigarette.

She was smoking again when the detectives left the room.


"His specialty is banks," Carella said.

"Just what I was thinking," Brown said.

They were driving crosstown and downtown to Elizabeth Turner's apartment and they were talking about the Deaf Man.

"That's if you consider two out of three a specialty," Carella said.

He was remembering that once, and only once, had

the Deaf Man's attempts at misdirection been designed to conceal and simultaneously reveal an elaborate extortion scheme. On the other two occasions it had been banks. Tell the police beforehand, but not really, what you're planning to do, help them dope it out, in fact, and then do something different but almost the same—it all got terribly confusing when the Deaf Man put in an appearance.

Eight black horses, five walkie-talkies, and one white lady who probably had nothing whatever to do with the Deaf Man, except for the fact that she had worked in a bank.

"Banks have security officers, you know," Brown said.

"Yeah," Carella said.

"And they carry walkie-talkies, don't they?"

"I don't know. Do they?"

"I guess they do," Brown said. "Do you think there might be a bank someplace in this city that's got five security guards carrying walkie-talkies?"

"I don't know," Carella said.

"Five walkie-talkies, you know?" Brown said. "And she worked in a bank."

"The only *real* thing we've got . . ."

"*If* it's a connection."

"Which it probably isn't."

"That's the trouble with the Deaf Man," Carella said.

"He drives you crazy," Brown said.

"What's that address again?"

"Eight-oh-four."

"Where are we now?"

"Eight-twenty."

"Just ahead then, huh?"

"With the green canopy," Brown said.

Carella parked the car at the curb in front of the building and then threw down the visor on the driver's side. A sign was attached to it with rubber bands. Visible through the windshield, it advised any overzealous foot patrolman that the guys who'd parked the car here were on the job. The city's seal and the words ISOLA P.D. printed on the sign were presumably insurance against a parking ticket. The sign didn't always work. Only recently they had busted a cocaine dealer who'd stolen an identical sign from a car driven by two detectives from the Eight-One. In this city it was sometimes difficult to tell the good guys from the bad guys.

It was difficult, too, to tell a good building from a bad building.

Usually a building with an awning out front indicated that there would be a doorman or some other sort of security. There was neither here. They found the superintendent's apartment on the street level floor, identified themselves, and asked him to unlock the door to Elizabeth Anne Turner's apartment. On the way up in the elevator Brown asked him if she'd lived here alone.

"Yep," he said.

"Sure about that?" Carella said.

"Yep," the super said.

"No girlfriend living with her?"

"Nope."

"No boyfriend?"

"Nope."

"No roommate at all, right?"

"Right."

"When'd you see her last?"

"Beginning of October, musta been."

"Going out or coming in?"

"Going out."

"Alone?"

"Alone."

"Carrying anything?"

"Just her handbag."

"What time was this?"

"In the morning sometime. I figured she was on her way to work."

"And you didn't see her again after that?"

"Nope. But I don't keep an eye out twenty-four hours a day, you know."

There is a feel to an apartment that has been lived in.

Even the apartment of a recent homicide victim can tell you at once whether anyone had been living there. There was no such sense of habitation in Elizabeth Turner's apartment.

The windows were closed tight and locked—not unusual for this city, even if someone were just going downstairs for a ten-minute stroll. But the air was still and stale, a certain indication that the windows hadn't been opened for quite some time. Well, after all, Elizabeth Turner had been found dead eight days ago, and perhaps that was a long enough time for an apartment to have gone stale.

But a slab of butter in the refrigerator had turned rancid.

And a package of sliced Swiss cheese had mold growing on it.

And a container of milk was sour to the smell; the SELL-BY date stamped at the top of the carton read "OCT. 1."

There were no dishes on the drainboard, none in the dishwasher.

The ashtrays were spotlessly clean.

The apartment revealed none of the detritus of living—even if the living had been done by a compulsive housekeeper.

There was only one coat hanging in the hall closet.

The double bed in the bedroom was made.

A framed picture of Elizabeth was on the dresser opposite the bed. She looked prettier alive.

The three top drawers of the dresser were empty.

The middle row of drawers contained one blouse.

The bottom row of drawers contained two sweaters and a handful of mothballs.

Only a suit, a pair of slacks, and a ski parka were hanging in the bedroom closet. There were two pairs of high-heeled pumps on the closet floor. They could find no suitcases anywhere in the apartment.

The roll of toilet paper in the bathroom holder was almost all gone.

They could not find a toothbrush in the medicine cabinet.

Nor a diaphragm. Nor a birth control pill dispenser. Nor any of the artifacts, cosmetic or otherwise, they normally would have found in an apartment actively occupied by a woman.

They went back into the bedroom and searched the desk for an appointment calendar.

Nothing.

They looked for a diary.

Nothing.

They looked for an address book.

Nothing.

"What do you think?" Carella asked.

"Flew the coop, looks like," Brown said.

Another envelope was waiting when they got back to the squadroom.

Kling handed it to Carella and said, "It looks like your pen pal again."

Carella's name was typewritten across the face of the envelope.

No return address.

The stamp was postmarked November 1.

"Shouldn't we be checking these for fingerprints or something?" Brown said.

"If it's the Deaf Man," Kling said, "we'd be wasting our time."

He looked very blond standing alongside Brown. He *was* very blond, but Brown made him look blonder. And younger. And more like a shit-kicking farmboy than usual. Born and raised in this city, he nonetheless exuded an air of innocence, a lack of guile or sophistication that automatically made you think he'd migrated from Kansas or someplace like that, wherever Kansas was—the detectives on the 87th Squad all thought Kansas was "out there someplace."

Kling looked as if he'd come from out there in the boondocks of America someplace, where you drove your car two hundred miles every Saturday night to a hamburger stand. Kling looked as if he still necked in the back seat of an automobile. Hazel-eyed and clean-shaven, blond hair falling loose over his forehead, he looked like a bumpkin who had wandered into the police station to ask directions to the nearest subway stop. He was very good at the Mutt and Jeff ploy. In much the same way that any cop teamed with Brown automatically became Jeff, any cop teamed with Kling automatically became Mutt. Together Kling and Brown were perhaps the best Mutt and Jeff act to be found anywhere in the city. It was almost unfair to the criminal population of this city to foist such a Mutt and Jeff team upon it. There was no way you could win, not with Brown playing the heavy and Kling playing the good-natured soul trying to keep his partner from chewing you to bits. No way.

"Even so," Brown said.

"Been handled by ten thousand people already," Kling said. "Postal clerks, letter carriers . . ."

"Yeah," Brown said, and shrugged.

"You going to open it or what?" Kling said.

"You open it," Carella said, and extended the envelope to him.

"It's not my case," Kling said.

"It's everybody's case," Carella said.

"Throw it away," Kling said, backing away from the envelope. "He gives me the creeps, that guy."

"*I'll* open it, for Christ's sake," Brown said, and took the envelope from Carella.

He tore open the flap. He unfolded the single white sheet of paper that was inside:

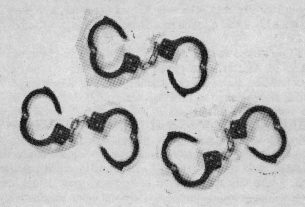

"Huh?" he said.

# 3

THE CITY FOR WHICH THESE MEN WORKED WAS divided into five separate geographical sections.

The center of the city, Isola, was an island; hence its name: *isola* means "island" in Italian. In actual practice the *entire* city was referred to as Isola, even though the other four sections were separately and more imaginatively named.

Riverhead came from the Dutch, though not directly. The land up there had once been owned by a patroon named Ryerhurt, and it had been called Ryerhurt's Farms, which eventually became abbreviated and bastardized to Riverhead.

No one knew why sprawling, boisterous Calm's Point was called that. Maybe at one time, when the British were still there, it had indeed been a peaceful pastoral place. Nowadays it was worth your life to wear a gold chain in some sections of Calm's Point.

Majesta had without question been named by the British; the name rang with all the authority, grandeur, greatness, and dignity of sovereignty, its roots being in the Middle English word *maieste*, from the Old French *majeste*, from the Latin *mājestās*, which was a long way around the mulberry bush.

Bethtown had been named for the virgin queen Elizabeth, but undoubtedly by a British official with a lisp; it was *supposed* to have been called *Bess*town.

Isola was the hub of the city.

Some people who lived there thought it was the hub of the entire *universe*, a belief that did much to contribute to its reputation for rudeness. Even people who lived elsewhere in the city held Isola in awe, invariably referring to it as "the City," as though they lived in the middle of a wheat field on its outer fringes.

There were no wheatfields in any part of this city.

But there *were* a hell of a lot of banks.

In Isola there were 856 banks.

In Majesta there were 296 banks.

In Calm's Point there were 249 banks.

In Riverhead there were 127 banks.

And in Bethtown there were 56 banks.

That came to 1,584 banks, more than a quarter of all the banks in the entire state.

On Thursday morning, November 3, a flyer from the Eight-Seven went out to the main branch of every bank in the city, requesting information on a homicide victim named Elizabeth Anne Turner, who may have been employed as a cashier sometime during the past three years. A photograph and description accompanied the flyer together with the social security number the detectives had got from Suncoast Federal in Los Angeles, where Elizabeth had worked before coming east.

On Friday morning, November 4, a call came from the branch manager of the First Fidelity Trust on Beverly Street downtown.

Carella and Brown were in his office not twenty minutes later.

Arnold Holberry was a man with a summer cold. He thought it was ridiculous to have a summer cold when it was already four days into November.

"I *hate* this weather," he told the detectives, and blew his nose. Outside the windows of his office November looked like June. "This is supposed to be *autumn*," he said. "The first day of autumn was September twenty-first. We are already into the last *quarter* of the year," he said. "The winter *solstice* is almost upon us. We are not supposed to be having this kind of weather. This kind of weather is dangerous for human beings at this time of year."

He blew his nose again.

He was a trim man in his late fifties, his hair graying at the temples, a gray mustache under his nose—which was very red at the moment. A bottle of cold tablets was on his desk. A box of tissues was on his desk as well. He looked thoroughly miserable, but he told the detectives he was willing to give them all the time they needed. He remembered Elizabeth Turner quite well and had been inordinately fond of her.

"How long did she work here, Mr. Holberry?" Brown asked.

"Almost two years. She used to live in California, excellent credentials out there. Well, a marvelous person all around. I was sorry to have her leave us."

"When was that?" Carella asked.

He was afraid he would catch Holberry's cold. He didn't want to bring a cold home to the kids just when the holidays were about to begin. Thanksgiving was only a few weeks off, and after that Christmas would be right around the corner. He was unaware of it, but his posture in the chair opposite Holberry's desk was entirely defensive. He sat leaning all the way back, his arms folded across his chest. Each time Holberry blew his nose, Carella winced, as if a battery of nuclear missiles were rushing out of their silos, aimed at his vulnerable head.

"In February," Holberry said.

"This past February?"

"Yes."

"When, exactly, in February?" Brown asked.

"On February fourth," Holberry said, and reached for a tissue and blew his nose again. "These pills don't work at all," he said. "Nothing works when you've got a cold like this one."

Carella hoped he would not sneeze.

"We gave her a wonderful reference," Holberry said.

"She left for another job, is that it?" Brown asked.

"Yes."

"Here in the city?"

"No. Washington, D.C."

The detectives looked at each other. They were thinking she had left for Washington in February, and she was back here in October—dead.

"Would you know when she came back here?" Brown asked.

"Gentlemen, I didn't know she *was* back until I got your request for information. You can't know how shocked I was." He shook his head. "Lizzie was such a . . . kind, generous, soft-spoken . . . *elegant* person, that's the word, elegant. To think of her life ending in violence . . ." He shook his head again. "Shot, you said?"

"Shot, yes," Carella said.

"Unimaginable."

Her sister had used the same word.

"Mr. Holberry," Brown said, "we've talked to the super at her building and also to many of her neighbors, and they told us she was living there alone . . ."

"I really wouldn't know about that," Holberry said.

"They described her as a very private sort of person, said they'd rarely seen her with friends of any kind, male or female . . ."

"Well, I wouldn't know about that, either," Holberry said. "She was certainly outgoing and friendly here at the bank. Gregarious, in fact, I would say."

"You didn't know her on a social level, did you, sir?" Carella asked.

"No, no. Well, that wouldn't have been appropriate, you know. But . . . gentlemen, it really is difficult to describe Lizzie to someone who didn't know her. She was simply a . . . *marvelous* person. Always a kind word for everyone, always a smile on her face. Crackerjack at her job, never complained about anything, nothing was too big for her to tackle. When she told me she was leaving for Washington, I was shattered. Truly. She could have gone quite far with this bank. Quite far. Excuse me," he said, and blew his nose again, and again Carella winced.

"You say she asked for a reference," Brown said.

"Yes. Actually she'd told me beforehand she was looking for employment elsewhere. It was not in Lizzie's nature to lie about anything. She was unhappy here, she said, and she . . ."

"Unhappy why?" Carella asked at once.

"She felt she wasn't advancing rapidly enough. I told her these things took time, we all had our eye on her, and we knew what a valuable employee she was . . . but you see, she'd been offered an assistant managership in Washington, and I can understand how that must have appealed to her."

"Which bank was that, sir?"

"The Union Savings and Trust."

"Would you know which branch?"

"I'm sorry, no."

"But it's your understanding that when she left here last February, it was to become an assistant manager at a Union Savings and Trust bank in Washington?"

"Well, yes. Of course. That's what I've been saying, isn't it?"

"What I meant, sir," Carella said, "is whether to your knowledge she actually *took* the job she'd been offered."

"I would have no way of knowing that. I assume . . ."

"Because you see, sir, she was here in this city nine months later . . ."

"Oh, yes, I see what you mean. I'm sorry, but I don't know. I suppose . . . I really don't know. Perhaps she was unhappy in Washington. Perhaps she came back to . . . I don't know." He paused. "This city has a way of luring people back, you know."

A sneeze was coming.

Carella wanted to run for the underground bunker.

Holberry grabbed for a tissue.

Carella hunched up his shoulders.

The sneeze did not come. Holberry blew his nose.

"Sorry," he said.

"Would you know where she was living when she worked here?" Brown asked.

"I'm sure we have the address in our files," Holberry said, and picked up the telephone receiver. "Miss Conway," he said, "can you bring in the file on Elizabeth Turner, please?" He put the phone back on its cradle. "It'll just be a moment," he said.

Carella knew exactly where Brown was headed.

In this city the new phone books came out on the first day of September each year. From past investigations the detectives knew that the closing date for any new listing was June 15. If a phone had not been installed by that date, it would not be listed in the new September 1 directory. Elizabeth's name, address, and number, however, *were* listed in the directory when her sister arrived here on October 27—even though Elizabeth had left the city on February 4. Which meant she'd either kept her old apartment and her old phone when she'd left the city or . . .

The door to Holberry's office opened.

A woman came in and put a file folder on his desk.

He opened it.

He began leafing through papers, stopped to blow his nose, and then began leafing again.

"Yes, here it is," he said, and looked up. "Twelve twenty-four Dochester Avenue."

Which meant that Elizabeth Turner had taken a new apartment when she'd come back to the city—sometime *before* June 15, the closing date for the telephone directory. The carton of sour milk in her refrigerator had been stamped with an October 1 SELL-BY date. In this city the legal shelf life for milk was eight to ten days; she had to have bought it sometime between September 22 and October 1. On October 29 the super at 804 Ambrose had told Inge Turner that he hadn't seen her sister in three or four weeks. That would make it about right. She had packed her bags and flown the coop, either temporarily or for good, sometime at the beginning of October.

But why?

And where had she gone?

"Thank you very much, sir," Carella said, "you've been very helpful."

Holberry rose and extended his hand.

Carella felt he was gripping the hand of a plague victim.

There were a lot of parks in the city, most of them inadequately lighted after sundown and therefore prime locations for anyone wishing to dispose of a corpse. That this *particular* park—directly across the street from the Eight-Seven's station house—had been chosen was a matter of some concern to the detectives. It indicated either daring or insanity.

Elizabeth Turner had been found naked in the park across the street.

Elizabeth Turner had worked for a bank in Los Angeles, had worked for another bank in this city, and had left employment here to work for yet another bank in Washington, D.C.

The Deaf Man's specialty was banks.

Something was in the wind.

And it smelled mightily of the Deaf Man.

Something was in the mail as well, and it arrived in the squadroom that Friday afternoon, while Carella was on the phone with the manager at the main branch of Union Savings and Trust in Washington.

When Carella saw the white envelope in Sergeant Murchison's hand, he almost lost track of the conversation. Murchison was wearing a long-sleeved blue woolen sweater over his uniform shirt, a sure sign that Indian summer was gone. Outside the squadroom windows the sky was gray and a sharp wind was blowing. The forecasters had promised rain. Shitty November was here at last. And so was another envelope from the Deaf Man, if that's what it was. From the look on Murchison's face, that's what it was.

". . . clash of personalities, you might say."

"I'm sorry, sir," Carella said. "What did you . . . ?"

"I said you might describe the differences between Miss Turner and Mrs. Hatchett as a clash of personalities."

"And Mrs. Hatchett, as I understand it, is a manager with Union Savings and Trust?"

"Yes, at our Sixteenth Street branch."

"And, as such, was Miss Turner's immediate superior?"

"Exactly."

Murchison was waving the white envelope in Carella's face. Carella covered the mouthpiece, said, "Thanks, Dave," and uncovered the mouthpiece again.

"It's him again," Murchison whispered.

Carella nodded sourly. His name was staring up at him from the envelope. Why *me?* he wondered.

"I recognize the typewriter," Murchison whispered.

Carella nodded again. Murchison kept hanging around, curious about what was in the envelope. Into the phone Carella said, "What sort of personality clash *was* this, Mr. Randolph?"

"Well, Miss Turner was a very gentle person, you know, soft-spoken, easygoing, very . . . well . . . different in every way from Mrs. Hatchett. Mrs. Hatchett is . . . uh . . . aggressive, shall we say? Competitive? Abrasive? Sharp-edged? Appropriately named, shall we say?"

Carella was sure he detected a smile in Randolph's voice.

"In any event," Randolph said, "it became apparent almost immediately that Miss Turner and she would not get along. It was merely a matter of time before the tension between them achieved its full potential, that's all."

"How long did it take?"

"Well, longer than most. Miss Turner gave us notice in April."

"Left the job in April?"

"No. Told us she was quitting. Gave us two weeks' notice in April."

"And left when?"

"At the beginning of May."

"Then she was there in Washington for three months."

"Yes. Well, a little less actually. She began work here on the seventh of February. Actually it was something of a record. We've had nine assistant managers working under Mrs. Hatchett in the past eighteen months."

"She sounds like a dreamboat, your Mrs. Hatchett."

"She's the daughter-in-law of one of our board directors."

"Oh," Carella said.

"Yes," Randolph said drily.

"And that was the only reason Elizabeth Turner left the job? This personality clash with Mrs. Hatchett?"

"Well, Mr. Carella, I'm afraid you'd have to *know* Mrs. Hatchett in order to appreciate the full horror of a personality clash with her."

"I see."

"Yes," Randolph said, again drily.

"Thank you very much, Mr. Randolph," Carella said. "I appreciate your time."

"Not at all," Randolph said, and hung up.

Carella replaced the receiver on its cradle and looked at the white envelope. Murchison was still standing by his desk.

"So open it," Murchison said. "It ain't a bomb."

"How do you know?" Carella said, and nudged the envelope with his pencil. It suddenly occurred to him that the Deaf Man was something of a sideshow for the cops of the Eight-Seven, something that broke the monotony of routine. The Deaf Man arrived, and suddenly the circus was back in town. With a small shock of recognition he realized that he himself was not immune to the sense of excitement the Deaf Man promised. Almost angrily he picked up the envelope and tore off the end on its long side.

Murchison was right. It wasn't a bomb. Instead, it was:

And suddenly it began raining outside.

The rain lashed the windows of the bar on Jefferson Avenue, some three and a half miles southwest of the station house. The tall blond man with the hearing aid in his right ear had just told Naomi he was a cop. A police *detective*, no less. She didn't know the police department was hiring deaf people nowadays. Antidiscrimination laws, she supposed. They allowed you to hire *anybody*. Next you'd have detectives who were midgets. Not that a hearing aid necessarily meant you were deaf. Not stone *cold* deaf anyway. Still she guessed any degree of hearing loss could be considered an infirmity, and she was far too polite to ask him how a man wearing a hearing aid had passed the physical examinations she supposed the police department required. Some people were sensitive about such things.

He was good-looking.

For a cop.

"So what's your name?" she asked.

"Steve," he said.

"Steve what?"

"Carella," he said. "Steve Carella."

"Really?" she said. "Italian?"

"Yes," he said.

"Me too," Naomi said. "Half."

"What's the other half?"

"Wildcat," she said, and grinned, and then lifted her glass. She was drinking C.C. and soda, which she thought was sophisticated. She looked up at him seductively over the rim of her glass, which she had learned to do from one of her women's magazines, where she had also learned how to have multiple orgasms, occasionally.

Actually she was half-Italian and half-Jewish, which she guessed accounted for the black hair and blue eyes. The tip-tilted nose was Irish, not that her parents could claim any credit for that. The nose's true father was Dr. Stanley Horowitz, who had done the job for her three years ago, when she was twenty-two years old. She'd asked him at the time if he didn't think she should get a little something done to her boobs as well, but he'd smiled and said she didn't need any help in *that* department, which she supposed was true.

She was wearing a low-cut blue nylon blouse that showed her breasts to good advantage and also echoed the color of her eyes. She noticed that the deaf man's eyes—what'd he say his name was?—kept wandering down to the front of her blouse, though occasionally he checked out her legs, too. She had good legs. That's why she was wearing very high-heeled, ankle-strapped shoes, to emphasize the curve of the leg. Lifted the ass, too, the high heels did, though you couldn't tell that when she was sitting. Dark blue shoes and smoky blue nylons. Sexy. She felt sexy. Her legs were crossed now, her navy blue skirt riding up over one knee.

"I'm sorry, *what* was your name again?" she asked.

"Steve Carella," he said.

"I got so carried away with your being *Italian*," she said, rolling her eyes, "that I . . ."

"A lot of people forget Italian names," he said.

"Well, *I* certainly shouldn't," Naomi said. "My mother's maiden name was Giamboglio."

"And your name?" he said.

"Naomi Schneider." She paused and then said, "That's what the other half is . . . Jewish." She waited for a reaction. Not a flicker on his face. Good. Actually she enjoyed being a Big City Jewish Girl. There was something special about the Jewish girls who lived in this city—a sharpness of attitude, a quickness of tongue, an intelligence, an awareness that came across as sophisticated and witty and hip. If anybody didn't like her being Jewish—well, *half* Jewish—then so long, it was nice knowing you. He seemed to like it, though. At least he kept staring into her blouse. And checking out the sexy legs in the smoky blue nylons.

"So, Steve," she said, "where do you work?"

"Uptown," he said, "at the Eight-Seven. Right across the street from Grover Park."

"Rotten neighborhood up there, isn't it?"

"Not the best," he said, and smiled.

"You must have your hands full."

"Occasionally," he said.

"What do you get up there? A lot of murders and such?"

"Murders, armed robberies, burglaries, rapes, arsons, muggings . . . you name it, we've got it."

"Must be exciting, though," Naomi said. She had learned in one of her women's magazines to show an intense interest in a man's work. This got difficult when you were talking to a dentist, for example. But police work really *was* interesting, so right now she didn't have to fake any deep emotional involvement with a left lateral molar, for example.

"Are you working on anything interesting just now?" she asked.

"We caught a homicide on the twenty-fifth," he said. "Dead woman in the park, about your age."

"Oh my," Naomi said.

"Shot in the back of the head. Totally naked, not a stitch on her."

"Oh my," Naomi said again.

"Not much to go on yet," he said, "but we're working on it."

"I guess you see a lot of that."

"We do."

She lifted her glass, sipped at her C.C. and soda, looking at him over the rim, and then put the glass down on the bartop again, empty. The bar at five-thirty in the afternoon was just beginning to get crowded. She'd come over directly from work, the long weekend ahead, hoping she might meet someone interesting. *This* one was certainly interesting; she'd never met a detective before. Good-looking, too. A naked dead girl in the park, how about that?

"Would you care for another one?" he asked.

"Oh, thank you," she said. "It's C.C. and soda." She waited for a reaction. Usually you said C.C. and soda to a wimp, he asked, "What's that, C.C.?" *This* one didn't even bat an eyelash. Either he knew what C.C. was, or he was smart enough to pretend he knew. She liked smart men. She liked handsome men, too. Some men, you woke up the next morning, it wasn't even worth the shower.

He signaled to the bartender, indicated another round, and then turned to her again, smiling. He had a nice smile. The jukebox was playing the new McCartney single. The rain beat against the plate glass windows of the bar. It felt cozy and warm and comfortably crowded in here, the hum of conversation, the tinkle of ice cubes in glasses, the music from the juke, the brittle laughter of Big City women like herself.

"What sort of work do *you* do, Naomi?" he asked.

"I work for CBS," she said.

It usually impressed people when she said she worked for CBS. Actually what she did, she was a receptionist there, but still it was impressive, a network. Again nothing registered on his face. He was a very cool one, this one, well-dressed, handsome, a feeling of . . . absolute certainty about him. Well, he'd probably seen it all and done it all, this one. She found that exciting.

Well, maybe she was looking for a little excitement.

This morning, when she was dressing for work, she'd put on the lingerie she'd ordered from *Victoria's Secret.* Blue, like the blouse. A demicup underwire bra designed for low necklines, a lace-front string bikini with a cotton panel at the crotch, a garter belt with V-shaped lace panels. Sat at the desk in the lobby with the sexy underwear under her skirt and blouse, thinking she'd hit one of the bars after work, find some excitement. "CBS, good morning." And under her clothes, secret lace.

"Actually I'm just a receptionist there," she said, and wondered why she'd admitted this. "But I do get to meet a lot of performers and such. Who come up to do shows, you know."

"Uh-huh," he said.

"It's a fairly boring job," she said, and again wondered why she was telling him this.

"Uh-huh," he said.

"I plan to get into publishing eventually."

"I plan to get into *you* eventually," he said.

Normally she would have said, "Hey, get lost, creep, huh?" But he was looking at her so intently, not a smile on his face, and he appeared so . . . *confident* that for a moment she didn't know *what* to say. She had the sudden feeling that if she told him to disappear, he might arrest her or something. For what, she couldn't imagine. She also had the feeling that he knew exactly what she was wearing under her skirt and blouse. It was uncanny. As if he had X-ray vision, like Superman. She was nodding before she even realized it. She kept nodding. She hoped her face was saying, "Oh, yeah, wise guy?" She didn't know what her face was saying. She just kept nodding.

"You're pretty sure of yourself, aren't you?" she asked.

"Yes," he said.

"Walk into a bar, sit down next to a pretty girl . . ."

"You are," he said.

"Think all you have to do . . ."

"Yes," he said.

"Man of few words," she said. Her heart was pounding.

"Yes," he said.

"Mmm," she said, still nodding.

The record on the juke changed. Something by the Stones. There was a hush for a moment, one of those sudden silences, all conversation seeming to stop everywhere around them, as though E. F. Hutton were talking. And then a woman laughed someplace down the bar, and Mick Jagger's voice cut through the renewed din, and Naomi idly twirled her finger in her drink, turning the ice cubes, turning them. She wondered if he liked sexy underwear. Most men liked sexy underwear. She visualized him tearing off her blouse and bra, getting on his knees before her to kiss her where the cotton panel covered her crotch, his big hands twisted in the garters against her thighs. She could feel the garters against her thighs.

"So . . . uh . . . where do you live, Steve?" she asked. "Near the precinct?"

"It doesn't matter where I live," he said. "We're going to *your* place."

"Oh, *are* we?" she said, and arched one eyebrow. She was jiggling her foot, she realized. She sipped at the drink, this time looking into the glass and not over the rim of it.

"Naomi," he said, "we are . . ."

"Bet you can't even spell it," she said. "Naomi."

Her magazines had said it was a good idea to get a man to spell your name out loud. That way, he would remember it. But it was as if he hadn't even heard her, as if her statement had been too ridiculous to dignify with a reply.

"We *are*," he repeated, giving the word emphasis because she'd interrupted him, "going to your apartment, *wherever* it is, and we are going to spend the weekend there.''

"That's what . . . what you think," she said.

She was suddenly aware of the fact that her panties were damp.

"How do you know I'm not married?" she said.

"Are you?"

"No," she said. "How do you know I'm not living with someone?"

"Are you?"

"No, but . . ."

"Finish your drink, Naomi."

"Listen, I don't like men who come on so strong, I mean it."

"Don't you?" he said. He was smiling.

"No, I don't."

"You do," he said.

"Do all detectives come on so strong?" she said.

"I don't know what *all* detectives do," he said.

" 'Cause, you know, you really *are* coming on very strong, Steve. I don't usually like that, you know. A man coming on so strong."

"I'm giving you sixty seconds to finish that drink," he said.

God, I'm soaking *wet,* she thought, and wondered if she'd suddenly got her period.

"Are *you* married?" she asked.

"No," he said, and pushed back the cuff on his jacket. He was wearing a gold Rolex. She wondered briefly how come a detective could afford a gold Rolex.

"Sixty seconds," he said. "Starting *now.* "

"What if I *don't* finish it in sixty seconds?"

"You lose," he said simply.

She did not pick up her glass.

"Fifty-five seconds," he said.

She looked into his face and then reached for her glass. "I'm drinking this because I *want* to," she said. "Not because you're looking at your watch."

"Fifty seconds," he said.

Deliberately, she sipped at the drink very slowly, and then suddenly wondered if she could really *finish* the damn thing in whatever time was left. She also wondered if she'd made the bed this morning.

"Forty seconds," he said.

"You're really something, you know that?" she said, and took a longer swallow this time.

"In exactly thirty-eight seconds . . ." he said.

"Do you carry a gun?" she asked.

"Thirty-five seconds now . . ."

" 'Cause I'm a little afraid of guns."

"Thirty seconds . . ."

"What is this, a countdown?" she asked, but she took another hasty swallow of the drink.

"Twenty-six seconds . . ."

"You're making me very nervous, you know that?" she said.

"Twenty-seconds . . ."

"Forcing me to . . ."

"Fifteen . . ."

"Slow *down*, will . . . ?"

"In exactly twelve seconds . . ."

"I'm gonna *choke* on this," she said.

"Ten seconds . . ."

"Jesus!"

"You and I . . . eight seconds . . . are going to . . . five seconds . . . walk out of here . . . two seconds . . ."

"All *right*, already!" she said and plunked the empty glass down on the bartop.

Their eyes met.

"Good," he said, and smiled.

She had found the ribbons for him in her sewing box. He had asked her for the ribbons. By then she would have given him the moon. Silk ribbons. A red one on her right wrist. A blue one on her left wrist. Pink ribbons on her ankles. She was spread-eagled on her king-size bed, her wrists and ankles tied to the bars of the brass headboard and footboard. She was still wearing the smoky blue nylons, the high-heeled, ankle-strapped shoes, and the garter belt. He had taken off her panties and her bra. She lay there open and exposed, waiting for whatever he chose to do next, *wanting* whatever he chose to do next.

He had put his shoulder holster and gun on the seat of the armchair across the room. That was when he was undressing. Jokingly she had said, "Let me see your badge," which is what anybody in this city said when somebody knocked on your door in the middle of the night and claimed to be a cop. He had looked at her without a smile. *"Here's* my badge, baby," he'd said, and unzipped his fly. She knew she was in trouble right that minute. She just didn't know how *much* trouble. She had looked down at him and said, "Oh, boy, I'm in trouble," and had giggled nervously, like a schoolgirl, and suddenly she was in his arms, and his lips were on hers, and she was lost, she knew she was lost.

That had been four hours ago, before he'd tied her to the bed.

The clock on the dresser now read ten o'clock.

He had insisted that they leave the shades on the windows up, even though she protested that people in the building across the way might see them. There were lights on in the building across the way. Above the building the night was black. She wondered if anyone across the way could see her tied to the bed with silk ribbons. She was oozing below again, dizzy with wanting him again. She visualized someone across the way looking at her. Somehow it made her even more excited.

She watched him as he went to the armchair, picked up the holster, and took the pistol from it. Broad, tanned shoulders, a narrow waist, her fingernail marks still on his ass from where she'd clawed at him. She'd described herself to him, back there in the bar, as half-wildcat, but that was something she'd never believed of herself, even after she'd learned all about multiple orgasms. Tonight . . . Jesus! Afloat on her own ocean. Still wet with his juices and her own, still wanting more.

He approached the bed with the gun in his hand.

"Is there a burglar in the house?" she asked, smiling.

He did not smile back.

"A lesson," he said.

"Is that loaded?" she said. She was looking at his cock, not the gun, though in truth the gun did frighten her. She had never liked guns. But she was still smiling, seductively she thought. She writhed on the bed, twisting against the tight silken ribbons.

"Empty," he said, and snapped open the cylinder to show her. "A Colt Detective Special," he said. "Snub-nosed."

"Like me," she said. "Do you like my nose?"

"Are you ready for the lesson?" he asked.

"Oh my," she said, opening her eyes and her bound hands in mock fright. "*Another* lesson?" The gun was empty, she wasn't afraid of it now. And she was ready to play any game he invented.

"If you're ready for one," he said.

"I'm ready for anything you've got," she said.

"A lesson in combinations and permutations," he said, and suddenly opened his left hand. A bullet was in it. "Voilà," he said. "Six empty chambers in the . . ."

"There's an empty chamber right here," she said.

". . . cylinder of the pistol."

"Come fill it," she said.

"And one bullet in my left hand."

He showed her the bullet.

"I insert this into the cylinder . . ."

"Insert something in *me,* will you, please?"

". . . and we now have one full chamber and five empty ones. Question: what are the odds against the shell being in firing position when I stop twirling the cylinder?" He started twirling the cylinder, slowly, idly. "Any idea?" he said.

"Five to one," she said. "Come fuck me."

"Five to one, correct," he said, and sat on the edge of the bed, resting the barrel of the gun against the inside of her thigh.

"Careful with that," she said.

He smiled. His finger was inside the trigger guard.

"Really," she said. "There's a bullet in it now"

"Yes, I know."

"So . . . you know . . . move it away from there, okay?" She twisted on the bed. The cold barrel of the gun touched her thigh again. "Come on, Steve."

"We're going to play a little Russian roulette," he said, smiling.

"Like hell we are," she said.

But she was tied to the bed.

He rose suddenly. Standing beside the bed, looking down at her, he began twirling the cylinder. He kept twirling it. Twirling it. Smiling.

"Come on, Steve," she said, "you're scaring me."

"Nothing to be scared of," he said. "The odds are five to one."

He stopped twirling the cylinder.

He sat on the edge of the bed again.

He looked at her.

He looked at the gun.

And then, gently, he placed the barrel of the gun into the hollow of her throat.

She recoiled, terrified, twisting her head. The metal was cold against her flesh.

"Hey, listen," she said, and he pulled the trigger.

The silence was deafening.

She lay there sweating, breathing harshly, certain he would pull the trigger yet another time. The odds were five to one. How many times could he . . . ?

"It's made of wood," he said. "The bullet in the gun. You weren't in any danger."

He moved the barrel of the gun away from her throat. She heaved a sigh of relief.

And realized how wet she was.

And looked at him.

His erection was enormous.

"You . . . shouldn't have scared me that way," she said. She was throbbing everywhere.

"I can do whatever I *want* with you," he said.

"No, you can't."

"I own you," he said.

"No, you don't," she whispered.

But she struggled against the restraining ribbons to open wider for him as he mounted her again.

They did not budge from that apartment all weekend.

She did not know what was happening to her; nothing like this had ever happened to her in her life.

He left early Monday morning, promising to call her soon.

As soon as he was gone, she dressed as he had ordered her to.

Sitting behind the reception desk as CBS later that morning, she wore no panties under her skirt and no bra under her blouse.

"CBS, good morning," she said into the phone.

And ached for him.

## 4

IF A PERSON IS AN ARMED ROBBER AND HE moves to another state, chances are he'll continue the pursuit of his chosen career. He will not, for example, suddenly become a used-car salesman or a television producer, however similar to felony violators those two professionals might be. He will, instead, buy himself a gun that isn't hot—which is easy to come by in any city in the United States—find himself a mom-and-pop grocery store, and stick it up one fine night. If Mom and Pop are smart and cooperative, they will empty the contents of the cash register into his waiting hands and pray that he departs at once. If Mom and Pop feel that an armed intruder in their store is a *personal* as well as a criminal violation, they might foolishly resist this invasion of their turf, in which case they might lose more than the cash in the register. An armed robber isn't armed because he belongs to the National Rifle Association. He is armed because he knows he is looking at twenty years down the pike if he's caught doing his job, and he is quite ready—and often eager—to use the pistol in his fist. In America the most recent annual figure for deaths caused by handguns was thirty-four thousand nationwide, second only to deaths caused in automobile accidents. That is a whole lot of dead people. Carella sometimes wondered if the members of the NRA, while happily shooting deer in the forest, ever said a silent prayer for all those victims.

Elizabeth Turner had worked for a bank in Los Angeles. She had worked for a bank here in this city, and she had also worked for a bank in Washington, D.C.

Honest citizens, like criminals, will most often seek the same line of work when they move from one state to another. Wasn't it likely, in fact almost mandatory, that Elizabeth would have sought a job in yet another bank upon her return here?

The detectives knew that in this state all employers had to fill out a so-called WRS-2 form, which was a quarterly report of wages that had to be filed with the state's Department of Taxation and Finance on April 30, July 31, October 31, and January 31. The WRS-2 form listed the name and social security number of each employee, together with the gross wages earned in that quarter. The detectives were in possession of Elizabeth Turner's social security number. They knew she had left the job in Washington on May 1. They further knew that she had been found dead in Grover Park on October 25. Wasn't it a likelihood that at least one and perhaps two WRS-2 forms had been filed for her since her return to the city? Carella made a call upstate and spoke to a man named Culpepper there. Culpepper said he would check the WRS-2 forms filed on July 31 and October 31 and get back to him.

He did not get back to him until November 11, a dismally gray, wet, and cold Friday, by which time the case was already seventeen days old. He told Carella that none of the forms filed on July 31 reported wages for an Elizabeth Turner in that quarter.

"How about the October thirty-first forms?" Carella asked.

"Those haven't been processed yet."

"Haven't you got a computer up there?"

"Not for these quarterly forms," Culpepper said.

"Well, when do you think they *will* be processed?"

"When we get to them."

"When will that be?"

"When we get to them," Culpepper said again. "Sometime before the next quarter's filing is due."

"You mean in January? Next *year?*"

"The WRS-2's are due on January thirty-first, that's right."

"This is a homicide here," Carella said. "I'm trying to find out where this girl *worked*. Can't you do something to expedite this?"

"It'd be different if the forms were filed under an *employee's* name," Culpepper said. "Or even his or her social security number. But they're not. They're filed under the *employer's* name. You don't know how long it took us to check all those July forms, looking for this Elizabeth Turner. And *those* forms had already been processed."

Carella knew exactly how long it had taken. He had made his request six days ago. "Look," he said, "it's very important for us to find out where . . ."

"I'm sorry," Culpepper said. "I'll have the October thirty-first forms checked once they've been processed, but I can't do better than that."

"Okay, thanks," Carella said, and hung up.

He sat staring at his typewriter for a moment, and then he rolled a D.D. Supplementary Report form into it. He had typed almost a full page when Alf Miscolo came from the clerical office down the hall. There was a plain white envelope in his hand. This one was postmarked November 10. As with the four that had preceded it, the letter was addressed to Detective Stephen Louis Carella, the name neatly typewritten on the face of the envelope.

"I thought maybe he'd forgotten us," Miscolo said.

"No such luck," Carella said and tore open the flap of the envelope.

The same single white sheet of paper inside.

And pasted to it:

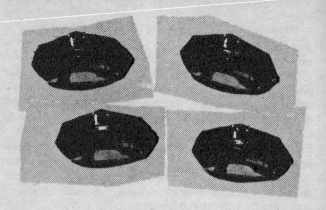

"That looks to me like four police hats," Miscolo said.

"Yes," Carella said.

"You think he's a cop?" Miscolo asked.

"I don't think so."

"Then why's he sending us pictures of all this police shit? Walkie-talkies, shields, handcuffs? Police hats?" He shook his head. "I don't like the idea of somebody sending us pictures of police paraphernalia," he said. "It's spooky."

He was not a handsome man, Miscolo. His nose was massive and his eyebrows were bushy, and there was a thickness about his neck that created the impression of head sitting directly on shoulders. But normally there was an animation to his face and a sparkle to his dark eyes—never more evident than when he was defending the truly abominable coffee he brewed in his office—and this was totally lacking now as he stared disconsolately at the sheet of paper in Carella's hand.

A police station was sacrosanct to men like Miscolo and Carella. Whatever happened out there on the streets, it did not come into the station house except in handcuffs

Although once—as they both remembered well—a woman with a gun and a bottle of nitroglycerin had held this very room hostage for more hours than either of them cared to count. For the most part, though, the precinct was as much a castle to these men as was a shabby row house to a British miner. It was enormously troubling to Miscolo that someone was using *police* equipment to make whatever the hell point he was trying to make. He felt as if he'd wandered into a filthy subway toilet and found his wife's monogrammed towels on one of the sinks.

He knew what the other four messages had—well, *advertised*, if that was the correct word. They were all posted side by side on the squadroom bulletin board in the order in which they'd been received:

Eight black horses.

Five walkie-talkies.

Three pairs of handcuffs.

Six police shields.

And now this.

Four police hats.

Except for the horses, it was as if somebody was putting together a policeman piece by piece.

"They all got to do with cops, you realize that?" he said. "Except the horses."

"Cops still ride horses in this city," Carella said.

"Them shields on the hats got no numbers on them, you realize that? He prolly cut out a picture of a hat someplace and then Xeroxed it."

"There's a number on this picture of the shields, though."

"You suppose that's a real shield?"

"I don't know."

" 'Cause you can Xerox anything nowadays," Miscolo said. "You lay something on the glass there, you close the cover, you press the button, you get a pretty good picture of it."

"Yeah," Carella said.

"If it *is* a real one . . . where'd he get it?" Miscolo asked.

"Maybe I oughta check it out," Carella said. "Trouble is . . ."

"Yeah, I know. You'd feel like a jerk."

"I mean, we're getting these dumb letters . . ."

"I know . . ."

"I make a call to Personnel, ask if a cop lost a potsie with the number seventy-nine on it . . ."

"You'd feel like a jerk."

"Which is how we're supposed to feel," Carella said.

"I don't like this guy, I really don't like him," Miscolo said, and looked at the picture of the four police hats again. "What's he trying to tell us anyway?"

"I don't know," Carella said, and sighed heavily.

"You want some coffee?" Miscolo asked.

"Thanks, not right now," Carella said.

"Yeah, well," Miscolo said, and shrugged and left the squadroom.

The rain lashed the windows.

Carella wondered if he should call Personnel to run a check on shield number seventy-nine.

He looked at the D.D. form in his typewriter. Years ago you had to use carbon paper to make duplicate, triplicate, even quadruplicate copies. Now you just ran down the hall and asked Miscolo to run off Xerox copies for you. The way the Deaf Man—it *had* to be the Deaf Man—had Xeroxed the pictures he'd been sending them. The form—just as he'd typed it, errors, overscoring, and all—read:

| DETECTIVE DIVISION SUPPLEMENTARY REPORT | SQUAD 87 | PRECINCT 87 | PRECINCT REPORT NUMBER 68-8946 | DETECTIVE DIVISION REPORT NUMBER DD 72 H-203 | PAGE NUMBER 1 |
|---|---|---|---|---|---|

| NAME AND ADDRESS OF PERSON REPORTING | DATE OF ORIGINAL REPORT |
|---|---|
| RE HOMICIDE VICTIM ELIZABETH ANNE TURNER (See Jane Doe L-4129) | 10/25 |

| SURNAME | GIVEN NAME | INITIALS | NUMBER | STREET | VILLAGE |
|---|---|---|---|---|---|

**DETAILS**

Subsequent to reports 10/25, 11/2, 11/4.

1) INGE /TURner, sister of deceased, ELIZABETH ANNE TURNER, returned to Los Angeles, California ᵃⁿⁿⁿⁿ on 11/6.

2) Further canvass of tenants at 804 South Ambrose Street revealed no additional significant details regarding deceased's habits or relationships with other men or women.

3) Despite gangland nature of slaying, precinct informers have heard nothing significant regarding the murder.

4) Second pass at banks, brokerage firms, other financial instituutions this city incomplete, but majority reporting no employment record Elziabeth Anne Turner May 1-October 25.

5) Check with State Department Taxation and ᵐᵐᵐᵐᵐᵐᵐᵐ Finance reveals no record of wages paid Elizabeth Anne Turner as per WRS-2 forms filed July 31. October 31 search pending.

6) Considering lack of further evidence, absence of ballistics data, witnesses, or motive for murder, it is respectfully submitted that ᵐᵐᵐᵐᵐ investigation be tempoerarily

| DATE OF THIS REPORT | |
|---|---|

| RANK | SURNAME | INITIALS | SHIELD NUMBER | COMMAND | SIGNATURE OF COMMANDING OFFICER |
|---|---|---|---|---|---|

That was as far as he'd got.

He was about to throw the Elizabeth Turner case into the Open File. Open. A euphemism for dead end. A case waiting for a miracle to happen. Open. In that years from now, by some impossible stroke of luck, they might arrest a man dropping another dead woman in yet another park, and he would confess to the first murder and perhaps a dozen murders before that one.

He looked at the form again.

He looked at the Deaf Man's most recent message.

Four police hats.

No faces under them.

Anonymous hats.

The form in Carella's typewriter was about to be thrown into the vast anonymity of the Open File, another piece of paper in a maze of information that confirmed the ineffectiveness of the police in a city where far too many murders were committed. The Open File was a gaping maw that swallowed victims. And in the process swallowed victimizers as well.

The proximity of the Deaf Man's anonymous hats and the imminently anonymous form in the typewriter made him suddenly angry. It was entirely possible that there was no connection whatever between Elizabeth Turner and the Deaf Man. Seeking such a connection would most certainly be time-consuming and, in the long run, perhaps foolish. But she had been found dead in the park across the street. And there had been five letters from the Deaf Man to date, and if he wasn't sticking his finger in their collective eye, then it certainly *seemed* that way. Throw Elizabeth Turner's corpse into the Open File, and he'd be throwing the Deaf Man into it as well.

He ripped the D.D. report from his typewriter.

He carried the Deaf Man's most recent greeting to the bulletin board and was about to tack it up with the others there, when it suddenly occurred to him that perhaps they were meant to be read in *numerical* rather than *chronological* order.

He began shifting them around, retacking them to the board in a single horizontal line.

Three pairs of handcuffs. Four police hats. Five walkie-talkies. Six police shields. Eight black horses.

So what? he thought.

They still meant nothing.

Not realizing how close he'd come to at least a *beginning,* he walked back to his desk, checked his book of police department phone listings, and then dialed Personnel downtown on High Street.

"Personnel, Sergeant Mullaney," a voice answered.

"Detective Carella at the Eight-Seven," he said. "I need a name and address for a possible police officer."

"A *possible* officer?" Mullaney said.

"Yes. All I've got is a shield number."

"What's the number?" Mullaney asked.

"Seventy-nine."

"You gotta be kidding," Mullaney said.

"What do you mean?"

"Seventy-*nine?* You know what number we're up to now? Don't even ask. You know how many cops been through this system since the police department was started? Don't ask."

"Check it anyway, okay?"

"This guy's got to be kidding," Mullaney said to no one. "Where'd you get this number?"

"On a picture of a shield."

"A *picture* of a shield?"

"Yes."

"And it says seventy-nine on it?"

"Yes."

"What's *your* number, Coppola?"

"Seven-one-four, five-six, three-two. And it's Carella."

"That'll give you some idea where we are now with the shield numbers. So you want me to check a shield some guy was a kid when the fuckin' *Dutch* were still here?"

"Just do me the favor, okay? This is a homicide we're working."

"I ain't surprised. A guy with shield number seventy-nine, he's been dead for at least three centuries. Hold on, okay?"

Carella held on.

Mullaney came back onto the line some five minutes later.

"No active shield number seventy-nine," he said. "Just like I figured."

"How about past records?"

"We don't go back to Henry Hudson," Mullaney said.

"Check your past records," Carella said impatiently. "This is a goddamn homicide here."

"Don't get your ass in an uproar, Coppola," Mullaney said, and left the phone again.

Carella waited.

When Mullaney came back, he said, "I got a badge number seventy-nine from 1858. There were eight-hundred thousand people in this city then, and we had a police force of fourteen hundred men. You'll be interested in learning, no doubt, that in those days the police department was also charged with cleaning the streets."

"So what's changed?" Carella said.

"Nothing," Mullaney said. "You want this guy's name?"

"Please," Carella said.

"Angus McPherson," Mullaney said. "He died in 1872. You'll be interested in learning, no doubt, that by then we had a population of a million-four and a police force of eighteen hundred men. Also, by then, there was a street cleaning department. Cops didn't have to shovel horse manure anymore. All they had to worry about was getting shot. Which was what happened to this guy McPherson. Where'd you get a picture of his shield? In an antiques shop?"

"I wouldn't be surprised," Carella said. "Thanks a lot, Maloney."

He had told Charlie Henkins that his name was Dennis Dove, and had asked him to make it "Den" for short. Charlie didn't realize it, but the words *den döve* were Swedish. In Swedish the word *den* meant "the," but *döve* was not a white bird of peace. The word wasn't even pronounced the way it was in English. In Swedish *döve* meant "deaf man." Den Dove, then, was the Deaf Man.

"The thing I still don't understand," Charlie said, "is why you want to do it on Christmas Eve. I mean, the situation is exactly the same on *any* night. The money'll be there in the vault *any* night we pick."

"Yes, but that's when I want to do it," the Deaf Man said.

Charlie scratched his head. He was not a particularly bright human being, but then again most armed robbers weren't. The Deaf Man had chosen him because he knew how to use a gun and was not afraid to use it. Charlie had, in fact, served a great deal of time at Castleview Prison upstate *precisely* because he'd used a gun while holding up a liquor store. The owner of the store was now confined to a wheelchair for life, a minor detail that disturbed Charlie not in the least. The way Charlie figured it, he'd *had* to burn the owner of the store because the man was reaching for his own gun under the counter. Charlie hadn't considered the fact that two cops in a cruising police car up the street would hear the shots and would, within the next three minutes, have Charlie in handcuffs. Those were the breaks. He who hesitates is lost, dog eat dog, and easy come, easy go. Charlie knew all the proverbs and tricks of the trade, and he had learned a few more of them while serving his time upstate. Everybody learned a few tricks in the slammer. The Deaf Man figured Charlie was perfect for the job he'd planned. Charlie had twinkling blue eyes and a little round pot belly.

"What I usually like to do on Christmas Eve," Charlie said, "is I like to watch television. They do a lot of specials on Christmas Eve. Last Christmas Eve I watched Perry Como on television. He used to be a barber, you know that? My cousin Andy used to be a barber, too, before he got into doing burglaries. Not that Perry Como does burglaries."

"You'll be home by seven-thirty," the Deaf Man said. "You can watch television all night long, if you like."

"I go in at a quarter to seven, huh?" Charlie said.

"Into the *vault* at a quarter to seven," the Deaf Man said.

"Yeah, sure, that's what I meant." He scratched his head again. "You sure Lizzie gave you the right numbers?"

"Positive."

"The combinations, I mean."

"Yes, I know what you mean. The numbers are absolutely correct."

"And there's this little push-button pad on the outer door, right?" Charlie said.

"Yes. Set in a panel to the right of the door."

"Steel door, huh?"

"Steel."

"And another door after that one."

"Yes, with another pad and a second set of numbers."

"And inside there's the safe with still *more* numbers."

"Yes."

"Think it was fuckin' Fort Knox they got there," Charlie said.

"Not quite," the Deaf Man said, and smiled.

"Still. Three sets of fuckin' numbers."

"Don't worry about the numbers," the Deaf Man said. "You'll have them memorized long before you actually use them."

"Yeah," Charlie said.

"Before we're through, you'll know those numbers the way you know your own name."

"Well, yeah," Charlie said.

"Does that bother you? Learning the numbers?"

"No, no, I just don't want anything to go wrong, that's all."

"Nothing'll go wrong if we're prepared for the *eventuality* of something going wrong. It's possible, of course, that you'll forget those combinations even after we've gone over them a thousand times. But it's not probable."

"I don't even know what that means, probable," Charlie said.

"A possibility is something that is *capable* of happening or being true without contradicting proven facts, laws, or circumstances. A *probability*, on the other hand, is something that is *likely* to happen or to be true. To put it in simpler terms . . ."

"Yeah, please," Charlie said.

"It is *possible* that our Christmas Eve adventure may go terribly awry, in which case we will both spend a good deal of time behind bars. It is *probable,* however, that all will go as planned, and we'll come out of it richer by half a million dollars."

"Which we split three ways, right?" Charlie said. "You, me, and Lizzie."

"Three ways, yes," the Deaf Man said.

Charlie nodded, but he looked troubled. "Just two broads inside the vault there, huh?" he said.

"Just the cashier and her assistant, yes."

"And you want me to take care of both of them, huh?"

"Immediately. As soon as you're in the vault."

"Well, that's the easy part, taking care of them," Charlie said.

"What's the *hard* part?" the Deaf Man asked.

"Well . . . learning the combinations, I guess. There's eighteen numbers to learn, you know. Six on each of those pads."

"You'll learn them, don't worry. You mustn't think of them as a single set of eighteen numbers. They'll be easier to remember if you think of them as three separate sets of six numbers each."

"Yeah," Charlie said.

"Three separate and distinct combinations."

"Yeah."

"In fact," the Deaf Man said, smiling, "combinations are a good way of differing between possibility and probability."

Charlie looked at him blankly.

"Let's start with something simple," the Deaf Man said. "Take two numbers. How many possible ways are there of arranging those two numbers?"

"Two?" Charlie asked uncertainly.

"Exactly. If the numbers are, for example, one and two, you can either arrange them as one-two or two-one. There are no other possibilities capable of being true without con-

tradicting proven facts, laws, or circumstances. Now let's
add another number. The number three. We now have three
numbers. One, two, and three. How many possible ways
can we arrange those three numbers?''

"Easy," Charlie said. "Three ways."

"Wrong. They can be arranged in six different ways.
Here," he said, and picked up a pencil and moved a pad
into place on the table. Writing swiftly, he listed the six
possible combinations of the numbers one, two, and three:

$$1\text{-}2\text{-}3$$
$$1\text{-}3\text{-}2$$
$$2\text{-}1\text{-}3$$
$$2\text{-}3\text{-}1$$
$$3\text{-}1\text{-}2$$
$$3\text{-}2\text{-}1$$

"Hey, how about that?" Charlie said.

"The way one calculates the possible ways of arranging
*any* amount of numbers is to multiply the highest number
by the one below it and then multiply the result by the
number below that, and so on. For example, we have three
numbers: one, two, and three. All right, we multiply three
by two and we get six. Then we multiply six by one, and
we get six again. The answer is six. And, as we just saw,
there *are*, in fact, only six possible ways of arranging
three numbers.''

"I was never good in arithmetic," Charlie said.

"It gets more complicated when there are more numbers," the Deaf Man said. "For example, those pads outside each of the doors have nine numbers on them. Do you
realize how many possible ways there are of arranging those
nine numbers?''

Again Charlie looked at him blankly.

"Well," the Deaf Man said, "do the multiplication.
Nine by eight by seven by six by five by four and so on
down to one. Nine times eight is seventy-two. Seventy-two
times seven is five hundred and four. Five hundred and

four times six is three thousand and twenty-four. And so on. If you carry it all the way through, you'll discover that there are three hundred and sixty-two thousand, eight hundred and eighty *possible* ways of arranging nine numbers. What, I ask you, is the *probability*—the likelihood—of anyone accidentally hitting upon the combination of six numbers that will unlock the outer door? And a different combination of six numbers for the inner door? And yet a third combination for the safe itself?"

"There ain't no way to figure that," Charlie said, shaking his head.

"Well, there is, but it would take forever. Which is exactly why combination locks were invented."

"Which is why *Lizzie* was invented, you mean."

"Yes, of course," the Deaf Man said, smiling. "To *provide* us with the combinations."

"For which she gets a third of the take," Charlie said, looking troubled again. "You think that's fair?"

"Do I think *what's* fair?"

"Her getting a third."

"Without her we wouldn't be going in at all."

"Yeah, well," Charlie said, "it ain't *us* going in, it's *me* going in."

"I know that."

"Yeah, but you just said *we'd* be going in."

"One of us has to be outside," the Deaf Man said. "You know that." He hesitated and then asked, "Would you rather *I* went in?"

"Well, I guess I look more the part," Charlie said.

"Exactly."

"Still."

"What is it, Charlie?" the Deaf Man said. "Tell me everything that's troubling you. I don't want any problems, not now and not later either."

"Okay, here's what's botherin' me," Charlie said. "I'm the one goes in the vault with a gun. I'm the one has to take care of the two broads in there. You're waitin' outside, and Lizzie ain't nowhere even *near* the scene. So, okay, it was your idea, the whole heist. I ain't begrudgin' you your share, especially since you're the one takes the fall if they catch you with the loot, by which time I'm already home free. But where does Lizzie come off takin' a third when all she done is give us the layout?"

"*And* the combinations."

"Yeah, well, the combinations."

"Without which there wouldn't be a job at all."

"It's just a question of what's fair, that's all," Charlie said. "You and me are takin' the biggest risks . . ."

"In a sense, Charlie," the Deaf Man said gently, *"you're* the one who's taking the greatest risk."

"Well, thank you," Charlie said, "I'm glad you said that, I really am. But it's your job, and fair is fair. And also you're taking a risk, too. It's that Lizzie ain't takin' no risk at all."

"Maybe you've got a point."

"I think I do."

"I'll have to talk to her. What would you suggest, Charlie?"

"Well, there's five hundred K in that vault, *supposed* to be five hundred K, anyway . . ."

"Perhaps more."

"So I thought, if we gave Lizzie a hundred thou for setting it up, then you and me split the rest."

"I'll tell you what I'll do," the Deaf Man said. "Fair is fair."

"It is."

"We'll give Lizzie a flat hundred, as you suggest. But I'll take only a hundred and fifty, and you'll get the lion's share, *two* hundred and fifty."

"Hey, no, I wasn't suggesting nothing like that," Charlie said.

"Fair is fair, Charlie."

"Well," Charlie said.

"Does that please you?"

"Well, if it's okay with you."

"It's fine with me."

" 'Cause I didn't want to say nothin' about like I'm the one lookin' at two counts of murder, you know what I mean?"

"I know exactly what you mean. And I appreciate it."

"And I appreciate what you're doin', too, the jester you just made. I really appreciate that, Den."

"Good. Are we agreed then?"

"I couldn't be happier," Charlie said, and then looked troubled again.

"What is it?" the Deaf Man asked.

"You think she'll go along with it? Lizzie?"

"Oh, I'm sure she will."

"I hope so. I wouldn't want her blowin' the whistle 'cause she thinks she ain't gettin' what she *should* be gettin'."

"No, don't worry about that, Charlie."

"Where is she, anyway?" Charlie asked. "Shouldn't she be here when we go over all this shit?"

"She's done her job already," the Deaf Man said. "She's no longer needed."

He looked at Charlie, wondering if he even suspected that once he carried that cash out of the vault he'd have done *his* job and he, too, would no longer be needed.

"Now then," he said, "the combinations."

"Yeah, the fuckin' combinations," Charlie said.

"Think of them as three different sets, Charlie. Forget that there are eighteen numbers in all."

"Okay, yeah."

"Can you give me the first set? The six numbers for the outer door?"

"Seven-six-one, three-two . . .

"Wrong."

"Seven-six-one . . .''

"Yes?"

"Three-two . . .''

"No."

"No?"

"No."

"Three-two . . ."

"No, it's two-three."

"Oh. Yeah. Two-three, yeah. Two-three-eight."

"And the inner door?"

"Nine-two-four, three-eight-five."

"Correct. And the safe?"

"Two-four-seven, four-six-three."

"Good, Charlie. Try it from the top again."

"Seven-six-one, two-three-eight."

"Again."

"Seven-six-one, two-three-eight."

"Again."

"Seven-six-one, two-three-eight."

"And the inner door?"

"Nine-two-four . . ."

# 5

EIGHT, FOUR, THREE, BROWN THOUGHT.

He was looking at the squadroom bulletin board where the Deaf Man's little billets-doux were tacked in a row under the wanted flyers and a notice advising that the Detective Division's annual Misletoe Ball would be held on Wednesday night, December 14.

Eight black horses, four police hats, and three pairs of handcuffs.

Six, five, he thought.

In police radio code, 10-5 meant REPEAT MESSAGE.

But this was a *six*-five.

Six police shields and five walkie-talkies.

Goddamn Deaf Man, Brown thought, and went to the coatrack in the corner of the room. He had dressed this morning in a bulky red plaid mackinaw, which made him look even bigger and meaner than he normally did. Blue woolen watch cap on his head. Bright red muffler around his throat. Only the fourteenth day of November, and already it was like Siberia out there. Idly he wondered if the Deaf Man had anything to do with it. Maybe the Deaf Man was a Russian spy. Manipulating the weather the way he manipulated everything else.

The clock on the squadroom wall read ten minutes to eight, but only one man from the graveyard shift was still there. Must've been a quiet night, Brown thought. "Cold as a witch's tit outside," he said to O'Brien, who looked up from his typewriter, grunted, glanced at the wall clock and then said, "You had a coupla calls last night. The messages are on your desk."

Outside the grilled squadroom windows the wind was

blowing leaves and hats and newspapers and skirts and all
kinds of crap all over the streets. Made a man happy to be
inside. Just walking from the subway station to the precinct, Brown thought he'd freeze off all his fingers and
toes. Should've worn his long johns this morning. Nice
and toasty in the squadroom, though. Even Miscolo's coffee, brewing down the hallway, smelled good. He took off
his mackinaw and hung it on the rack, tossing the red muffler over it. He left the blue watch cap on his head. Made
him feel like Big Bad Leroy just out of Castleview, where
he done time for arson, murder, and rape. Yeah, watch it,
man. Cross my path today, you go home with a scar. Smiling, he sat at his desk and looked at the pile of junk the
men on the graveyeard shift had dumped there.

The squadroom was quiet except for the howling of the
wind outside and the clacking of O'Brien's typewriter.
Brown leafed through the papers on his desk. A note from
Cotton Hawes telling him that a burglary victim had called
late last night to ask if Detective Brown had been able to
find his stolen television set. Fat Chance Department. That
television set had disappeared into the world's biggest bar-
gain basement. The thieves in this city, they gave you a
bigger discount than if you were buying wholesale. Some
thieves even stole things to *order* for you. Want a brand-
new video cassette player? What make? RCA? Sony? See
you tomorrow night this time. Coming up with that man's
stolen TV would be like finding a pot of gold in the sewer.
He wondered if it was true there were alligators down there
in the sewers. He once had to chase a thief down a sewer,
never wanted to do that again in his life. Dripping water,
rats, and a stink he couldn't wash out of his nostrils for the
next ten days.

Hawes had been complaining lately that the midnight-
to-8:00 A.M. was ruining his sex life. His sex life these
days was a lady Rape Squad cop named Annie Rawles.
Brown wondered what it was like to go to bed with a De-
tective/First Grade. Excuse me, ma'am, would you mind
unpinning your potsie, it is sticking into my arm. Six police

shields. Carella had told him shield number seventy-nine had belonged to a guy named Angus McPherson, long dead and gone. So where had the Deaf Man found it? Goddamn Deaf Man, he thought again. He was looking through the other messages on his desk when the telephone rang.

"Eighty-seventh Squad, Brown," he said.

"Hello, yes," the voice on the other end said. A young woman. Slightly nervous. "May I speak to Detective Carella, please?"

"I'm sorry, he's not here just now," Brown said. "Should be in any minute, though." He looked up at the wall clock. Five minutes to eight. "Can I take a message for him?"

"Yes," the woman said. "Would you tell him Naomi called?"

"Yes, Miss, Naomi who?" Brown said. O'Brien was on his way out of the squadroom. He waved to Brown, and Brown waved back.

"Just tell him Naomi. He'll know who it is."

"Well, Miss, we like to . . ."

"He'll know," she said, and hung up.

Brown looked at the telephone receiver.

He shrugged and put it back on its cradle.

Carella walked into the squadroom not three minutes later.

"Your girlfriend called," Brown said.

"I told her never to call me at the office," Carella said.

He looked like an Eskimo. He was wearing a short woolen car coat with a hood pulled up over his head. The hood was lined with some kind of fur, probably rabbit, Brown thought. He was wearing leather fur-lined gloves. His nose was red, and his eyes were tearing.

"Where'd summer go?" he asked.

"Naomi," Brown said, and winked. "She said you'd know who."

The phone rang again.

Brown picked up the receiver.

"Eighty-seventh Squad, Brown," he said.

"Hello, it's Naomi again," the voice said, still sounding nervous." I'm sorry to bother you, but I'll be leaving for work in a few minutes, and I'm not sure he has the number there."

"Hold on, he just came in," Brown said, and held the phone out to Carella. "Naomi," he said.

Carella looked at him.

"Naomi," Brown said again, and shrugged.

"You kidding?" Carella asked.

"It's Naomi," Brown said. "Would I kid you about Naomi?"

Carella walked to his own desk.

"What extension is she on?" he asked.

"Six. You want a little privacy? Shall I go down the hall?"

Carella pushed the six button on the base of his phone and lifted the receiver. "Detective Carella," he said.

"Steve?" a woman's voice said. "It's Naomi."

"Uh-huh," he said, and looked at Brown.

Brown rolled his eyes.

"You promised you'd call," she said.

"Uh-huh," Carella said, and looked at Brown again. The way he figured it, there were only two possible explanations for the youngish-sounding lady on the phone. One: she was someone he'd dealt with before in the course of a working day, an honest citizen with one complaint or another, and he'd simply forgotten her name. Or two, and he considered this more likely: the witty gents of the Eight-Seven had concocted an elaborate little gag, and he was the butt of it. He remembered back to last April, when they'd asked a friendly neighborhood hooker to come up here and tell Genero she was pregnant with his child. Now there was Naomi. City-honed voice calling him "Steve" and telling him he'd promised to call. And Brown sitting across the room, watching him expectantly. Okay, he thought, let's play the string out.

"Steve?" she said. "Are you still there?"

"Yep," he said. "Still here. What's this in reference to, Miss?"

"It's in reference to your pistol."

"Oh, I see, my pistol," he said.

"Yes, your big pistol."

"Uh-huh," he said.

"When am I going to see you again, Steve?"

"Well, that all depends," he said, and smiled at Brown. *"Who'd* you say this was?"

"What is it?" she said. "Can't you talk just now?"

"Yes, Miss, certainly," he said. "But police regulations require that we get the name and address of anyone calling the squadroom. Didn't they tell you that?"

"Didn't *who* tell me that?"

"Whoever put you up to calling me."

There was a long silence on the line.

"What is it?" she said. "Don't you *want* to talk to me?"

"Miss," Carella said, "I would *love* to talk to you, truly. I would love to talk to you for hours on end. It's just that these jackasses up here"—he looked meaningfully at Brown—"don't seem to understand that a dedicated and hardworking policeman has better things to do at eight o'clock in the morning than . . ."

"Why are you acting so peculiarly?" she said.

"Would you like to talk to Artie again?" Carella said.

"Who's Artie?"

"Or did Meyer set this up?"

"I don't know what you're talking about," she said.

"Cotton, right? It was Cotton."

"Am I talking to the right person?" she asked.

"You are talking to the person they asked you to talk to," he said, and winked at Brown. Brown did not wink back. Carella felt suddenly uneasy.

"Is this Detective Steve Carella?" she asked.

"Yes," he said cautiously, beginning to think he'd made a terrible mistake. If this *was* an honest citizen calling on legitimate police business . . .

"Who ties girls to beds and plays Russian roulette," she said. "With a wooden bullet."

Uh-oh, he thought, a bedbug. He signaled to Brown to pick up the extension, and then he put his forefinger to his temple and twirled it clockwise in the universal sign language for someone who'd lost his marbles.

"Can you let me have your last name, please?" he said. He was all business now. This was someone out there who might need help. Brown had picked up the phone on his desk. Both men heard a heavy sigh on the other end of the line.

"Okay," she said, "if you want to play games, we'll play games. This is Naomi Schneider."

"And your address, please?"

"You know my address," she said. "You spent a whole goddamn weekend with me."

"Yes, but can you give it to me again, Miss?"

"No, I won't give it to you again. If you've forgotten where I *live,* for Christ's sake . . ."

"Are you alone there, Miss?" he asked. They sometimes called in desperation. They sometimes asked the department sergeant to put them through to the detectives, and sometimes the sergeant said, "Just a moment, I'll connect you to Detective Kling," or Brown or whoever the hell—Detective *Carella* in this case—but how did she know his first name?

"Yes, I'm alone," she said. "But you can't come over just now, I'm about to leave for work."

"And where's that, Miss? Where do you work?"

"I'm wearing what you told me to wear," she said. "I've been wearing it every day."

"Yes, Miss, where do you work?"

"The garter belt and stockings," she said.

"Can you tell me where you work, Miss?"

"No panties," she said seductively. "No bra."

"If you'll tell me where you work . . ."

"You know where I work," she said.

"I guess I've forgotten."

"Maybe you weren't listening."

"I was listening, but I guess I . . ."

"Maybe you should have turned up your hearing aid," she said.

"My *what?*" Carella asked at once.

"What?" Naomi said.

"What makes you mention a hearing aid?" Carella said. There was a long silence on the line.

"Miss?" he said.

"Are you *sure* this is Steve Carella?" she said.

"Yes, this is . . ."

"Because you sound strange as hell, I've got to tell you."

"Listen, I'd like to see you," Carella said, "really. If you'll give me your address . . ."

"I told you I'm leaving for work in a few minutes . . ."

"And where's that? I'd like to talk to you, Naomi . . ."

"Is that all you'd like to do?"

"Well, I . . ."

"I thought you might want to fuck me again."

Brown raised his eyebrows. Jesus, Carella thought, he thinks I really *know* this girl! But she had mentioned a hearing aid, and right now he didn't give a damn *what* Brown thought.

"Yes, I'd like to do that, too," he said.

"At *last,*" she said, and sighed again. "It's like pulling teeth with you, isn't it?"

"Tell me where you work," he said.

"You already know where I work. Anyway, why would you want to come *there?*"

"Well, I thought . . ."

"We couldn't *do* anything there, could we, Steve?" she said, and giggled. "We'd get arrested."

"Well, what time do you get off tonight?" he asked.

"Five."

"Okay, let me have your address, I'll come by as soon as . . ."

"No," she said.

"Naomi . . ."

"You try to *remember* my address, okay?" she said. "I'll be waiting for you. I'll be wide open and waiting for you."

There was a click on the line.

"Miss?" he said.

The line was dead.

"Shit," he said.

Brown was staring at him.

Carella put the receiver back on its cradle. "Listen," he said, "if you're thinking . . ."

"No, I'm not," Brown said. "I'm thinking the Deaf Man."

If this had been a smaller city, the man from the telephone company might have been more conspicuous, arriving as he did at precincts all over town and claiming he was there to clear the trouble on the line. But this was a bigger city than most, one of the biggest cities in the world, in fact, and not many cops paid too much attention to a telephone repairman in their midst. Noticing a telephone repairman would have been like noticing an electrician or a plumber. The man who came and went at will was virtually invisible.

There were rules and regulations, of course, that pertained to anyone entering a police station. Ever since the bomb scares several years back, a uniformed cop stood at the entrance door to every precinct, and he asked any visitor what his business there might be. Or at least he was *supposed* to ask. Not many of them bothered. That was because most cops hated pulling what they called "door duty." They had not joined the force so that they could stand around with their thumbs up their asses waiting for terrorist attacks that never came. Police work meant *action*. There was as much action standing outside a precinct door as there was in an undertaker's shop.

So most cops on door duty, they gauged a citizen coming up the steps, nodded him in, and went back to watching the street, where—if they were lucky—the wind would blow a girl's dress up every now and then. Besides, if a guy was wearing coveralls that had the telephone company's name on the back and if there was a little plastic telephone company ID card pinned to the pocket of those coveralls and if there was a yellow lineman's phone hanging from his belt together with a lot of other wires and crap and if he was carrying a canvas bag with tools in it (some of the door-duty cops actually looked inside the bag to see if there was a bomb or something in it), then they automatically figured the guy was just what he claimed to be, a telephone company repairman there to clear the trouble on the line.

When Henry Caputo entered the Twelfth Precinct downtown, he stopped at the muster desk, just as the sign behind the desk advised him, and he stated his business to the desk sergeant.

"Telephone company," he said. "Here to clear the trouble on the line."

"*What* trouble on the line?" the desk sergeant asked. He had been answering the telephone all morning, and he wasn't aware of any trouble on the line.

Henry reached into a pocket, pulled out a white slip of paper, read it silently, and said, "This the Twelfth Precinct?"

"You got it, pal," the sergeant said.

"Okay, so there's trouble on the line. You want me to fix it or what?"

"Be my guest," the sergeant said, and Henry disappeared into the busy precinct boil.

Henry had hair the color of iodine and eyes the color of coal, and even in his telephone company coveralls he looked like a man who would slit your throat if you didn't hand over your watch the instant he asked for it. He *had*, in fact, once slit a man's throat, which was why he'd served time in a maximum security prison in Oklahoma. He had not slit the man's throat over anything as inconsequential as a watch. He had slit the man's throat because he'd interrupted a conversation Henry was having with a hooker in a bar in downtown Tulsa. The hooker had been a true racehorse, the hundred-dollar variety, not one of your scaly legged dogs who'd do a ten-dollar blowjob in a pickup truck. Henry had not enjoyed having his train of thought interrupted, especially when he had a hard-on. The man was very surprised to find his throat open and blood spilling down the front of his white shirt. All he'd said was, "Excuse me, sister, would you please pass the . . ." and the knife had appeared suddenly in Henry's hand, and the next thing the man knew he was trying to talk through a bubbling red froth in his mouth, and he never did get out the word "peanuts."

Fortunately, for both of them, the man didn't die. Henry was only locked up for the equivalent of what in this city would have been First-Degree Assault, a Class-C felony punishable by a minimum of three and a maximum of fifteen. Henry was now out on the street again, back east again, where he'd been born and raised—the hell with all them cowboys and Indians out west, people with no manners, who interrupted a conversation a person was having with a lady. Henry was ready to take his place in civilized society again, and a good way to start seemed to be the job—or, more accurately, the *series* of jobs—this guy Dennis Dove had asked him to do. Henry did not particularly like cops. Henry thought all cops were crooks with badges. So the idea of *stealing* from cops tickled the shit out of him.

The only thing Henry couldn't dope out was why this Dennis Dove character with the hearing aid in his ear *wanted* all this stuff Henry was stealing from police stations all over town. And paying pretty good for it besides. Two grand up front—plus *another* two grand when Henry delivered all the stuff—wasn't exactly potato chips. Actually Henry would have done the job for much less. A fun job like this one was difficult to come by these days. Besides, being in police stations, he was learning a lot about cops. He was learning they were all pricks, which is just what he'd thought all along. It was terrific to be stealing from these pricks, especially since they kept asking him all the time how the phones were coming along.

He'd go in and unscrew the mouthpiece from a phone, fiddle with the wires, check out some panels in the basement, and then come upstairs again and go into this room and that room and say hello to the prisoners in the holding cells and the squadroom detention cage and pop into the men's room to take a leak and go back to another phone and unscrew another mouthpiece, and meanwhile he was lifting little things here and there and dropping them in his canvas bag, while the cops kept telling rotten jokes about all the crooks out there in the city, never once realizing that a crook was right there in the police station with them, stealing them blind.

So far, Henry had stolen four walkie-talkies from the charging racks they had on the ground floor of the precincts on the far wall past the muster desk, and he had stolen three badges from uniform tunics in locker rooms while some guy was taking a shower or a nap, and he had a nightstick and a whole stack of Detective Division forms from the clerical office in one of the precincts, and he had stolen two police hats and a pair of handcuffs, and when he walked out of here today, he hoped to have another walkie-talkie, which would make five altogether, and maybe another badge or two and also some wanted flyers from one of the bulletin boards, though it was pretty risky to take something from a bulletin board, the fuckin' cops were always reading the bulletin boards like there was something important on them.

He wondered what this Dennis Dove character with the hearing aid in his ear wanted with seven different wanted flyers. That was on the list he'd given Henry: seven wanted flyers. If Henry had known wanted flyers were so valuable, he'd have asked the cops to send him the one of him that had been in a couple of post offices after he'd killed that hooker in New Orleans. They were still looking for him for that one. That one was after he'd got out of prison for slitting that guy's throat in Tulsa. He'd headed back east

by way of New Orleans, and he'd got into an argument
with this hooker who kept insisting he'd given her a phony
C-note, which happened to be true, but it wasn't fuckin'
polite to tell a man he was passing Monopoly money, not
after you'd just blown him. So he'd slapped her around a
little, and when she started screaming she was gonna get
her pimp to beat the shit out of him, he juked her, plain
and simple. Served her right, the dumb cunt. Accusing him
of handing her a phony bill, true or not. A customer was
a customer. And anyway it had been a lousy blowjob.

He wondered if there were any wanted flyers of him up
here in any of the precincts. Be a real gas if he walked into
a station house in his telephone company suit and saw his
own face looking down at him from a bulletin board. Well,
that's what made his line of work so interesting. You never
knew what was gonna happen next.

"Where you got your primary terminal?" he asked a cop
who was taking a walkie-talkie from the charging rack in
the muster room. Henry didn't know what a primary terminal was. He'd made that up on the spot.

"How the fuck do I know?" the cop said.

"They're usually in the basement," Henry said.

"So go down the basement," the cop said, and hung the
walkie-talkie on his belt.

Henry waited until he turned his back. He took a quick
look at the muster desk, lifted a walkie-talkie from the
rack, and dropped it into his canvas bag.

"Hey, you," somebody said.

His blood froze.

He turned.

A huge guy was standing near the iron-runged steps
leading to the second floor. He was in his shirt-sleeves,
and a pistol was hanging in a shoulder holster on his chest.

"While you're here," he said, "the buttons on my phone
ain't workin'. The extension buttons. Upstairs in the
squadroom."

"I'll take a look," Henry said. "You know where the
primary terminal is?"

* * *

The sixth letter from the Deaf Man arrived in that afternoon's mail.

It was addressed to Carella, but Carella was out of the squadroom, and all the detectives knew it was from their old pal, so they debated opening it for about thirty seconds, and then nominated Meyer as the person to intrude upon their colleague's right to private communication.

There was, to no one's great surprise, a single folded white sheet of paper inside the envelope.

Meyer unfolded the sheet of paper.

The other detectives crowded around him.

What they were looking at was:

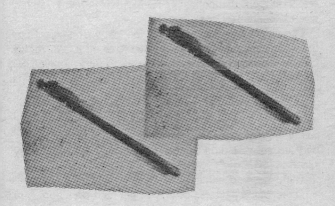

# 6

THANKSGIVING DAY ALWAYS FELL ON THE
fourth Thursday in November, and this year it would fall
on November 24.

Every detective on the squad wanted Thanksgiving Day
off. On Christmas or Yom Kippur it was possible for detectives of different faiths to swap the duty so that they could
celebrate their own holidays. Thanksgiving Day, however,
was nondenominational.

The detectives of the Eight-Seven knew of a squad farther uptown that had an Indian detective on it. An *Indian*
Indian. Come Thanksgiving, he was in very popular de-
mand because he had come to this country only four years
ago—after having served as a captain of police in Bom-
bay—and he did not understand the peculiar ways of the
natives here, and he did not celebrate Thanksgiving.
Everyone always wanted him to take the Thanksgiving Day
duty because he didn't know from turkeys and cranberry
sauce.

There were no Indian detectives on the 87th Squad.

There was a Japanese detective, but he'd been born here
and knew all about Thanksgiving, and no one would have
*dreamed* of asking him to forego his turkey dinner.

Genero asked him to forego his turkey dinner.

"You're a Buddhist, ain't you? Genero said.

"No, I'm a Catholic," Fujiwara said.

"This is a nondeterminational holiday," Genero said.

"So what's your point?"

"My point is I got the duty tomorrow," Genero said,
"and I'd like to swap with you."

"No," Fujiwara said.

"You people don't celebrate Thanksgiving, do you?" Genero said, "Buddhists?"

"Go fuck yourself," Fujiwara said.

Genero figured he was sensitive about being the only Jap on the squad.

Genero asked Andy Parker if he would like to swap the Thanksgiving Day duty with him.

"You got no family to eat turkey with," Genero said.

"Go fuck yourself," Parker said.

Genero tried Kling.

"You just been through a divorce," Genero said. "Holidays are the worst time of year for people just been through a divorce."

Kling merely looked at him.

Genero figured everybody on this goddamn squad was all of a sudden getting very touchy.

The cops working the day shift on November 24 were Genero, O'Brien, Willis, and Hawes. Genero was annoyed because his mother's big Thanksgiving Day dinner was at two o'clock. The other three detectives didn't mind working on Thanksgiving Day. Like Genero, they were all single, but they'd made plans for later on in the day. Hawes, in particular, was very much looking forward to the plans he'd made for later on in the day; he had not seen Annie Rawles for almost a week.

"Don't any of you guys have mothers?" Genero asked, still sulking.

The detectives on duty were thankful that there'd be no mail deliveries today.

They had not heard from the Deaf Man since the fourteenth, ten days ago. They all hoped they would not hear from him ever again. But they were certain they would not hear from him today. As they ate the turkey sandwiches they had ordered from the local deli, they thanked God for small favors.

The two men sitting at a corner table in a restaurant not ten blocks from the police station were eating turkey with all the trimmings. They were drinking the good white wine ordered by the one with the hearing aid in his right ear. They were talking mayhem.

"How'd you get onto me in the first place?" Gopher Nelson asked.

He'd been nicknamed Gopher during the Vietnam War. His first name was really Gordon. But he'd been a demolitions man back then, and whenever there was any kind of discussion as to whether it was feasible to blow up a bridge or a tunnel or a cache of Cong supplies, Gordon would say, "Let's go for broke," which is how he got the name Gopher. Nothing was too difficult or too risky for Gopher back then. A chopper would drop him and his gear in the boonies someplace, and he'd sneak into a deserted enemy enclave and wire the place from top to bottom and then sit in the jungle waiting for the little bastards in their black pajamas to come trotting back in. Little Gopher Nelson, all by himself in the jungle, waiting to throw the switch that would blow them all to smithereens. Gopher loved blowing up things. He also loved setting things on fire. In fact, Gopher thought back most fondly on the incendiary devices he had wired back then. There'd been something very satisfying about *first* seeing the flames and all them fuckin' gooks running for their lives, and *then* hearing the explosions when the fire touched off the ammo in the underground bunkers, all them fuckin' tunnels they'd dug clear across the country. Very satisfying. First you got your roast gook, and then you got the Fourth of July. Gopher wished the Vietnam War had never ended. It was hard for a civilian to find work that was as completely satisfying.

"Well, I make it my business to know what's going on," the Deaf Man said.

"What was it?" Gopher asked. "The Cooper Street job?"

"That, yes. And others."

"Like?"

"I heard you wired the break-in at First National Security."

"Oh, yeah. In Boston."

"Yes."

"Not many people know I was responsible for that one."

"Well, as I say, it's important for me to know such things."

"They're *still* lookin' for us up there."

"What was your end of the take?" the Deaf Man asked.

"Well, that's personal, ain't it?"

"I understand you went in for five percent."

"Ten. And it was just for wiring the place. I wasn't nowhere near it when they went in. There were four guys went in. They were expecting maybe eight hundred thou in the vault, but there was some kind of fuck-up, most of it was in non-negotiable securities. So they came away with two-fifty, which wasn't bad for an hour's work, huh? And I figured my end—at twenty-five—was fair. The other four guys netted a bit more than fifty-six each, and they took all the risk."

"I can't afford twenty-five on this one," the Deaf Man said.

"Then maybe you picked the wrong man."

"Maybe."

He poured more wine into Gopher's empty glass.

" 'Cause, like if you want a Caddy," Gopher said, "you can't expect to pay Chevy prices."

"All I can afford is ten."

"For *both* jobs?"

"A *total* of ten, yes."

"That's only five grand apiece."

"That's right."

"And the first one, that's a compound job, if you know what I mean. There's really nine *separate* jobs in the first one."

"Well, that's a bit of an exaggeration, isn't it?"

"How is it an exaggeration? By my count, nine is nine."

"You wouldn't have to do all nine at the same time."

"But you want them timed to go *off* at the same time, don't you?"

"Yes, of course."

"Or at least *approximately* the same time."

"Within an hour or so, yes. I don't care about the specific hour or minute."

"But all of them on January second, right?"

"Yes."

"Well, who knows what I'll be doin' next year? You're talkin' months ahead here. I was thinkin' I might go down to Miami right after Christmas."

"Well, that's up to you, of course. I thought you might be interested in picking up a quick ten thousand, but if you're not . . ."

"I didn't say I'm not interested. Would I be here if I wasn't interested? I'm saying you're talking low, is all. Especially for the second one. The second one's gonna be risky, all them fuckin' cops up there. Not to mention this'll be three days after the *first* one so they're gonna be on their guard, you know what I mean?"

"I'm not sure you understand," the Deaf Man said. "You won't be anywhere *near* the place when . . ."

"I understand, I understand, you want this all done in advance, I understand that. What I'm saying is after the *first* one they might start snooping around, they'll uncover what I done, they might get onto me somehow."

"How?"

"I don't know how. I'm only saying."

"I hardly think there's any likelihood of that."

"Well, with cops you never know. Also I may have to use a complicated timer. Something like what they used in the Thatcher bombing—something I can set at least a week in advance."

"Will you be using timers on the cars as well?"

"That depends. Does this have to happen during the daytime? Or can it be at night? The cars, I mean."

"That's irrelevant. So long as it's January second."

"And do they have to be totaled?"

"No, that's not important either."

"Well then, maybe I can use a five-pound charge. A

charge that size'll open all your doors, your hood, and your trunk and give you a pretty decent wreck. The IRA's been using hundred-pound, even two-hundred-pound charges for their car bombs, but we don't need anything that showy, huh? What they do, they fill their bombs with a mixture of chemical fertilizer and diesel fuel, which I don't like 'cause it's hard to detonate—you need a gun-cotton priming charge or else a few sticks of gelignite to set it off. What I was thinking, I figured a five-pound charge of dynamite would do the job very nice indeed. And if you don't care whether it's day or night, I think I know how I can detonate without a timer. But, for the other, you want a *fire* . . ."

"Exactly."

"Well, that's my point. I'll have to figure on an explosion that'll touch *off* a fire. What's in our favor, this is an old building we're dealing with here, it should go up pretty fast, your old wood and plaster. If I use napalm—which I ain't sure I'll be using yet—I can make it myself, put together the soap chips and the gasoline, make the jelly, you understand? That's if I . . ."

"You can make that yourself?"

"Oh, sure, if I decide to go the napalm route. All you need is your raw materials and a double boiler. Trouble with napalm, it don't like a delay time of more than an hour, 'specially in a hot room. Your gasoline evaporates. Also with napalm they can sometimes smell the gasoline, which is a tip-off. I gotta see. *Whatever* I use, I'm gonna have to figure a small explosion that'll touch off the incendiary, you understand? That's 'cause I'll be working with a timer, you understand? Think of it as a spark first, then an explosion, and *then* your fire. But what I'm saying, the second job ain't as easy as it looks. Even getting *in* there won't be . . ."

"There'll be no problem about getting in."

"That's provided you get me those maps."

"I already *have* the maps," the Deaf Man said. "Believe me, it's all very simple."

"Everything's simple to you," Gopher said, and smiled.

"Yes," the Deaf Man said. "If you choose the right people, everything's simple."

"For the right people," Gopher said, "you've got to pay the right money."

"How much do you want?" the Deaf Man asked.

"Dennis, I'll level with you," Gopher said. "The first job is risky as hell because there's nine of them and because of the proximity. It's not like I'll be working in some empty lot someplace. I'm gonna be right behind the fuckin' *police* station!"

"*Authorized* to work there."

"Sure, if these papers of yours pass muster."

"They will."

"Who's doing these papers for you?"

"You don't need to know that."

"It's my ass, not yours. They smell fish on those papers, the jig's up right that minute."

"All right, I'll grant you that. Someone who once worked for the CIA is preparing the papers for me."

"What *kind* of work for the CIA?"

"He was in their Documents Section.

"Phony passports and such?"

"Phony *everything.*"

"So, okay, I'll take your word for the papers."

"Which should calm any fears you have about the risk factor."

"It's *still* risky, papers or not. I can't do nine fuckin' cars in a single day."

"Why not?"

" 'Cause it's not that simple. I'm not talking about the wiring. If I do what I'm figuring on doing, it'll take me two minutes to wire each car. But the charge itself, there'll be nine five-pound charges, and I can't go in with a load like that without somebody noticing. Well, wait a minute, if I do what I'm figuring on doing, I'll *have* to do them all the same day. Yeah. I'll have to plan on making a few trips back to the truck. Yeah. So, okay, it's a day's work is all. But still, there'll be cops comin' and goin' all the time. All it takes is for one of them to ask me what the fuck I'm doin'."

"In which case you show the papers again."

"And pray he don't smell a rat."

The Deaf Man sighed.

"Listen, Den, I'm sorry all to hell, believe me. But like I said, this is my ass we're talkin' about."

"I asked you how much you wanted. I still haven't got an answer."

"For the first job, the nine cars. I want seventy-five hundred."

"And the second job?"

"That's the toughest one, *whatever* you think. I want ten grand for that one."

"So you're asking for seventeen-five total."

"Seventeen-five, right."

"I came here prepared to pay you ten."

"What can I tell you, Den? You were thinkin' too low."

"You've almost doubled the price."

"You can always look somewhere else. No harm done, we drink our wine, we shake hands and say good-bye."

"I'll give you a flat fifteen, take it or leave it."

"Make it sixteen, and we've got a deal."

"No. Fifteen is all I can afford."

"You're getting me cheap."

"Is it a deal?"

"It's a deal. Five up front, five when I'm done on the inside, another five when the cars are wired."

"You're robbing me blind," the Deaf Man said, but he was smiling. He had come here with an offer of ten, but had not expected to get off for less than thirty.

The man reached across the table and shook hands.

"When can you start?" the Deaf Man asked.

"As soon as you get me the maps and the papers and all the other shit. Also I want to look it over first, make sure I ain't steppin' into a lion's den. One question."

"Yes?"

"Why do you want this thing done? I mean . . ."

"Let's say it's personal," the Deaf Man said.

The Carella house in Riverhead was a huge white elephant they'd picked up for a song shortly after Teddy Carella gave birth to the twins. At about the same time, Teddy's father presented them with a registered nurse as a month-long gift while Teddy was getting her act together, and Fanny Knowles had elected to stay on with them at a salary they could afford, telling them she was tired of carrying bedpans for sick old men.

A lot of cops ribbed Carella about Fanny. They told him they didn't know any other cop on the force who was rich enough to have a housekeeper, even one who had blue hair and wore a pince-nez. They said he had to be on the take. Carella admitted that being able to afford live-in help was decidedly difficult these days; the numbers boys in Riverhead were always so late paying off. Actually Fanny was worth her weight—a hundred and fifty pounds—in pure gold. She ran the house with all the tenderness of a Marine Corps drill sergeant, and she was fond of saying, "I take no shit from man nor beast," an expression the ten-year-old twins had picked up when they were learning to talk and which Mark now used with more frequency than April. In fact, the twins' speech patterns—much to Carella's consternation—were more closely modeled after Fanny's than anyone else's; Teddy Carella was a deaf mute, and it was *Fanny's* voice the twins heard around the house whenever Carella wasn't home.

When the phone rang at three o'clock that Thanksgiving Day, Fanny was washing dishes in the kitchen. Her hands were soapy but she answered the phone anyway. Whenever she and Teddy were alone in the house, she *had* to answer the phone, of course. But even when Carella was home, she normally picked up because she wanted to make sure it wasn't some idiot detective calling about something that could easily wait till morning.

"Carella residence," she said.

"Yes, hello?" a woman's voice said.

"Hello?" Fanny said.

"Yes, I'm trying to get in touch with Detective Steve Carella. Have I got the right number?"

"This is the Carella residence, yes," Fanny said.

"Is there a Detective Steve Carella there?"

"Who's this, please?" Fanny said.

"Naomi Schneider."

"Is this police business, Miss Schneider?"

"Well . . . uh . . . yes."

"Are you a police officer, Miss Schneider?"

"No."

"Then what's this in reference to, please?"

It wasn't often that a civilian called here at the house, but sometimes they did, even though the number was listed in the book as "Carella, T. F.," for Theodora Franklin Carella. Not too many cops listed their home numbers in the telephone directories; this was because not too many crooks enjoyed being sent up the river, and some of them came out looking for revenge. The way things were nowadays, most of them got out ten minutes after you locked them up. These days, when you threw away the key, it came back at you like a boomerang.

"I'd rather discuss it with him personally," Naomi said.

"Well, he's finishing his dinner just now," Fanny said. "May I take a message?"

"I wonder if you could interrupt him, please," Naomi said.

"I'd rather not do that," Fanny said. "They're just having their coffee. If you'll give me your number . . ."

"They?" Naomi said.

"Him and Mrs. Carella, yes."

There was a long silence on the line.

"His mother, do you mean?" Naomi asked.

"No, his wife. Miss Schneider, he'll be back in the office tomorrow if you'd like to . . ."

"Are you sure I have the right number?" Naomi said. "The Detective Carella I have in mind isn't married."

"Well, this one is," Fanny said. She was beginning to get a bit irritated.

"Detective *Steve* Carella, right?" Naomi said.

"Yes, Miss, that's who lives here," Fanny said. "If you'd like to give me a number where he can reach you . . ."

"No, never mind," Naomi said. "Thank you."

And hung up.

Fanny frowned. She replaced the receiver on the wall hook, dried her hands on a dish towel, and went out into the dining room. She could hear the television set down the hallway turned up full blast, the twins giggling at yet another animated cartoon; Thanksgiving Day and all you got was animated cats chasing animated mice. Carella and Teddy were sitting at the dining room table, finishing their second cups of coffee.

"Who was that?" Carella asked.

"Somebody wanting a Detective Steve Carella," Fanny said.

"Well, who?"

"A woman named Naomi Schneider."

"What?" Carella said.

"Got the wrong Carella," Fanny said, and looked at him. "The one she wanted ain't married."

Teddy was reading her lips. She looked at Carella questioningly.

"Did you get a number?" he asked. "Did she leave a number?"

"She hung up," Fanny said, and looked at Carella again. "You ought to tell people not to bring police business into your home," she said, and went out into the kitchen again.

Josie was only fourteen years old. That was the problem. She shouldn't have been in the park in the first place, not at one o'clock in the morning, and certainly not doing what she'd been doing. She had told her parents she'd be spending the night at Jessica Cartwright's house, which was true, but she hadn't told them that Jessica's parents didn't care *what* time Jessica came in or that she and Jessica *wouldn't* be studying for a big French exam, as she'd told them, but instead would be out with two seventeen-year-old boys.

Seventeen-year-old boys were exciting.

Actually *all* boys were exciting.

She and Jessica and the two boys had gone to a movie and then Eddie—who was the boy Jessica had fixed her up with—suggested that they take a little stroll in the park, it being such a nice night and all. This was back in October, when the weather was acting so crazy and you could walk around in just a skirt and sweater, which was what Josie was wearing that night. October twenty-fourth, a Monday night. She remembered the date because the French exam wasn't until Wednesday, actually, the twenty-sixth, and she and Jessica *really* planned to study for it on Tuesday, but at *her* house instead of Jessica's. She also remembered the date because of what she had seen in the park.

Josie hadn't wanted to go into the park at all because if you were born and raised in this city, you knew that Grover Park after dark was like a cage of wild animals, which if you walked into it you could get chewed to bits, or even raped, which she supposed was worse, maybe. But Eddie said *this* part of the park was safe at night, which was probably true. In this city the neighborhoods changed abruptly. You could walk up Grover Avenue past buildings with awnings and doormen and security guards—like the building Jessica lived in—and then two blocks farther uptown you were all at once in a neighborhood with graffiti all over the buildings and minority groups hanging around in doorways because they were collecting welfare and didn't want to work. That was what her father told her when he explained why he was voting for Ronald Reagan. "Too many spics and niggers getting welfare," he'd said. Josie didn't know about that, but she thought Ronald Reagan was cute.

So what they did after the movie, they went into the park the way Eddie had suggested. This was around midnight, a little before midnight, and the park entrance they used was a few blocks *downtown* from Jessica's building, which meant this was still a safe neighborhood. Also there was a service road to the right of the entrance, and you could always see parks department trucks parked in there, so it had to be pretty safe if the city parked trucks there overnight. Farther *uptown,* where the police station was, the neighborhood was awful, and if you left your car parked on the street, you'd come back in the morning and find everything gone but the steering wheel. But Eddie promised they wouldn't be going anywhere *near* there; he knew some good spots right here near the service road.

He really knew a lot of things, Eddie. Well, seventeen, you know.

He knew, for example, that what you did, you found a spot that was *dark* but that was also near a *light.* The marauders in this city, they didn't like lights. Darkness was very good for marauders. "That's 'cause all of them are niggers," her father said. "They blend in nice." She didn't know about that, but she thought Eddie was awfully cute, the way he led the four of them past the service road, where she could see a truck parked at the end of it, and then along the path where the lampposts were spaced maybe fifteen, twenty feet apart, and then started climbing up onto a sort of bedrock shelf that had trees around it and was dark, but from which you could still see the path with the lights on it.

It was such a nice night.

Almost like springtime.

She couldn't get over it. She kept telling Eddie she couldn't get over how mild it was for October, almost the end of October.

She didn't even know where Jessica and Aaron—that was the other boy's name—went, they just disappeared in the bushes someplace.

Eddie spread his jacket on the ground for her.

It was very dark there on the rock.

This was now maybe ten after twelve, around then.

Lying on her back, she could look up through the yellowing leaves of the trees and see millions and millions of stars. Eddie told her all those stars were *suns,* he was so smart, Eddie. He had his hand inside her sweater when he told her that all those suns up there maybe had planets rotating around them, that maybe they were solar systems like our own, that maybe there were people like us up there, millions of light-years away, who were in a park just like this one, that maybe there was a green guy with lizard skin, trying to take off a green girl's bra, which was what he was trying to do with Josie's bra. She helped him unclasp it. Boys, even seventeen-year-old boys, could be very smart about a lot of things, but when it came to unhooking a bra they sometimes had trouble.

He started touching her breasts, and kissing them, and wondering out loud if the green girls up there had only *two* breasts—he called them "breasts," which she liked, and not "tits"—like the girls here on earth, or did they have *four* of them or how*ever* many—the mind boggled when you began thinking about alien life. He wondered, also, if the green guys up there on a planet millions and millions of light years away had a penis—he called it "penis" and not "cock," which she also liked—same as the guys on earth, or did they maybe ask a girl to grab hold of their nose or their armpit or maybe one of their *horns,* if they had horns, maybe they found *that* thrilling, you know?

"Would you like to grab hold of *my* penis?" he asked.

Well, one thing led to another, you know—he was really very experienced, Eddie—and it must have been around one in the morning when he showed her how to take him in her mouth, which she much preferred to going all the way since she didn't want to get pregnant and have to have an abortion, which her father said Ronald Reagan would do away with damn soon, you could bet on *that,* young lady. She had her head in his lap and was doing it the way he told her to do it when she heard the sound of an engine on the service road. She lifted her head to see if it was a parks department truck, but he whispered, "No, don't stop," and so she kept doing it, not liking very much that he had his hand on the back of her head and was pushing down on it because, as much as she thought this was better than getting pregnant, she sure as hell didn't want to *choke*. He had told her he wouldn't come in her mouth, but of course he did, and she was trying to decide whether she should swallow it or spit it out when she saw the man on the path.

He was very tall and very blond.

He was carrying a naked woman.

The naked woman was draped over his shoulder, like a sack.

The naked woman looked very white in the moonlight.

The man walked right past the rock ledge they were sitting on, five feet below them, no more than that. As he carried the girl under the lamppost, Josie saw blood at the back of the girl's head where her long blond hair was hanging downward.

Then the man moved past the lamppost and into the darkness, and all Josie could hear was the sound of leaves crunching under his feet as he disappeared.

"Did you see that?" she whispered.

In her excitement she had swallowed instead of spitting.

"That was terrific," Eddie said. "Where'd you learn to do that?" He seemed to have forgotten that *he* had taught her how to do that.

"Did you see that *guy?*" Josie said.

"What guy?" Eddie said.

"That guy with the . . . didn't you *see* him?"

"No, my eyes were closed," Eddie said.

"Holy shit, he had a dead girl over his shoulder!"

"Yeah?" Eddie said.

"You mean you didn't *see* him?"

"I saw stars," Eddie said, and grinned.

"Let's get out of here," she said, and got to her feet, and wiped the back of her hand across her mouth, and clasped her bra, and pulled down her sweater, and then whispered into the darkness, "Jessica?"

Before they left the park, she forced the others to walk

up the service road with her to where a blue Buick was parked behind the parks department truck. She looked at the license plate and read the number on it again and again, repeating it out loud until she'd memorized it. That was when she still thought she might go to the police and tell them what she had seen. That was before she realized that if she went to the police, she would also have to tell them she'd been in the park at one in the morning, doing something she shouldn't have been doing, which would have been bad enough even *without* swallowing it.

That was a month ago.

She hadn't seen anything on television about the dead lady in the park.

Maybe she'd imagined it.

She did not think she'd imagined it.

Standing outside the police station now, looking at the green globes with the white numerals 87 on each of them, she thought, *My father'll kill me.*

But the girl in the park was *already* dead.

She took a deep breath and climbed the precinct steps.

# 7

CARELLA GOT TO THE SQUADROOM FORTY
minutes after Hawes called him. Officially the homicide in
the park was his and Brown's, and Hawes had called them
both at home the moment Josie Sears came into the office
with her story. She was only fourteen years old, and the
law specified that juveniles could not be interviewed or
interrogated anywhere in the proximity of adult offenders.
Hawes had talked to her initially in Lieutenant Byrnes's
empty office. That was where Carella found them at ten
minutes to four that Thanksgiving Day.

Hawes looked like a sunset against the gunmetal gray of
the sky outside. He stood by the meshed window in the
lieutenant's corner office, his red hair streaked with white
over the left temple, a purple tie hanging on what appeared
to be a lavender shirt with a little polo pony over the left
pectoral muscle. He was dressed for his date with Annie
Rawles, for which he was already late. He had hoped to
be out of here by a quarter to four, at which time the shift
was relieved. Genero had shot out of the squadroom like a
launch from Canaveral. Hawes was stuck with a fourteen-
year-old girl who'd maybe witnessed a man carrying a body
on the night of October 24.

"So you got this now?" he asked Carella.

"I've got it."

"See you," Hawes said, and disappeared.

Carella looked at the young, dark-eyed, dark-haired girl
sitting in the chair opposite the lieutenant's desk. "I'm
Detective Carella," he said. "Detective Hawes told me on
the phone that you saw something happen in the park last
month. I wonder if . . ."

"Well, I didn't see anything *happen,* actually," Josie said.

"As I understand it, you saw a man carrying a dead body."

"Well, I guess she was dead," Josie said. She was biting the cuticles on her right hand. Carella squelched a fatherly urge to tell her to quit doing that.

"Can you tell me what you *did* see?" he asked gently.

"This man parked his car on the service road . . ."

"You saw him parking his car?"

"No, but I heard the car come in, and then the engine went off."

"Go ahead."

"And then he walked past us on the . . ."

She stopped suddenly.

"Yes?"

"We were on this sort of rock. Above the path," Josie said.

"Who?" Carella said. "You and who?"

"Me and this boy."

"I see. What time was this, Josie?"

"Around one o'clock."

"One o'clock in the morning?"

"Well, yeah."

"Go on."

"And this man came by," Josie said, and shrugged.

"What did he look like, this man?"

"He was tall and blond."

"Was he wearing a hearing aid?"

"I don't know. I didn't see any hearing aid."

Of all the detectives on the squad Carella and Willis were the only ones who'd ever seen the Deaf Man face to face. Willis had glimpsed him only fleetingly, in the midst of a shoot-out in the back of a tailor shop. But Carella had remembered him from their *first* meeting . . .

*The Deaf Man turning from the hi-fi unit against the living room wall, Carella seeing the hearing aid in his right ear and then the shotgun in his hands. And suddenly*

*it was too late, suddenly the shotgun exploded into sound.
Carella whirled away from the blast. He could hear the
whistling pellets as they screamed across the confined space
of the apartment, and then he felt them lash into his shoulder like a hundred angry wasps, as he fired a shot at the
tall blond man who was already sprinting across the apartment toward him. His shoulder felt suddenly numb. He
tried to lift the hand with the gun and quickly found he
couldn't and just as quickly shifted the gun to his left hand
and triggered off another shot, high and wide as the Deaf
Man raised the shotgun and swung the stock at Carella's
head. A single barrel, Carella thought in the instant before
the stock collided with the side of his head, a single barrel,
no time to reload, and a sudden flashing explosion of rock-
eting yellow pain, slam the stock again, suns revolving, a
universe slam the stock . . .*

"Sorry I'm late," Brown said, coming into the office
and closing the door behind him.

"This is my partner, Detective Brown," Carella said.
"Artie, this is Josie Sears. She was just telling me what
she saw in the park last month." He turned to Josie. "That
was on October twenty-fourth, is that right?"

"Well, the twenty-fifth, actually," she said. "It was one
o'clock in the morning, you know."

"Right," Carella said. "And this tall blond man you
just described . . ."

"Was he wearing a hearing aid?" Brown asked at once.

"I didn't see any," Josie said. She was looking at
Brown, remembering all the things her father had said
about niggers and wondering if he was a genuine detective. She didn't want to be telling any nigger about what
she and Eddie had been doing when she saw the man
carrying the body. She hoped they wouldn't ask her what
she and Eddie had been doing.

"What was he doing?" Carella asked.

For a panicky moment she thought he was referring to
Eddie. Then she realized he meant the man she'd seen.

"He was carrying a girl over his shoulder," Josie said.

"What color was she?" Brown asked.

"White," Josie said, and wondered if that was a trick question.

"What color hair did she have?" Brown asked.

"Blond."

"How old would you say she was?" Carella asked.

"I don't know."

"But you called her a girl."

"Well, yeah. I mean, she didn't look like a *lady,* if that's what you mean. Not like my *mother* or anything."

"How old is your mother?" Carella asked.

"Thirty-eight," Josie said.

He almost sighed. "And this woman was younger than that?" he asked.

"Yeah."

"Can you estimate how old she was?"

"Well, in her twenties, I guess. I only had that glimpse of her when they passed the light."

"How far away from you were they? This man and woman."

"Five feet, something like that."

"You were *where?*" Brown asked.

"On this rock. Above the path."

"Doing what?" Brown asked.

Here we go, Josie thought.

"Sitting with this boy," she said.

"What boy?"

"A boy I know."

"What's his name?"

"Eddie."

"Eddie what?"

"Hogan."

"Did he see this man, too? This man carrying a woman over his shoulder?"

"No, he . . . he didn't see her."

"He was sitting with you, wasn't he?" Brown asked.

"Yes, but . . ."

"Both of you five feet from where the man . . ."

"His eyes were closed," Josie said.

"Eddie's eyes?"

"Yes."

"Was he sleeping?"

"No, but his eyes were closed."

Josie looked away. Brown looked at Carella. Carella nodded almost imperceptibly.

"So you're the only one who saw this man carrying the woman," he said.

"Yes."

"And you say you guess she was dead. What made you think that?"

"There was blood at the back of her head."

"Where?"

"Right here," Josie said, and lifted her hair and touched the nape of her neck.

"You saw blood?"

"Yes."

"At the back of her head?"

"Yes. Her head was hanging down, you know? He was carrying her over his shoulder with her head hanging down. And her hair was hanging, too, and I could see blood at the back of her head."

"Then what?"

"Well, he just kept walking. I mean, I didn't see him after that."

"Where was this?" Brown asked. "What part of the park?"

"You know where the service road is?" Josie said. "Near Macomber?"

"Yes?"

"Right near there. The entrance there. We were a little bit past the service road. That's how come I heard the car when it drove in."

"Did Eddie hear the car?"

"I don't think so."

"Didn't hear the car, didn't see the man."

"No."

"But he wasn't sleeping."

"No, he was awake."

*Wide* awake, she thought, and remembered the salty taste in her mouth.

"So you were near the Macomber Street service road," Carella said.

"Yes."

"About ten blocks west of here."

"Well, whatever."

"When the man walked off, did he head in *this* direction? Or did he go west?"

"What do you mean?"

"Was he heading *toward* the police station here or *away* from it?"

"Toward it."

"What did you do then?"

"Well, I yelled to Jessica . . ."

"Who's Jessica?" Brown asked.

"My girlfriend. She was with another boy."

"Same place?"

"Well, I don't know where exactly. But nearby."

"Did *she* see this man?"

"No."

"Did her boyfriend?"

"No."

"Okay, you yelled to Jessica . . ."

"Yes, and we went to look at the car. The one that came in the service road."

"You saw the car?" Carella said.

"Yes. A blue car. Eddie said it was a Buick Century."

"Did you happen to look at the license plate?"

"I did."

"Would you happen to remember . . . ?"

"WL-seven," Josie said, "eight-one-six-four."

Brown and Carella looked at each other in surprise.

"Are you sure that's the number?" Carella asked.

"Positive."

"You wrote it down?" Brown asked.

"I memorized it," Josie said.

"Smart girl," Carella said, and smiled.

It was beginning to snow lightly.

Naomi stood under the lamppost across the street from the old house and wondered for perhaps the tenth time whether she should go in or not. Her shrink, whom she used to see three years ago, would have said she was conflicted. That had been one of Dr. Hammerstein's favorite words, "conflicted." If she couldn't decide between the vanilla or the chocolate ice cream, that was because she was conflicted. She once protested about his use of the word "conflicted," and he said, "Good, ve are making progress." That wasn't what he'd really said, he didn't even have a German accent. But Naomi always *thought* of him as having a German accent.

The house across the street looked cozy and warm.

Well, Thanksgiving.

The reason Naomi felt conflicted was because she didn't want to lay this heavy stuff on this bastard Carella's wife, but at the same time nobody should have the right to do to her what he'd done to her, which she wouldn't have let him do if she'd known he was married, which he'd lied about. A cop, no less! A *detective!* Lying to her, taking advantage of her, doing disgusting things to her, and then not even calling her again. She'd called every damn Carella in the Isola phone book and had come down to six Carellas in the Riverhead directory before she'd struck pay dirt earlier today with T. F. Carella. Who the hell was T. F. Carella? Was Steve even his right name? She'd never have gone to bed with somebody who didn't even give a person his right name. A married man. She'd never have gone to bed with a married man who'd picked her up in a bar. Well, maybe she would have. Isadora Wing went to bed with married men, didn't she? That wasn't the point. This wasn't a question of her *own* morality here, this was a question of whether a man sworn to uphold the laws of the city, state, and nation should be allowed to get away with not calling up a person after the person had allowed him to do such things to her. You weren't even supposed to take your gun out of your *holster* without justification, were you? No less what *he* had done with it.

She could imagine telling that to Hammerstein.

Ja? Dot is very inner-estink. Are you avare vot a symbol der gun is?

She wondered what Hammerstein was doing these days, the crazy old bastard.

Conflicted, she thought, and started across the street toward the house.

The snow was sticking. She shouldn't have come all the way up here. If the snow got really bad, it would raise hell with mass transit. Well, some things simply had to be done. One thing she'd learned about being conflicted was that if you took action, the confliction disappeared. Better you than me, Steve, she thought, and knocked on the door.

A short fat lady with blue hair answered it.

Is *this* his wife? Naomi thought. No wonder he picks up girls in bars.

"Yes?" the woman said.

"I'm looking for Steve Carella," Naomi said.

"I'm sorry, he's not here just now," the woman said.

"He was here an hour and a half ago," Naomi said. "He was here having coffee with his wife."

The woman studied her more closely.

"Are you the person who called here?" she asked.

"I'm the person who called here," Naomi said. "I'm Naomi Schneider. Are you his wife?"

"No, I'm not his . . ."

Another woman appeared suddenly behind her. Dark eyes and hair the color of a raven's wing, good breasts and legs, an inquisitive look on her face. God, she's *gorgeous!* Naomi thought. Why is that son of a bitch fooling around?

"Mrs. Carella?" she asked.

The woman nodded.

"I'm Naomi Schneider," she said. "I'd like to talk to you about your husband. May I come in?"

The other woman was studying her mouth as she spoke. All at once, Naomi realized she was deaf. Oh God, she thought, what am I doing here? But the woman was gesturing her into the house.

She stepped inside.

I'm going to bring this house down around your ears, Steve, she thought, and followed the woman into the living room.

The man from Motor Vehicles got back to them not ten minutes after they'd called.

"Blue Buick Century," he said, "tag number WL-seven, eight-one-six-four. Registered to a Dr. Harold Lasser, One-twenty-seven Hall Avenue."

"One-twenty-seven . . ." Carella repeated, writing.

"This is marked with an 'Auto' flag," the man from Motor Vehicles said. "May have been recovered by now, I don't know. You'd better check with them."

"Thanks," Carella said.

Teddy listened motionless as Naomi told her all about the man she'd met in a bar some three weeks ago, a man she claimed was Steve Carella. Detective Carella had told her he was not married. They had gone to her apartment afterward. Naomi detailed all the things they had done together in her apartment, her eyes unflinching, the words spilling soundlessly from her lips. They had spent the entire weekend together. He had told her he wanted her to go to work on Monday morning without anything under her . . .

Teddy held up her hand. Not *quite* like a traffic cop, but with much the same effect. She rose, crossed the room to a rolltop desk standing near a Tiffany-type floor lamp, and took from it a pencil and pad. She walked back to where Naomi was sitting.

On the pad she wrote: *Are you sure the name was Detective Stephen Louis Carella?*

"He didn't give me his full name," Naomi said. "He just said Steve Carella."

*Did he say where he worked?* Teddy wrote.

Naomi began talking again.

Teddy watched her lips.

The man—she kept referring to him as "your *husband*"—had told her he worked uptown at the Eight-Seven, right across the street from Grover Park. He'd told her he was working a homicide he'd caught on the twenty-fifth of October. Dead woman in the park, about your age, he'd said.

"I'm twenty-five," Naomi said, a challenging look on her face.

Told her the woman had been shot in the back of the head. Totally naked, not a stitch on her. Not much to go on, he'd told her, but we're working on it.

*How can she know all this?* Teddy wondered.

On the pad she wrote: *When was this?*

"November fourth," Naomi said. "A Friday night. He left on Monday morning, the seventh. When I went to work that morning—does your husband ask *you* to run around naked under your dress? Does he tie *you* to the bed and stick his goddamn . . ."

Teddy held up the traffic-cop hand again. She rose and went to the desk again. She picked up her appointment calendar. On Friday night, November 4, she and Carella had had dinner with Bert Kling and his girlfriend, Eileen. They had talked about the plastic surgery Eileen was considering. It had been painful for Eileen to discuss the scar a rapist had put on her left cheek. On Saturday, November 5, she and Carella had taken the kids to see a magic show downtown. On Saturday, November 6, they had gone to visit Carella's parents. She went back to where Naomi was sitting. On the pad she wrote, *Please wait,* and then went down the hall to fetch Fanny.

* * *

The man at Auto Theft said, ''This vehicle is still missing, Carella.''

''When was it stolen?'' Carella asked.

''We got it down for October twenty-third.''

''From what location?''

''Outside the doctor's office. One-twenty-seven Hall.''

''What time?''

''Six P.M. Well, that's when he discovered it was missing. He was going home from work, thought at first it might've been towed away by *us*. He had it parked in a no-parking zone. He called Traffic, they told him they hadn't towed his fuckin' car away, and he shouldn't have parked it in a no-parking zone to begin with. He told them he was an M.D. Big deal. They told him to call Auto, which is what he done. Anyway it ain't been recovered yet.''

''Thanks,'' Carella said.


''Mrs. Carella would like me to translate for her,'' Fanny said. She looked at Naomi sternly, her arms folded across her ample bosom. ''Save a lot of time that way.''

''Fine,'' Naomi said, looking just as stern.

Teddy's fingers moved.

Fanny watched them and then said, ''This man who picked you up wasn't my husband.''

''*Your* husband?'' Naomi said, looking suddenly puzzled.

''Mrs. *Carella's* husband,'' Fanny said. ''I'm translating exactly what she signs.''

Teddy's fingers were moving again.

''My husband and I were together on the weekend you're talking about,'' Fanny said.

''You're trying to protect him,'' Naomi said directly to Teddy.

Teddy's fingers moved.

''What did this man look like?'' Fanny asked.

''He was tall and blond . . .''

Watching Teddy's hands, Fanny said, ''My husband has brown hair.''

"What color eyes does he have?" Naomi asked.

"Brown," Fanny said, ahead of Teddy's fingers.

Naomi blinked. She realized all at once that she couldn't remember what color his eyes were. Damn it, what color were his *eyes?* "Does he wear a hearing aid?" she asked in desperation.

This time Teddy blinked.

"No, he doesn't wear no damn hearing aid," Fanny said, though Teddy hadn't signed a thing. "You've got the wrong man. Now what I suggest you do is get out of here before I . . ."

Teddy was signing again. Very rapidly. Fanny could hardly keep up.

"This man you met is a criminal," Fanny said, translating. "My husband will want to talk to you. Will you please wait here for him? We'll call him at once."

Naomi nodded.

She suddenly felt as if she were in a spy novel.

Carella did not get back to the house until six that night.

Naomi Schneider was still waiting there for him. Fanny had brought her a cup of tea, and she was sitting in the living room, her legs crossed, chatting with Teddy as Fanny translated, the two of them behaving like old college roommates, Teddy's hands and eyes flashing, her face animated.

Naomi thought Carella was very good-looking, and wondered immediately if he fooled around. She was happy when Teddy excused herself to see how the children were doing. Twins, she explained with her hands as Carella translated. A boy and a girl. Mark and April. Ten years old. Naomi listened with great interest, thinking a good-looking man like this, burdened with a handicapped wife and a set of twins, probably *did* play around a little on the side. She waited for Fanny to leave the room, grateful when she did. She was going to enjoy telling the *real* Steve Carella all about what the *fake* Steve Carella had done to her. She wanted to see the expression on his face when she told him.

The real Steve Carella didn't want to know what the fake Steve Carella had done to her.

Instead he started questioning her like a detective.

Which he was, of course, but even so.

"Tell me exactly what he looked like," he said.

"He was tall and . . ."

"*How* tall?"

"Six-one, six-two?"

"Weight?"

"A hundred and eighty?"

"Color of his eyes?"

"Well, actually I don't remember. But he did terrible things to . . ."

"Any scars or tattoos?"

"I didn't see any," Naomi said. "Not anywhere on his body." She lowered her eyes like a maiden, the way she had learned in her magazines.

"Did he say where he lived?"

"No."

"What was he wearing?"

"Nothing."

"Nothing?"

"Oh, I thought you meant when he was doing all those . . ."

"When you met him."

"A gray suit," she said. "Sort of a nubby fabric. An off-white shirt, a dark blue tie. Black shoes. A gold Rolex watch, *all* gold, not the steel and gold one. A gun in a shoulder holster. He used the gun to . . ."

"What kind of gun?"

"A Colt Detective Special."

"You know guns, do you?"

"That's what he told me it was. This was just before he . . ."

"And you met him where?"

"In a bar near where I work. I work for CBS. On Monday morning, when I went to work, he forced me to . . ."

"What's the name of the bar?"

"The Corners."

"Where is it?"

"On Detavoner and Ash. On the corner there."

"Do you go there a lot?"

"Oh, every now and then. I'll probably drop by there tomorrow after work." She raised one eyebrow. "You ought to check it out," she said.

"Had you ever seen him in that bar before?"

"Never."

"Sure about that?"

"Well, I would have noticed. He was very good-looking."

"Did he seem familiar with the neighborhood?"

"Well, we didn't discuss the neighborhood. What we talked about mostly, he gave me sixty seconds to finish my drink, you see, because he was in such a hurry to . . ."

"Did you get the impression he knew the neighborhood well?"

"I got the feeling he knew his way around, yes."

"Around that particular neighborhood?"

"Well, the city. I got the feeling he knew the city. When we were driving toward my apartment later, he knew exactly how to get there."

"You drove there in his car?"

"Yes."

"What kind of car?"

"A Jaguar."

"He was driving a Jaguar?"

"Yes."

"You didn't find that surprising? A detective driving a Jaguar?"

"Well, I don't know any detectives," she said. "You're only my second detective. My *first,* as a matter of fact, since he wasn't a real detective, was he?"

"What year was it?"

"What?"

"The Jag."

"Oh. I don't know."

"What color?"

"Gray. A four-door sedan. Gray with red leather uphol-stery."

"I don't suppose you noticed the license plate number."

"No, I'm sorry, I didn't. I was sort of excited, you see. He was a very exciting man. Of course, later, when he started doing all those things to me . . ."

"And you say he knew how to get there? From the bar on Detavoner and Ash to where you live?"

"Oh, yes."

"Where *do* you live, Miss Schneider?"

"On Colby and Radner. Near the circle there. If you'd like to come over later, I can show you . . ."

"Did you ask him for any sort of identification? A shield? An ID card?"

"Well, when he was undressing, I said, 'Let me see your badge.' But I was just kidding around, you know. It never occurred to me that he might not be a real detective."

"*Did* he show you a badge?"

"Well, what he said was, '*Here's* my badge, baby.' And showed me his . . . you know."

"You simply accepted him as a cop, is that right?"

"Well . . . yeah. I'd never met a cop before. Not so-cially. Of course, *you* must meet a lot of young, attractive women in your line of work, but I've never had the op-portunity to . . ."

"Did he say anything about coming *back* to that bar? The Corners?"

"No, he just said he'd call me."

"But he never did."

"No. Actually I'm glad he didn't. Now that I know he wasn't a real detective. And, also, I might never have got to meet you, you know?"

"Miss Schneider," Carella said, "if he *does* call you, I want you to contact me at once. Here's my card," he said, and reached into his wallet. "I'll jot down my home num-ber, too, so you'll have it . . ."

"Well, I already know your home number," she said, but he had begun writing.

"Just so you'll have it handy," he said, and gave the card to her.

"Well, I doubt if he'll call me," she said. "It's already three weeks, almost."

"Well, in case he does."

He looked suddenly very weary. She had an almost uncontrollable urge to reach out and touch his hair, smooth it back, comfort him. She was certain he would be very different in bed than the *fake* Steve Carella had been. She suddenly wondered what it would be like to be in bed with both of them at the same time.

"How are you getting home?" he asked.

End of interview, she thought.

Or was he making his move?

"By subway," she said, and smiled at him. "Unless someone offers to drive me home."

"I'll call the local precinct," he said. "See if I can't get a car to take you down."

"Oh," she said.

"Thanksgiving Day, they might not be too busy."

He rose and started for the phone.

"Miss Schneider," he said, dialing, "I really appreciate the information you've given me."

Yeah, she thought, so why the fuck don't you come home with me?

The man who arrived at the station house at a quarter past eight that night was wearing a shabby overcoat and a dilapidated felt hat. The desk sergeant on duty looked at the envelope he handed across the muster desk, saw that it was addressed to Detective Stephen Louis Carella, and immediately said, "Where'd you get this?" The Deaf Man was famous around here. There wasn't a cop in the precinct who didn't know about those pictures hanging on the bulletin board upstairs.

"Huh?" the man said.

"Where'd you get this?"

"Guy up the street handed it to me."

"What guy?"

"Guy up the street. Blond guy with a hearing aid."

"What?" the desk sergeant said.

"You deaf, too?" the man said.

"What's your name?" the desk sergeant asked.

"Pete MacArthur. What's yours?"

"Don't get smart with me, mister," the desk sergeant said.

"What *is* this?" MacArthur said. "Guy gives me five bucks, asks me to deliver this for him, that's a crime?"

"Sit down on the bench over there," the desk sergeant said.

"What for?"

"Sit down till I tell you it's okay to go."

He picked up a phone and buzzed the squadroom. A detective named Santoro picked up the phone.

"We got another one," the desk sergeant said.

"There ain't no mail deliveries today," Santoro said.

"This one came by hand."

"Who delivered it?"

"A guy named Pete MacArthur."

"Hold him there," Santoro said.

Santoro talked to MacArthur until they were both blue in the face. MacArthur kept repeating the same thing over and over again. A tall blond guy wearing a hearing aid had handed him the envelope and offered him five bucks to deliver it here. He'd never seen the guy before in his life. He'd taken the five bucks because he figured an envelope so skinny couldn't have a bomb in it and also because it was a cold, snowy night, and he thought maybe he could find an open liquor store, even though it was Thanksgiving, and buy himself a bottle of wine. Santoro figured MacArthur was telling the truth. Only an exceedingly stupid accomplice would march right into a police station. He took his address—which happened to be a bench in Grover

Park—told him to keep his nose clean, and sent him on his way.

These days Carella's mail was everybody's mail.

Santoro took the envelope up to the squadroom and opened it.

He looked at what was inside, shrugged, and then tacked it to the bulletin board:

# 8

CARELLA HAD BEEN SHOT TWICE SINCE HE'D been a cop, one of those times by the Deaf Man. He did not want to get shot ever again. It hurt, and it was embarrassing. There was something even more embarrassing than getting shot, however, and the Deaf Man had been responsible for *that*, too.

Once upon a time, when the Deaf Man was planning a bank holdup for which he'd fairly and scrupulously prepared the Eight-Seven far in advance, two hoods jumped Carella and Teddy on their way home from the movies. The men got away with Teddy's handbag and wristwatch as well as Carella's own watch, his wallet with all his identification in it, and—most shameful to admit—his service revolver.

The most recent message from the Deaf Man depicted eleven Colt Detective Specials.

The pistol the Deaf Man had shown to Naomi Schneider had been a Colt Detective Special, probably the same one he'd photographed and then Xeroxed for his pasteup. The pistol Carella had been carrying for some little while now was *also* a Colt Detective Special. In fact, this was the pistol of choice for most of the cops on the squad.

Pinned to the bulletin board, slightly to the left of the picture of the eleven revolvers, was the picture of the six police shields.

Carella's shield and his ID card had been used during the bank job the day after they'd been stolen from him. The man who'd gone in claiming to be Detective Carella was also carrying the gun he had taken from Carella the night before.

114

Was there some connection between that long-ago theft of pistol and shield and the current messages depicting pistols and shields?

There were now seven messages in all, each posted to the bulletin board in ascending numerical order:

Two nightsticks.

Three pairs of handcuffs.

Four police hats.

Five walkie-talkies.

Six police shields.

Eight black horses.

Eleven Colt Detective Specials.

One thing Carella knew for certain about the Deaf Man was that he worked with different pickup gangs on each job, rather like a jazz soloist recruiting sidemen in the various cities on his tour. In the past any apprehended gang members did not know the true identity of their leader; he had presented himself once as L. Sordo, another time as Mort Orecchio, and—on the occasion of his last appearance—simply as Taubman. In Spanish *el sordo* meant "the Deaf Man." Loosely translated, *mort'orecchio* meant "dead ear" in Italian. And in German *der taube Mann* meant "the Deaf Man." If indeed he *was* deaf. The hearing aid itself may have been a phony, even though he always took pains to announce that he was hard of hearing. But whatever he was or whoever he was, the crimes he conceived were always grand in scale and involved large sums of money.

Nor was conceiving crimes and executing them quite enough for the Deaf Man. A key element in his M.O. was telling the police what he was going to do long before he did it. At first Carella had supposed this to be evidence of a monumental ego, but he had come to learn that the Deaf Man used the police as a sort of *second* pickup gang, larger than the nucleus group, but equally essential to the successful commission of the crime. That he had been thwarted on three previous occasions was entirely due to chance. He was *smarter* than the police, and he *used* the police, and he let the police *know* they were being used.

Knowing they were being used but not knowing *how*, knowing he was telling them a great deal about the crime but not *enough*, knowing he would do what he predicted but not *exactly*, the police generally reacted like hicks on a Mickey Mouse force. Their behavior in turn strengthened the Deaf Man's premise that they were singularly inept. Given their now-demonstrated ineffectiveness, he became more and more outrageous, more and more daring. And the bolder he became, the more they tripped over their own flat feet.

And yet, he always played the game fair.

Carella hated to think of what might happen if all at once he decided *not* to play the game fair.

What if those seven messages on the bulletin board had nothing whatever to do with the crime he was planning this time around? What if each of them taken separately had nothing to do with all of them as a whole? In short, what if he was *cheating* this time?

There seemed no question now—if ever there had been—that the man who'd dropped Elizabeth Turner's corpse in the park across the street was the Deaf Man. Josie Sears hadn't seen a hearing aid in the man's ear, but she'd described him as tall and blond. Given the circumstances, that was close enough. No cigar, but damn close.

It was also clear that someone of the same description, and definitely wearing a hearing aid this time, had passed himself off to Naomi Schneider as Detective Steve Carella of the 87th Squad.

The Deaf Man had been driving a stolen blue Buick Century on the night Josie spotted him and a gray Jaguar sedan on the night he'd driven Naomi home. Even before Carella called Auto Theft, he suspected the Jaguar had been stolen, too.

His call to Auto disclosed that a dozen Jaguars, apparently popular cars with thieves, had been stolen in this city since the beginning of November. Four of them had been sedans. One of those had been gray. It had not yet been recovered. Carella now had a license plate number for the car the Deaf Man might still be driving. *If* the same license plate was still on it. And if the car hadn't already been dumped in some empty lot in the next state.

The Deaf Man was a one-man crime wave.

But what was he up to?

What was the goddamn significance of these pictures he kept sending them? Did the numbers themselves mean something? Why all this police paraphernalia, with eight black horses thrown in for good measure?

Come on, Carella thought, play it fair. Give us a break, willya?

The next break in the case—if in retrospect it could be considered that—came on the third day of December, a Saturday. It came with a phone call from Naomi Schneider at twenty minutes past three.

"Did you just call me?" she asked Carella.

"No," he said. And then at once, "Have you heard from him again?"

"Well, somebody named Steve Carella just called me," she said.

"Did it sound like him?"

"I guess so. I've never heard his voice on the phone."

"What'd he want?"

"He said he wants to see me again."

"Did he say when?"

"Today."

"Where? Is he coming there?"

"Well, we didn't arrange anything actually. I thought I'd better call you first."

"How'd you leave it?"

"I told him I'd call him back."

"He gave you a number?"

"Yes."

"What is it?"

Naomi gave him the number.

"Stay right there," Carella said. "If he calls again, tell him you're still thinking it over. Tell him you're hurt because you haven't heard from him in such a long time."

"Well, I already told him that," Naomi said.

"You told him . . . ?"

"Well, I really *was* hurt," Naomi said.

"Naomi," Carella said, "this man is a very dangerous criminal. Don't play games with him, do you hear me? If he calls again, tell him you're still considering whether you want to see him again, and then call me here right away. If I'm not here, leave a message with one of the other detectives. Have you got that?"

"Yes, of course, I've got it. I'm not a child," Naomi said.

"I'll get back to you later," he said, and hung up. He checked his personal directory, dialed a number at Headquarters, identified himself to the clerk who answered the phone, and told her he needed an address for a telephone number in his possession. The new hotline at Headquarters had been installed because policemen all over the city had been having trouble getting information from the telephone company, whose policy was not to give out the addresses of subscribers, even if a detective said he was working a homicide. Carella sometimes felt the telephone company was run by either the Mafia or the KGB. The clerk was back on the line three minutes later.

"That number is for a phone booth," she said.

"On the street or where?" Carella asked.

"Got it listed for something called the Corners on Detavoner and Ash."

"Thank you," Carella said, and hung up. "Artie!" he yelled. "Get your hat!"

When the knock sounded on the door to Naomi's apartment, she thought it might be Carella. He had told her he'd get back to her later, hadn't he? She went to the door.

"Who is it?" she asked.

"Me," the voice said. "Steve."

It did not sound like the *real* Carella. It sounded like the *fake* Carella. And the *real* Carella had told her the *fake* Carella was a very dangerous man. As if she didn't know.

"Just a second," she said, and unlocked the door and took off the night chain.

There he was.

Tall, blond, handsome, head cocked to one side, smile on his face.

"Hi," he said.

"Long time no see," she said. She felt suddenly weak. Just the sight of him made her weak.

"Okay to come in?"

"Sure," she said, and let him into the apartment.

The Corners at three-thirty that Saturday afternoon was—thanks to the football game on the television set over the bar—actually more crowded than it would have been at the same time on a weekday. Carella and Brown immediately checked out the place for anyone who might remotely resemble the Deaf Man. There was only one blond man sitting at the bar, and he was short and fat. They went at once to the men's room. Empty. They knocked on the door to the ladies' room, got no answer, opened the door, and checked that out, too. Empty. They went back outside to the bar. Carella showed the bartender his shield. The bartender nodded.

"Tall blond man," Carella said. "Would have used the phone booth about forty minutes ago."

"What about him?" the bartender said.

"Did you see him?"

"I saw him. Guy with a hearing aid?"

"Yes."

"I saw him."

"He's been in here before, hasn't he?"

"Coupla times."

"Would you know his name?"

"I think it's Dennis, I'm not sure."

"Dennis what?"

"I don't know. He was in here with a guy one night, I heard the guy calling him Dennis."

"There's just this one room, huh?" Brown said.

"Just this one."

"No little side rooms or anything."

"Just this."

"Any other toilets? Besides the rest rooms back there?"

"That's all," the bartender said. "If you're lookin' for him, he already left."

"Any idea where he went?"

"Nope."

"Did he leave right after he made his phone call?"

"Nope. Sat at the bar for ten minutes or so, finishing his drink."

"What was he drinking?" Carella asked.

"Jim Beam and water."

Carella looked at Brown. Brown shrugged. Carella went to the phone booth and dialed Naomi Schneider's number.

"Let it ring," the Deaf Man said.

She was naked. They were on her bed. She would have let it ring even if it was the fire department calling to say the building was on fire. The phone kept ringing. Spread wide beneath him, her eyes closed, she heard the ringing only distantly, a faraway sound over the pounding of her own heart, the raging of her blood. At last the phone stopped.

All at once *he* stopped too.

"Hey," she said, "don't . . ."

"I want to talk," he said.

"Put it back in," she said.

"Later."

"Come on," she said.

"No."

"Please, baby, I'm almost there," she said. "Put it back in. Please."

He got off the bed. She watched him as he walked to the dresser, watched him as he shook a cigarette free from the package on the dresser top. He thumbed a gold lighter into flame, blew out a wreath of smoke. Everything was golden about him. Gold watch, gold lighter, golden hair, big magnificent golden . . .

"There's something we have to discuss," he said. "Something I'd like you to do for me."

"Bring it here, I'll show you what I can do for you."

"Later," he said, and smiled.

They were in the unmarked sedan, heading back toward the precinct. The heater, as usual, wasn't working. The windows were frost-rimed. Brown kept rubbing at the windshield with his gloved hand, trying to free it of ice.

"I told her to stay home," Carella said. "I specifically told her to . . ."

"We don't own her," Brown said.

"Who owns you?" the Deaf Man said.

"You do."

"Say it."

"You own me."

"Again."

"You own me."

"And you'll do anything I want you to do, won't you?"

"Anything."

"You think we ought to stop by there?" Brown asked. "It's on the way back."

"What for?" Carella said.

"Maybe she just went down for a newspaper or something."

"Pull over to that phone booth," Carella said. "I'll try her again."

The phone was ringing again.

"You're a busy little lady," the Deaf Man said.

"Shall I answer it?"

"No."

The phone kept ringing.

Carella came out of the booth and walked back to the car. Brown was banging on the heater with the heel of his hand.

"Any luck?" he asked.

"No."

"So what do you want to do?"

"Let's take a spin by there," Carella said.

"I need you on Christmas Eve," the Deaf Man said.

"I need you right now," Naomi said.

"I want you to be a very good little girl on Christmas Eve."

"I promise I'll be a very good little girl," she said, and folded her hands in her lap like an eight-year-old. "But you really owe me an apology, you know."

"I owe you nothing," he said flatly.

"I mean for not calling me all this . . ."

"For *nothing*," he said. "Don't ever forget that."

She looked at him. She nodded. She would do whatever he asked her to do, she would wait forever for his phone calls, she would never ask him for explanations or apologies. She had never met anyone like him in her life. She almost said out loud, "I'll bet you've got girls all over this city who'll do anything you want them to do," but she caught herself in time. She did not want him walking out on her. She did not want him disappearing from her life again.

"I want you to dress up for me," he said. "On Christmas Eve."

"Like a good little girl?" she said. "In a short skirt? And knee socks? And Buster Brown shoes? And white cotton panties?"

"No."

"Well, whatever," she said. "Sure."

"A Salvation Army uniform," he said.

"Okay, sure."

That might be kicks, she thought, a Salvation Army uniform. Nothing at all under the skirt. Sort of kinky. Little Goodie-Two-Shoes tambourine-beating virgin with her skirt up around her naked ass.

"Where am I supposed to get a Salvation Army uniform?" she asked.

"I'll get it for you. You don't have to worry about that."

"Sure," she said. "You know my size?"

"You can give me that before I leave."

"Leave?" she said, alarmed. "I'll *kill* you if you walk out of here without . . ."

"I'm not walking out of here. Not until we discuss this fully."

"And not until you . . ."

"Be quiet," he said.

She nodded. She had to be very careful with him. She didn't want to lose him, not ever again.

"Where do you want me to wear this uniform?" she said. "Will you be coming here?"

"No."

"Then where? Your place?"

"Uptown," he said. "Near the precinct."

"Uh-huh," she said, and looked at him. "Is that where you live? Near the precinct?"

"No, that's not where I live. That's where you'll be wearing the uniform. On the street up there. A few blocks from where I work."

"We're gonna do it on the street?" she asked, and smiled.

"You have a very evil mind," he said, and kissed her. She felt the kiss clear down to her toes. "This is a stakeout," he said. "Police work. Both of us in Salvation Army uniforms."

"Oh, *you're* gonna be wearing one, too."

"Yes."

"Sounds like fun," she said. "But what do you *really* have in mind?"

"That's what I have in mind," he said.

"A stakeout, huh?"

"Yes, a stakeout."

"Even though you're not a cop, huh?"

"What do you mean?"

"I mean, I know you're not a cop."

"I'm not, huh?"

"I know you're not Steve Carella."

He looked at her.

"And how do you know that?" he said.

" 'Cause I know the *real* Steve Carella," she said.

He kept looking at her.

"I do," she said, and nodded. "I called the station house," she said. "I called the Eighty-seventh Precinct."

"Why'd you do that?"

" 'Cause you told me you worked there."

"You spoke to someone named Carella?"

"Steve Carella, yes. In fact, I met him. Later."

"You met him," he said.

"Yes."

"And?"

"He told me you're not him. As if I didn't know. I mean, the minute I saw him I knew he wasn't . . ."

"What else did he tell you?"

"He said you're very dangerous," Naomi said, and giggled.

"I am," he said.

"Oh, I *know*," she said, and giggled again.

"And what'd you tell him?"

"Oh . . . how we met . . . and what we did . . . and like that."

"Did you tell him *where* we met?"

"Oh, sure, the Corners," she said.

He was very silent.

"What else did you tell him?" he asked at last.

A good way for a statistician to discover how many policemen are on duty in any sector of the city is to put a 10-13 call on the radio. Every cop in the vicinity will immediately respond. Sometimes even cops from other precincts will respond. That is because the 10-13 radio code means ASSIST POLICE OFFICER, and there is no higher priority.

Carella and Brown were a block from Naomi's apartment when the 10-13 erupted from the walkie-talkie on the seat between them. Neither of the men discussed or debated it. The cop in trouble was ten blocks from where they were, in the opposite direction from the one they were traveling. But Brown immediately swung the car around in a sharp U-turn, and Carella hit the siren switch.

The Deaf Man sat up straight the moment he heard the siren. Like an animal sensing danger, Naomi thought. God, he is *so* beautiful. But the siren was moving away from her street, and as it faded into the distance, he seemed to relax.

"What else did you tell him?" he asked again.

"Well . . . nothing," she said.

"Are you sure?"

"Well . . . I told him what you looked like and what you were wearing . . . he was asking me questions, you see."

"Yes, I'm sure he was. How did he react to all this information?"

"He seemed interested."

"Oh, yes, I'm sure."

"He told me to keep in touch."

"And have you kept in touch?"

"Well . . ."

"Have you?"

"Look, don't you think you should tell me who you *really* are?" she said.

"I want to know whether you and Steve Carella have kept in touch."

"He said you're a dangerous *criminal* is what he actually said. *Are* you a criminal?"

"Yes," he said. "Tell me whether you've stayed in touch."

"What kind of criminal are you?"

"A very good one."

"I mean . . . like a burglar . . . or a robber . . .
or . . ." She arched her eyebrows, the way her magazines
had taught her. "A rapist?"

"When did he tell you I was a criminal?" he asked.

"Well, when I saw him, I guess. At his house."

"Oh, you went to his house, did you?"

"Well, yeah."

"When was that?"

"On Thanksgiving Day."

"And that was when he told you I was a criminal?"

"Yes. And again today. A *dangerous* criminal is what
he . . ."

"Today?" the Deaf Man said. "You spoke to him today?"

"Well, yes, I did."

"When?"

"Right after you called. "

Four patrol cars were already angled into the curb when
Carella and Brown got to the scene. At least a dozen
patrolmen with drawn guns were crouched behind the
cover of the cars, and more patrolmen were approaching
on foot, at a run, their guns magically appearing in their
hands the moment they saw what the situation was. Again
neither Carella nor Brown discussed anything. They immediately drew their guns and stepped out of the car.

A sergeant told them a cop was inside there. "Inside
there" was a doctor's office. The cop and his partner had
responded to a simple radioed 10-10—INVESTIGATE SUSPI-
CIOUS PERSON—and had walked into the waiting room to
find a man holding a .357 Magnum in his hand. The man
opened fire immediately, missing both cops, but knocking
a big chunk of plaster out of the waiting room wall and
scaring the patients half to death. The point-cop had thrown
himself flat on the floor. The backup-cop had managed to
get out the door and radio the 10-13. The sergeant figured
the man inside there was a junkie looking for dope. Doc-

tors' offices were prime targets for junkies. Carella asked
the sergeant if he thought he needed them there. The sergeant said, "No, what I think I need here is the hostage
team."

Carella and Brown holstered their guns and went back
to the car.

The Deaf Man was putting on his clothes. Naomi
watched him from the bed.

"I didn't tell him you were coming here, if that's what's
bothering you," she said.

"Nothing's bothering me," he said.

But he was tucking the flaps of his shirt into his trousers.
He sat again, put on his socks and shoes, and then went to
the dresser for his cuff links. He put on the cuff links and
then picked up the gun in its holster. He slipped into the
harness and then came back to the chair for his jacket.

She kept watching him, afraid to say anything more. A
man like this one, you could lose him if you said too much.
Instead, she opened her legs a little wider, give him a better
look at her, he was only human, wasn't he? He went to
the closet, took his coat from a hanger, and shrugged into
it.

He walked back to the bed.

He smiled and reached under his coat, and under his
jacket, and pulled the gun from its holster.

Naomi returned his smile and spread her legs a little
wider.

"Another game with the gun?" she asked.

It took Carella and Brown five minutes to clear the immediate area around the doctor's office. The police had
cordoned off the scene, so they had to stop at the barricade
to identify themselves. It took them another ten minutes to
get uptown to Naomi's apartment.

They were twelve minutes too late.

The door to Naomi's apartment was wide open.

Naomi was lying on the bed with a bullet hole between her eyes.

The pillow under her head was very red.

Well, now they had a bullet.

The bullet had entered Naomi Schneider's skull just above the bridge of her manicured nose, and angled up slightly and exited at the back of her head, and had gone through the down pillow under her head to lodge in the mattress, where the lab technicians dug it out.

The bullet told them that the murder weapon was a Colt Detective Special—similar to any one of the eleven on the picture the Deaf Man had sent them.

But that was all they had.

And until they were in possession of an actual weapon they could test-fire for comparison purposes, the bullet was virtually useless to them.

On Monday morning, December 12, another message from the Deaf Man arrived in the mail:

They were looking at seven wanted flyers.

"Beautiful people, each and every one of them," Meyer said.

"Maybe he's telling us who the gang is," Brown said.

"He wouldn't be *that* crazy, would he?" Carella said. "To *name* them for us?"

"Why not?" Brown said. "If these guys are still loose, their pictures are in every precinct in town."

Which was just the problem.

Even before they tacked the latest message to the bulletin board, the pictures were already there. All seven of them. Plus a dozen more like them. The detectives looked at *all* the Deaf Man's messages now, marching across the bulletin board in a single, inscrutable horizontal line:

Two nightsticks. Three pairs of handcuffs. Four police hats. Five walkie-talkies. Six police shields. Seven wanted flyers. Eight black horses. Eleven Colt Detective Specials.

"What's missing?" Carella asked.

*"Everything's* missing," Brown said.

"I mean . . . there's no *one*, right? Nothing for the number one. And nothing for nine or ten either."

"Assuming he plans to stop at eleven," Meyer said. "Suppose he plans to go to twenty? Or a *hundred* and twenty? Suppose he plans to keep sending these damn things *forever?*"

"Fun is fun," Lieutenant Byrnes said, "but we happen to have two dead bodies."

He was sitting behind a desk in his corner office, the blinds open to the parking lot behind the police station. Inside the cyclone fence with its barbed wire frosting, pale December sunlight glanced off the white roofs of the patrol cars parked below. Carella thought the lieutenant looked tired. His hair seemed a bit grayer, his blue eyes a bit more faded. Am *I* going to look that way in a few years? he wondered. Is that what the job does to you? Burns you out, grinds you down to graying cinders?

"Technically," Carella said, "the Schneider murder . . ."

"It's linked, it's ours," Byrnes said flatly. "Wherever the hell it actually . . ."

"The Four-One," Carella said.

"So? Are *they* working it?"

"No, Pete. They were happy to turn it over."

"Sure. Christmas coming up . . ."

He let the sentence trail. He was thinking, Carella knew, that there'd be enough headaches ahead in the next two weeks. All the bad guys doing their Christmas shopping. The bad guys didn't need cash or credit cards or charge accounts. The bad guys only needed nimble fingers. He wondered if the bad guys ever got to look as gray and as pale as Byrnes did. Send them to jail, they complained that the swimming pool wasn't properly filtered. If you can't do the time, don't do the crime. They laughed at the old police adage and did their time standing on their heads, laughing. Came out looking healthier than when they went in, all that weight lifting in the prison gym. Came out ready to victimize again. Laughing all the way. Oh what fun it is to ride . . .

"So what've you got?" Byrnes asked.

"Nothing," Carella said.

"Don't tell me *nothing*," Byrnes said, "I'm starting to get heat on this. The cops in New York, they get a dead Harvard graduate, they wrap it in forty-eight hours. We got *two* dead girls, and you tell me *nothing*."

"Well, we know it's the Deaf Man, but . . ."

"Then find him."

"That's the trouble, Pete. We . . ."

"What's all this crap he keeps sending us? What's any of it got to do with the victims?"

"We don't know yet."

"According to this . . ." He picked up the D.D. report on his desk. "According to this, the second girl knew him, is that right?"

"Yes, sir. But only as Steve Carella. That's the name he gave her."

"Used your name."

"Yes, sir."

"Why'd she let him in that apartment? You told her he was dangerous, didn't you?"

"Yes, sir."

"So why'd she let him in? Was she crazy or something? Man like that, she lets him in her apartment?" He shook his head. "What about the first victim? Did this . . . what's her name?" He began leafing through the other D.D. reports.

"Elizabeth Turner, sir."

"Did *she* know him, too?"

"We don't know, Pete. We're assuming she did."

"Still don't know where she worked, huh?"

"No, sir."

"But you're assuming it was a bank."

"That's the line we're taking, yes."

"Which would tie in. His M.O., I mean."

"Yes."

"Maybe planning an inside job, is that what you figure?"

"Something like that."

"Use the girl."

"Yes."

"But you don't know which bank."

"We've checked them all, Pete."

"If he planned to use her, why'd he kill her?"

"We don't know."

"Same gun?"

"We don't know."

"This picture of the guns . . . the one he sent. All Colt Detective Specials, huh?"

"Yes, sir."

"And the Schneider girl was killed with a Colt Detective Special, huh?"

"Yes, sir."

"Eleven of them, huh? In the picture."

"Eleven, yes, sir."

"You think he plans to kill *eleven* girls?"

"We don't know, sir."

''What the hell *do* you know?'' Byrnes said, and then immediately said, ''I'm sorry, Steve,'' and washed his open hand over his face and sighed heavily. ''I got a call from Inspector Cassidy this morning,'' he said. ''The girl's father—the Schneider girl—her father's a big wheel at some temple in Calm's Point, he's yelling like it's the Holocaust all over again. You think there's an anti-Semitic angle here?''

''I doubt it.''

''The other girl wasn't Jewish, was she?''

''No, sir.''

''Yeah, well . . . also the Schneider girl worked for CBS, which the newspapers figure to be a glamour job . . .''

''She was a receptionist there, Pete.''

''You think he's planning a heist at CBS?''

''Well . . . I'll tell you the truth, that never occurred to us.''

''I don't know, do they have cash laying around there?''

''I doubt it.''

''Anyway, you get a girl working for a television network, the media automatically makes a big deal of it. Well, you've seen the papers, you've seen television.''

''Yes, sir.''

''What I'm saying is we're getting a lot of heat on this, Steve. From departmental rank *and* the media. I'd like to be able to tell somebody *something*. And *soon.*''

''We're doing our best, Pete.''

''Yeah, I know, I know. It's just . . . with Christmas coming . . .''

He let the sentence trail again.

# 9

CHRISTMAS WAS INDEED COMING.

And as far as Detective Lloyd Andrew Parker was concerned, it was coming too damn soon. In fact, it *started* coming sooner and sooner each year. This year the stores were already decorated for Christmas a few days before Thanksgiving. You woke up one morning, it wasn't even turkey time yet, and there was Santa Claus in the store windows.

Parker hated Christmas.

He also hated his first name. He doubted that anyone on the squad knew his first name was Lloyd. Maybe no one in the entire world knew his first name was Lloyd. He himself had almost forgotten that his first name was Lloyd. Well, maybe Miscolo in the clerical office knew because he was the one who made out the pay chits every two weeks. Lloyd was a piss-ant name. Andrew was better because Andrew was one of the twelve apostles, and anybody with a twelve-apostle name was a good guy. If you were reading a book—which Parker rarely did—and you ran across a guy named Luke, Matthew, Thomas, Peter, Paul, James, like that, you knew right off he was supposed to be a good guy. That was in books. In real life you sometimes got the scum of the earth named for apostles, criminals who'd slit your throat for a nickel.

Parker hated criminals.

He also hated being called Andy. Made him sound like fuckin' Andy Hardy or something. Little piss-ant twerp having heart-to-heart chats with his Judge Hardy father. Parker hated judges. It was judges who let criminals go free. He would have preferred being called Andrew, which

133

was his true and honorable middle name. Andrew had some respect attached to it. Andy sounded like a good old boy you patted on the back: Hey, Andy, how's it goin', Andy? Parker hated his mother for having named him, first of all, Lloyd, and then having reduced his middle name, which he'd got when he was confirmed, to Andy. Parker hated his father for not having stood up to his mother when she decided to name him first Lloyd and then Andrew. Parker was glad both his mother and his father were dead.

Parker wished Santa Claus was dead, too.

Parker wished Rudolph the Red-Nosed Reindeer would get shot some starry Christmas Eve and be served as venison steak on Christmas Day. Or, better yet, venison stew. If he heard that dumb song on the radio one more time, he would take out his pistol and *shoot* the fuckin' radio. The person Parker liked most at Christmastime was Ebenezer Scrooge. Scrooge would've made a good cop. Parker thought of himself as a good cop, but he knew most of the guys on the squad thought he was a lousy cop. He also knew they didn't like him much. Fuck 'em, he wasn't running in any fuckin' popularity contest.

The Christmas songs had started on the radio a couple of days ago, as if all the disc jockeys just couldn't *wait* to start playing them. Same old songs every year. This was only the fifteenth of December, and already he'd heard all the Christmas songs a hundred times over. "Silent Night" and "God Rest Ye Merry Gentlemen" and "Little Drummer Boy"—he wished the little drummer boy would get shot together with Rudolph the Red-Nosed Reindeer—and "The First Noel" and "Joy to the World" and "White Christmas" and "I'll Be Home for Christmas" and "Deck the Halls" and "Jingle Bells" and the worst fuckin' Christmas song ever written in the history of the world: "All I Want for Christmas Is My Two Front Teeth." If Parker ever met the guy who wrote that song, he'd give him his two front teeth all right, on a platter after he knocked them out of his mouth.

Parker hated Christmas songs.

He hated everything about this city at Christmastime.

He hated the city *all* the time, but he hated it most at Christmastime.

All those phony Santa Clauses standing on street corners ringing bells and asking for donations. All the Salvation Army piss-ants blowing trumpets and shaking tambourines. All the fake fuckin' beggars who crowded the sidewalks, guys with signs saying they were blind or deaf and dumb like Carella's wife, or guys on little trolleys with signs saying they lost their legs, all of them phonies like the phony Santa Clauses. Fuckin' phony blind man went home at night, all of a sudden he could see when he was counting the money in his tin cup. Parker hated the street musicians and the break dancers. He hated the guys selling merchandise on the sidewalks outside department stores. If he had his way, he'd lock up even the ones who had vendor's licenses, cluttering up the sidewalks that way, most of them selling stolen merchandise. Parker hated the out-of-towners who flocked to this city before Christmas. Gee, looka the big buildings, Mama. Fuckin' greenhorns, each and every one of them, cameras clicking, oohing and ahhing, prime targets for pickpockets, caused more trouble than they were worth. Suckers for all the guys driving horse-drawn carriages around Grover Park. He hated the way those guys decorated their carriages for the holidays, garlands of pine hanging all over them, wreaths, banners saying SEASONS GREETINGS, all the phony trappings of Christmas, when all they were after was the buck, the long green. Hated horses, too. All they did was shit all over the streets, make the job harder for the sanitmen. Hated the idea that there were still some horse-mounted cops in this city, more horses to shit on the city streets, had their stable right up here in the Eight-Seven, the old armory on the corner of First and Saint Sab's, saw them heading downtown each and every morning, a fuckin' parade of horses in different colors, cops sitting on them like they were a fuckin' Roman legion. Hated horses and hated mounted cops and hated tourists who should have stayed home in Elephant Shit, Iowa.

Most of all, Parker hated Alice Patricia Parker.

None of the guys on the squad knew that Parker had once been married. Fuck 'em, it was none of their business.

Around Christmastime he always wondered where Alice Patricia was. He hated her, but he wondered where she was, what she was doing.

Probably still hooking someplace.

Probably L.A. She'd always talked about going out to California. Maybe San Francisco. Hooking someplace out there in California.

On Thanksgiving Day he'd sat alone in his garden apartment in Majesta and watched the Gruber's Thanksgiving Day parade. Watched it on one of the local channels. Not as big or as famous as the Macy's parade in New York, but what the fuck, it was at least the city's *own* parade. Ate a frozen turkey dinner he'd heated up in his microwave oven. And wondered where Alice Patricia was.

And wondered what she was doing.

Blond hair and blue eyes.

A figure you could cry.

Whenever a blond, blue-eyed homicide victim turned up—like the one Carella and Brown had caught in October—Parker wondered where Alice Patricia was, wondered if she was lying dead in an alley someplace, her throat slit by some California pimp.

I'm only doing it as a sideline, she'd told him.

Well, listen, they'd warned him. This was when he was still working out of the Three-One downtown, not a bad precinct, still in uniform down there, learning what it was like to be a fuckin' cop in this fuckin' city. Filth and garbage, that was what you dealt with. Went home with the stink of it on your hands and in your nostrils. He'd met her in a bar, she was dancing topless there, the guys all warned him. These topless dancers, they said, you know what they are. They're either turning tricks already, or else they drift into doing massage parlors part-time, and before you knew it, they were full-fledged hookers. He told them to go fuck themselves. Alice Patricia was maybe dancing topless, but she had ambitions and ideals, wanted to dance someday in a legitimate show, make it here and then move on to Broadway and the big time. Took ballet lessons and voice lessons and acting lessons, wanted to make it big. She wasn't what they thought. Parker knew she wasn't. When he married her, he didn't invite any of the guys from the Three-One to the wedding.

It was going good, he thought it was going real good.

Then one night—he had the four to midnight—he went over to the club she was working at, a place called Champagne Bubbles or some such shit, and one of the girls told him Alice Patricia had gone out for an hour or so, and he said, "What do you mean she went out for an hour or so?" This was now twelve-thirty, one o'clock in the morning, the place was almost empty except for some sailors sitting at the bar watching a girl Alice Patricia called the Titless Wonder. "This time of night she went out for an hour or so?" Parker said. He knew what this city turned into after midnight. A fuckin' moonscape full of predators crawling the streets looking for victims. Filth and garbage, the stink of it. "Where'd she go?" he asked.

The girl looked at him.

She was topless. She kept toying with a string of pearls around her neck.

"Where'd she go?" he asked again.

"Leave it be, Andy," the girl said.

He grabbed the string of pearls, ripped them from her neck. The pearls clattered to the floor, rolled on the floor. The sound of the pearls was louder than the sound of the taped music the girl onstage was dancing to.

"Where?" he said.

So, you know, he found her in a hot-bed hotel three blocks from the club. He was in civvies, he had changed in the locker room when his tour ended, the room clerk thought he was a detective when he showed his shield. This was a year before he'd made Detective/Third. He'd made Detective/Third after the divorce, when he had nothing to concentrate on but police work. The room clerk told him a blond, blue-eyed girl had come in with a black man about fifteen minutes ago. The room clerk told him they were in room 1301. Parker would remember the number of the room always. And the stink of Lysol in the hallway.

He beat the black man to within an inch of his life. Kicked him down the stairs. Told him to get his black ass out of this city. He went back to the room. Alice Patricia was still on the bed, naked, smoking a cigarette.

He said, "Why?"

She said, "I'm only doing it as a sideline."

He said, "Why?"

"For kicks," she said, and shrugged.

"I loved you," he said.

It was already past tense.

Alice Patricia shrugged again.

He should have killed her.

He said, "This is it, you know."

"Sure," she said, and stubbed out the cigarette.

He walked out of the room and out of the hotel and into the city. He beat up two drunks who were singing at the tops of their lungs on Hastings Street. He threw an ash can through a plate glass window on Jefferson Avenue. He roamed the city. He was drunk himself when he got back to the apartment at four in the morning. He thought maybe he'd find Alice Patricia there. He thought if she was there, he would kill her. But she was already gone, took all of her clothes with her. Not even a note. Took his lawyer three months to find her. The divorce became final six months after that. And three months after that he made Detective/Third.

He still wondered about her whenever the holidays came around.

Hated her, but wondered about her.

Hated the fuckin' holidays.

Hated the thought of snow maybe coming for Christmas.

He hated snow. It started out white and pure and ended up filthy.

He hated Christmas trees, too. All they did was make a

garbage collection problem, even *more* work for the sanitmen, like the horseshit all over the streets. Right after
Christmas you had a dead forest of fuckin' Christmas trees,
trailing tinsel, stacked up outside the buildings with the
garbage. The garbage was bad enough in this city, he
sometimes thought it was a city of uncollected black plastic
bags. The leftover Christmas trees only made it worse. Saw
them all over the city. Dead. Trailing tinsel. She used to
dance with this little G-string that looked as if it was made
of Christmas tree tinsel, all sparkly and bright, her hips
rotating, dollar bills tucked into the waistband. I'm only
doing it as a sideline. Could've been a big fuckin' star.
He'd have gone backstage, talked to the other people in
the cast. Alice Patricia is my wife, he would've said. No
kidding? Yeah, I'm a cop. No kidding?

He hated being a cop.

Hated the notes from this guy who had the squadroom
in a fuckin' tizzy. The Deaf Man. Who gave a shit about
the Deaf Man? In Parker's world they were *all* thieves,
some of them smart thieves and some of them dumb ones.
Maybe the Deaf Man was a smart one, but he was still a
thief. So what was all this fuss about the notes he was
sending? Smart-ass thief was all.

Parker wondered what it was like to be young.

Wondered what it would be like to be called Andrew
again.

Alice Patricia used to call him Andrew.

He hated her.

Oh, Christ, how he loved her!

On Monday morning, December 19, another note from
the Deaf Man arrived.

They were beginning to get tired of him. In six days it
would be Christmas. They had other things to do besides
worrying about his foolishness. They did not know why he
had killed Elizabeth Turner—*if* he'd killed her—and they
did not know what his goddamn messages meant. They
figured he had killed Naomi Schneider because he may

have told her something she had not yet repeated to them, and this something would have been dangerous if revealed. The Deaf Man let them know only what he *wanted* them to know. Anything else was a risk, and he took no unpredictable risks. So good-bye, Naomi.

But both cases were as dead as this year's calendar would soon be, and the latest message from him was only an irritation. They merely glanced at it and then tacked it to the bulletin board with the others:

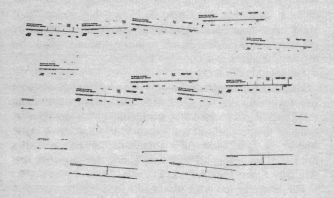

Cotton Hawes was in trouble.

He felt like calling in a 10-13.

Instead, he said, "I *do* have a Gruber's charge account."

He was embarrassed to begin with. He had just bought Annie Rawles two hundred dollars' worth of sexy lingerie as a Christmas gift. Two hundred and *thirteen* dollars *and* twenty-five cents with tax. He hoped he would not have to explain to this lady on the sixth floor of Gruber's new uptown store that he had bought the underwear for a Detective/First Grade. The store, not six blocks from the station house, was part of the mayor's new Urban Renewal Program. The *real* Gruber's was all the way downtown, on

Messenger Square. Hawes should have gone downtown. He should have known better than to shop anywhere in the precinct, even though the new store was very nice and—according to the mayor's office, at least—was doing a very good business and was serving as a model for redevelopment of shitty neighborhoods all over the city.

"Not according to our records," the woman behind the counter said.

Hawes wondered if she would be caught dead in the sort of sexy lingerie he had bought for Annie.

"I've had a Gruber's charge account for three years now," he said.

"Let me see your card again, please," the woman said.

He handed her the card.

He was in the sixth-floor credit office. The woman downstairs on the first floor—where Lingerie was—had told him to go up to the sixth floor to the credit office because when she'd tried to run his card through the computer, she had come up with an INVALID. He had taken the escalator up to the sixth floor and had seen a bristling array of signs pointing in different directions: MANAGER'S OFFICE. CASHIER'S OFFICE. CREDIT OFFICE. RETURNS. PERSONNEL OFFICE. TOY DEPARTMENT. SANTA CLAUS. TELEPHONE OFFICE. REST ROOMS. He had almost gotten lost, fine detective that he was. But here he was in the credit office, handing his card across the counter to a woman who had a nose like a broomstick. And eyes like dirt. Her eyes were dirty. Not brown, not black—just dirty. She looked at his card with her dirty eyes. She almost sniffed it with her broomstick nose.

"I have the new card," he said.

"Where is the new card, sir?" she asked.

"Home," he said. "I haven't put it in my wallet yet."

He realized, as he said this, that claiming to have the card at home was akin to a pistol-carrying thief claiming he had left his permit in a desk drawer someplace.

"If you planned to shop here," the woman said, "you should have put your card in your wallet."

Hawes opened his wallet. "This is where the new card should be," he said. "But I left it home."

He had really opened his wallet so she could see the gold- and blue-enameled detective shield pinned to it. She looked at the shield with her dirty eyes.

"You should have the new card with you at all times," she said.

"I didn't know I'd be shopping today," he said. "I have a lot of things to carry in my wallet," he said. "My police shield," he said. "My police ID card. I'm a detective," he said. "I don't like to carry more things in my wallet than I absolutely have to."

"But you're carrying the *old* card in your wallet," she said.

"Yes, I am. By mistake. The new one should be there."

"The old card went through our computer as invalid."

"Yes, I know. That's why I'm up here on the sixth floor. But if you run a check through your computer files up here, you'll see that I received a new card in May. And forgot to put it in my wallet."

"No wonder people get away with murder in this city," she said, and left the counter.

He waited.

She came back ten minutes later.

"Yes, you did indeed receive a new card," she said.

"Yes, I know," he said. "Thank you," he added.

"You understand, sir," she said, "that the charging of two hundred dollars' worth of lingerie could not go unquestioned when a card came up invalid."

"Yes, I understand that," he said.

She knew it was for lingerie. She had called downstairs. He wondered if she knew what *sort* of lingerie.

"There are a lot of crooks in this city, you know," she said.

"Yes, I'm aware of that," he said.

"If you'll go downstairs again to Lingerie," she said, "the card will go through this time. I hope you are aware, sir, that panties are not returnable."

"I didn't know that," he said.

"Yes. *Especially* our Open City line, which many women wear for special occasions only. I hope you have the right size."

"I have the right size, yes," he said.

"Yes, well," she said, and sniffed the air as if smelling something rank, and gave him a last look with her dirty eyes, and left him standing at the counter.

All the way home he thought about his encounter in Gruber's. He wished Gruber's would burn to the ground. He wished the mayor would take his Urban Renewal Program to Dallas, Texas. Or Vladivostok. All Gruber's did was encourage more crime in an area already crime-ridden. More damn pickpocket and shoplifting arrests in that store since it opened last February than in all the other stores along the Stem. Okay, it was making a lot of money. And maybe attracting other businesses to the area. But did the mayor ever stop to think how much time the cops up here were putting into Gruber's? On shitty little arrests? For which they had to travel all the way down to Headquarters to do the booking?

He was still fuming when he reached his building downtown. He stepped into the small entry foyer, took his keys from his pocket, and unlocked his mailbox. There was a sheaf of letters, *including* a bill from Gruber's. He did not look at the mail more closely until he was in his apartment. He was tempted to call Annie, tell her about the hassle uptown, but that would blow the surprise. Instead, he mixed himself a drink and then sat down and leafed through the envelopes. One of them seemed to be a Christmas card. He tore open the flap on the red envelope. It was not a Christmas card. It was an invitation. It read:

YOU ARE INVITED TO A PARTY

FOR: *Detective-Lieutenant Peter Byrnes*

DATE: *January 5*

TIME: *8:00 P.M.*

PLACE: *87th Precinct Squadroom*

Scrawled on the flap of the card in the same handwriting was the message:

*Cotton— I haven't been able to invite everyone, so please keep this a secret, won't you? Harriet.*

Harriet was Harriet Byrnes, the lieutenant's wife. Why in hell was she throwing a party for him in the squadroom? Was it Pete's birthday? An anniversary? Twenty years on the force? Thirty? A hundred?

Hawes shrugged and wrote down the date and time in his appointment calendar.

On Tuesday morning, December 20, the Deaf Man's tenth message arrived.

They knew by now that the number of items pasted to each blank sheet of paper had nothing whatever to do with the order in which the messages were received. The eight black horses, for example, were on the very first message. The six police shields were on the fourth message. The eleven Colt Detective Specials were on the seventh message. And so on. And now on the tenth message:

The detectives tacked the sheet of paper to the bulletin board. There were now:

Two nightsticks. Three pairs of handcuffs. Four police hats. Five walkie-talkies. Six police shields. Seven wanted flyers. Eight black horses. Nine patrol cars. Ten D.D. forms. And eleven Detective Specials.

They still didn't know what any of it meant.

*Did* he plan to stop at eleven?

Or would he go beyond that?

If he stopped at eleven, then the number one was still missing in the sequence.

The hell with it, they thought.

Christmas was only five days away.

Bert Kling was looking through his mail when Eileen Burke let herself in with the key he had given her.

It was close to four-thirty in the afternoon, and the lights on the Calm's Point Bridge—festooned for the holiday season and visible through his windows—were blinking red and green against the purple dusk. He sat under a floor lamp near the windows in an easy chair he'd bought in a thrift shop after his divorce. He had never discussed his

divorce with Andy Parker. He had never discussed anything but police work with Parker, and even that rarely.
He did not know Parker was himself divorced. He did not
know that the two men might have shared common thoughts
on the subject, did not know that Parker, like himself,
thought of divorce as a kind of killing.

The holidays, even now and even with Eileen, were the
most difficult time for Kling. Augusta would pop into his
mind whenever he shopped the stores, even when he was
shopping for Eileen. Well, the physical similarities, he
supposed. In trying to settle on a color, he'd tell a store
clerk that his girlfriend was a green-eyed redhead—describ-
ing Eileen, of course—and immediately Augusta would
come to mind. Or in trying to remember what size Eileen
wore, he'd say she was five feet nine inches tall, and immediately the image of Augusta would come again, unbid-
den, ghostlike, Augusta as he'd first seen her when he was
investigating a burglarly in her apartment . . .

*Long red hair and green eyes and a deep suntan. Dark
green sweater, short brown skirt, brown boots. High
cheekbones, eyes slanting up from them, fiercely green
against the tan, tilted nose gently drawing the upper lip
away from partially exposed, even white teeth. Sweater
swelling over breasts firm without a bra, the wool cinched
tightly at her waist with a brown brass-studded belt, hip
softly carving an arc against the nubby sofa back, skirt
revealing a secret thigh as she turned more fully toward
him . . .*

Augusta.

"Hi," Eileen said, and came to where he was sitting.

She kissed him on top of the head. Red and green lights
from the bridge blinked into the red and green of her hair
and her eyes.

"You look like Christmas," he said.

"I do, huh?" she said. "I feel like Halloween. When
did you get in? I called a little while ago."

"A little after four," he said. "I was doing some shopping. What'd the doctor say?"

"He said time heals all wounds."

She took off her coat, tossed it familiarly onto the bed, sat on the edge of the bed, eased off her high-heeled shoes, and reached down to massage one foot. Long legs, sleek and clean, full-calved and tapering to slender ankles. Eileen. Augusta. The knifing would have destroyed Augusta. She was a model, her face was her fortune. Eileen was only a cop. But she was a woman. And a beautiful woman. And she'd been cut on her face. The knifing had occured on October 21, two months ago. At the hospital they'd taken twelve stitches. The scar was still livid on her left cheek.

"He said I might not need plastic surgery at all," Eileen said. "Told me the hospital emergency room did a very good job. He said the scar may look awful now . . ."

"It doesn't really look bad at all," Kling said.

"Yeah, bullshit," Eileen said. "But it'll heal as a thin white line, he said, if I can live with that. He said it all depends on my 'acceptance level.' How do you like *that* for a euphemism?"

"When do you have to see him again?" Kling asked.

"Next month. He says I shouldn't even be *thinking* about plastic surgery just yet. He said the cut should be entirely healed within six months to a year, and I should wait till then to see how I feel. That's what he means by acceptance level, I guess. How much vanity I have. How ugly I'd care to look for the rest of my life."

"You don't look ugly," Kling said. "You couldn't *possibly* look . . ."

"I'm not winning any beauty contests these days, that's for sure," Eileen said. "You think there are any rapists out there who dig scars? Think they'd go for a decoy with a slashed left cheek?"

"I kind of like the look it gives you," he said, trying to joke her out of her dark mood. "Makes you look sort of dangerous."

"Yeah, dangerous," she said.

"Devil-may-care. Like a lady pirate."

"Like a three-hundred-pound armed robber," Eileen said. "All I need is a tattoo on my arm, Mom in a heart."

"You feel like Chinese tonight?" he asked.

"I feel like curling up in bed and sleeping for a month. Going to see him is exhausting. He's always so fucking *consoling*, do you know what I mean? It isn't *his* fucking face, so he thinks . . ."

"Hey," Kling said softly.

She looked up at him.

"Come on," he said, and went to her. He kissed the top of her head. He cupped his hand under her chin and kissed her forehead and the tip of her nose. He kissed the scar. Gently, tenderly.

"Kissing it won't make it go away, Bert," she said, and paused. "I hope you didn't buy me anything too feminine for Christmas."

"What?"

"I don't feel pretty," she said. "I wouldn't want any gifts that . . ."

"You're beautiful," he said. *"And* feminine. *And* sexy. *And . . ."*

"Sweet talker," she said.

"So where do you want to eat?" he said. "McDonald's?"

"Big spender, too," she said, pausing again. "And what?" she said.

"Huh?"

"Beautiful and feminine and sexy and what?"

"And I love you," he said.

"Truly?"

"Truly."

"With all the umpteen million other women in this city . . . ?"

"You're the only woman in this city," he said.

She looked at him. She nodded.

"Thank you," she said softly and rose from the bed. "Let me shower and change," she said. "Thank you," she said again and kissed him on the mouth and then went into the bathroom.

He heard the shower when she turned it on.

He picked up the stack of mail again. He opened several Christmas cards and then picked up a red envelope and tore open the flap. The card inside read:

**YOU ARE INVITED TO A PARTY**

FOR: *Detective-Lieutenant Peter Byrnes*

DATE: *January 5*

TIME: *8:00 P.M.*

PLACE: *87th Precinct Squadroom*

Scrawled on the flap on the card in the same handwriting was the message:

*Bert - I haven't been able to invite everyone, so please keep this a secret, won't you? Harriet.*

The door to the bathroom opened.

Eileen poked her head around the jamb.

"Wanna come shower with me?" she asked.

Christmas Day would fall on a Sunday this year.

This was good for the department stores. Normally sales fell off a bit on Christmas Eve. You had your last-minute shoppers, sure, and the stores all stayed open till six o'clock to accommodate even the tardiest, but the volume was nowhere as great as it was at any other time during that last hectic week before the big event. Unless Christmas Eve fell on a Saturday. Then, miraculously, sales perked up. This may have had something to do with the fact that working people were *used* to shopping on Saturdays. Maybe they felt this was just *another* Saturday, same as all the rest in the year, time to get out there and spend Friday's paycheck. Or maybe the Christmas bonuses had something to do with it, get that big fat extra wad of money on Friday, good time to spend it was Saturday, right? It was funny the way a Saturday Christmas Eve brought out the customers in droves. Statistics showed that it didn't work that way if Christmas Eve fell on a Sunday. Not as many shoppers. Even God rested on Sunday. This year, with prosperity lingering for yet a little while and with Christmas Eve coming on a Saturday, storekeepers all over the city were anticipating a banner day.

On Thursday, December 22, the detectives of the 87th Squad received what they surmised was almost the last of the Deaf Man's communications. It was Arthur Brown, in fact, who guessed this one was the penultimate one. The single white sheet of paper in the now-familiar typewritten envelope showed:

"Number twelve," Brown said.

"Twelve roast pigs," Carella said.

"Only one more to go," Brown said.

"How do you figure that?"

"It's the twelve days of Christmas, don't you get it?" Brown said. "Two nightsticks, three pairs of handcuffs, four police hats . . . the twelve days of Christmas."

"He's just wishing us a Merry Christmas, huh?" Carella said.

"Fat chance," Brown said. "But all that's missing now is the first day. It's the twelve days of Christmas, Steve. I'll bet next month's salary on it."

"So what'll the *first* day be?"

"Take a guess," Brown said, grinning.

Brown did not like putting up Christmas trees.

He also did not like what Christmas trees *cost* nowadays. When he was a kid, you could get a huge tree for five bucks. The seven-foot tree he'd bought this year had cost him thirty-five dollars. Highway robbery. He would not have bought a tree at all if it weren't for Connie, his eight-year-old daughter. Connie still believed in Santa Claus. There was no fireplace and hence no chimney in the Brown apartment, but Connie always left a glass of milk and a platter of chocolate-chip cookies under the tree for Santa. Every Christmas Brown had to drink the goddamn glass of milk before he went to bed. He also had to eat some of the chocolate-chip cookies.

The first thing he did not like about putting up a Christmas tree was the lights. It seemed to Brown that if the United States could put a man on the moon, then some brilliant scientist someplace could also figure out a way to make Christmas tree lights that didn't have wires. Brown was no brilliant scientist, but he himself had figured out a very simple way to do this, and if some starving inventor out there wanted to cash in on a bonanza, he was willing to divulge it for a hefty piece of the action. He knew just how it would work in principle, but he didn't have the

electrical engineering know-how to put it on paper. He had
never discussed his idea out loud with anyone because he
didn't want it stolen from him. There were a lot of crooks
in this world, as he well knew, and it seemed likely to him
that his multimillion-dollar idea would be stolen the moment he talked to anyone about it. He already had a name
for the product: No Strings. If he and somebody went part-
ners on it, they could sell billions and billions of Christmas
tree lights every year. No strings. No wires to loop around
branches. Each Christmas tree light an individual entity
that could be hung anyplace on the tree. All anybody had
to do was contact him, write to him care of the 87th Precinct, make him an offer. He was willing to listen.

Meanwhile, he struggled with the damn lights.

Nobody helped him.

That was the *second* thing he disliked about putting up
the tree.

His wife, Caroline, was in the kitchen baking the chocolate-chip cookies Connie would put under the tree on
Christmas Eve, some of which Brown would later have to
eat while he drank the goddamn glass of milk. Connie herself was in the den watching television. All alone in the
living room Brown struggled first with the lights and then
with the Christmas balls, which was the third thing he disliked about putting up a tree. Not the Christmas balls themselves—except when one fell off the tree and crashed to the
floor, leaving all those silvery splinters that were impossible to pick up—but the little *hooks* that held the balls to
the tree. Why was it that no matter how carefully you
packed all the ornaments away after Christmas, there were
always more balls than there were hooks? Brown suspected
there was an international ring of ornament-hook thieves.

The smell of baking cookies filled the apartment.

The sound of animated cartoon characters filled the
apartment.

Brown worked on the tree.

Only two more days to go, he thought.

His daughter, Connie, suddenly appeared in the doorway.

"How come there's no black Santa Clauses?" she asked.

Brown sighed.

The twelve days of Christmas.

Twelfth Night.

The eve of Epiphany.

The first day of Christmas was Christmas Day itself. On Christmas Day the detectives of the 87th Squad would no doubt be celebrating, opening their own meager gifts, and not for a moment expecting the first of *his* gifts. But receive it they would and perhaps recognize at last what all his advance publicity had been about. They would *not,* however—if his notes had been inaccessible enough—realize what lay in store for them on January 5, Twelfth Night, Epiphany Eve.

In lower case the word "epiphany" meant the sudden revelation of an underlying truth about a person or a situation. The English word was from the Greek *epiphaneia,* of course, the gods revealing themselves to mortal eyes, but the Irish novelist James Joyce—one of the Deaf Man's favorites—first popularized the word in modern literature by calling his early experimental prose passages "epiphanies." A sudden flash of recognition. Would the men of the 87th recognize at last? Before the sudden flash? During it? There would be no time for recognition afterward.

He smiled again.

Epiphany Day. January 6. In honor of the first time Jesus Christ manifested himself to the Gentiles. On Epiphany Eve, Twelfth *Night,* as it was called—oh what fun Shakespeare'd had with *that* one—the Deaf Man would reveal himself in spirit to the detectives, making it clear to them for the first, last, and only time that he would brook no further interference with his chosen profession. On three previous occasions he had given them every opportunity to thwart his plans, virtually laying them all out in advance— but never once realizing his plans actually *would* meet with disaster. Oh, not through any brilliant deduction on their part, no, that would be giving them far too much credit for intelligence. But rather through clumsy accidents. Accidents. The bane of the Deaf Man's existence.

Accidents.

The first time it had been a cop wanting to buy ice cream from the Deaf Man's stolen getaway truck. Wanted an ice cream pop. One of the specials with the chopped walnuts. Never once suspected the refrigerator compartment was stuffed with money stolen from the Mercantile Trust. But blew the job anyway—by accident.

The next time it had been two small-time hoods committing a holdup in a tailor shop on the very same night the Deaf Man had planned a little fillip-surprise to his big extortion scheme. There were two detectives in the back of the store, waiting for the hoods. The Deaf Man and his accomplices came in the front door at the very same moment. Fuzz! A stakeout for the two punks, and the Deaf Man had accidentally walked into it. Carella had shot him on that occasion; he would never forget Carella's shooting him, would never forgive him for it.

The last time—well, he supposed he could credit Carella with having doped that one out in advance, though he'd certainly given him enough help with it. That had been his mistake. Laid it all out too clearly, too fairly. Virtually *told* Carella he was planning to rob the same bank twice in the same morning, setting up an A-team for a fall and then going in with his B-team—to find Carella there and waiting.

Carella was smarter than the Deaf Man thought he was. He was maybe even smarter than he *himself* thought he was.

Accidents, not mistakes.

But now—no more Mr. Nice Guy.

There was nothing in the book that said he had to play the game fairly.

They were lucky he was playing it at *all*.

On the night before Christmas the Deaf Man would steal half a million dollars, perhaps more.

And get away with it this time, because this time he had not warned the police in advance. Well, yes, he had not been able to resist dropping Elizabeth's body in the park opposite the station house. Naked, though, and therefore unidentifiable. And that had been the only clue, if it could be considered one, to the job planned for Christmas Eve.

On *Epiphany* Eve, Twelfth Night, he would destroy the detectives—most of them anyway—who worked out of the old building facing Grover Park.

And get away with *that*, too.

Because, although he'd warned them, he had not warned them fairly.

They would die.

Horribly.

He smiled at the thought.

Tonight was December 23.

Tonight there was still some work to be done.


In this neighborhood you had to be careful, even with it being so close to Christmas. In fact, maybe even *more* careful this time of year; people did funny things around Christmastime. Lots of the street people around here, they could remember a time—well, this hadn't been Christmastime, it was in March sometime, years ago—they could remember some young kids setting fire to bums sleeping in doorways. Winos. Doused them with gasoline and set fire to them. Doug Hennesy hadn't lived in this city then, but he'd heard plenty about them long-ago roasts, and he knew you had to be more careful in this city than maybe in any city on earth. Not that Doug considered himself a bum. Or even a wino. Doug was a street person, is what he was.

He didn't particularly enjoy the holiday season because the streets were always too crowded, everybody rushing around, everybody selfish and concerned only with his ownself, never mind dropping a coin in the hand of someone needy like Doug. He'd managed to get four dollars and twenty-two cents today—two days before Christmas, could you imagine it? where was the spirit of giving?—but that had taken him from eight this morning till almost seven tonight. He kept wondering who had given him the two cents. Had it been that well-dressed guy in the raccoon coat and the beaver hat? Two cents. But the money Doug collected had been enough for three bottles of excellent wine at a dollar forty a bottle, including tax, with the two cents still left over. He'd already drunk one of the bottles and planned to savor the remaining two all through the night, huddled in the doorway here on Mason Avenue.

The hookers on Mason Avenue didn't like the idea of street people sleeping in doorways. They felt it made the neighborhood look shoddy, as if anything could make it look shoddier than it actually was. Felt it was bad for business. Downtown johns came up here looking for a little black or Puerto Rican ass, they didn't want to see wino bums sprawled in the doorways. The hookers on Mason Avenue were thinking of getting a petition signed against the street people who made their turf look shoddy. Well, Doug guessed he couldn't blame them much. They worked hard, those girls did. He tried to remember the last time he'd been to bed with a woman, hooker or otherwise. Couldn't remember for the life of him. Back in Chicago, wasn't it? Back when he used to be an accountant in Chicago? Another lifetime ago.

Some of your street people, the men, they took advantage of women living on the streets same as themselves. Found a bag lady curled up in a doorway, threw her skirts up, had their way with her. Doug would never in a million years do anything like that, take advantage of someone unfortunate. He'd seen—this was yesterday morning, it almost broke his heart. He'd seen this young street person, she couldn't have been older than twenty-eight or nine, wearing a pink sweater over a thin cotton dress, woolen gloves cut off at the fingers, Christ, she almost broke his heart. Standing in a doorway. Looking at herself in the plate glass window on the door. Hands clasped over her

belly. Exploring her belly. Fingers widespread in the
sawed-off woolen gloves. Touching her belly. Her belly as
big as a watermelon. And on her face a look of total be-
wilderment. For an instant Doug visualized her standing in
a bedroom someplace, the closet door open, a full-length
mirror on the closet door, imagined her standing in a silken
nightgown, her hands widespread over her pregnant belly,
just the way they were widespread over her belly in that
doorway, only with a different look on her face. A look of
pride, of pleasure. A young pregnant woman awed by the
wonder of it, her face glowing. Instead, a doorway on a
cold winter day near Christmas—and a look of utter confusion.

Ah, God, the poor unfortunates of this world.

He unscrewed the top of the second bottle of wine.

It was going to be another cold night.

Maybe on Christmas Day he'd wander over to the Salvation Army soup kitchen.

Well, he'd see. No sense making plans in advance.

He had the bottle tilted to his mouth when the man appeared suddenly out of the darkness. The street light was
behind the man; Doug couldn't see his face too clearly.
Only the blond hair whipping in the wind. And what looked
like a hearing aid in his right ear.

"Good evening," the man said pleasantly.

Doug figured he was a downtown john up here looking
for a little poontang.

"Good evening," he answered, and then—in the season's spirit of generosity—he extended the bottle of wine
and said, "Would you like some wine, sir?"

"No, thank you," the man said. "I'd like your ear."

At first Doug thought the man wanted to talk. Friends,
Romans, countrymen, lend me your ears. But then, suddenly and chillingly, he saw a switchblade knife snap open
in the man's hand, the blade catching the reflection of the
traffic light on the corner, the steel flashing red and then
green as the light changed, little twinkly Christmas pin-
points of light, and all at once the man's left hand was at

Doug's throat, forcing him onto his back in the doorway. The wine bottle crashed to the sidewalk—a dollar and forty cents!—splintered into a thousand shards of green glass as the man rolled him over onto his left side, the knife flashing yellow and then red as the traffic light changed again.

Doug felt a searing line of fire just above his right ear.

And then the fire trailed downward, spreading, the pain so sharp that Doug screamed aloud and instantly cupped his hand to his right ear.

His right ear was gone.

His hand came away covered with blood.

He screamed again.

The blond man with the hearing aid disappeared as suddenly as he had materialized.

Doug kept screaming.

A hooker swishing by in red Christmas satin and fake fur, heading for the bar up the street, her stiletto heels clattering on the sidewalk, looked into the doorway and shook her head and clucked her tongue.

## 10

CHRISTMAS EVE DAWNED BRIGHT AND CLEAR and sparklingly cold. The Deaf Man was pleased. Snow would not have upset his plans at all, but he preferred this kind of weather. It made the blood hum.

He loved Christmastime. Loved all the Santa Clauses jingling their bells on virtually every corner. Loved the horse-drawn carriages in the streets. Loved the big Christmas tree in Andover Square. Loved all the little runny-nosed toddlers ooohing and ahhhing at the sights and sounds. Loved the thought of all that money waiting to be stolen.

The streets were thronged with holiday shoppers.

That was good.

More cash in the till.

The Deaf Man smiled.

He had put Charlie Henkins up in a hotel some ten blocks from the 87th Precinct station house. Nothing to write home about, and probably a place frequented by a great many prostitutes, but the best to be found in the area. He himself had rented a brownstone miles from the precinct. Charlie had never been there. It was important that he not know where the Deaf Man lived. After the job, when Charlie realized nobody was going to come to the hotel with all that hard-earned cash, the Deaf Man didn't want him paying an unexpected visit. But even if Charlie went snooping, he would never find the brownstone. The Deaf Man had rented it as Dr. Pierre Sourd. In lower case *pierre* meant stone in French. *Sourd* meant deaf. Together and with a little license—the actual idiom would have been *complète-*

*ment sourd* or, more familiarly, *sourd comme un pot*—the words meant "stone deaf."

Elizabeth had moved into the brownstone with him at the beginning of October. He'd met her in September at the Isola Modern Art Museum, which the natives of this city affectionately called IMAM. In Moslem countries an imam was an Islamic prayer leader, but in this city it was a museum and a good place to meet impressionable young women. Chat them up over the Matisses and the Chagalls—would you care for some tea in the garden? Shy, she was, Elizabeth. A virgin, he'd thought at first—but there were surprises. There are always surprises.

Learned she'd been working as a cashier since sometime in August. Well, now. Learned she handled large sums of money. Really, Elizabeth? Called her Elizabeth, which she loved. Hated people calling her Lizzie or Liz. Three, four hundred thousand dollars a day, she said. Oh my, he said. Fucked her that very night. A screamer. The quiet ones were always screamers.

The hotel Charlie was staying at was called the Excelsior, a prime example of hyperbole, perhaps, in that the word derived from the Latin *excelsus*, from the past participle of *excellere*, which meant "to excel." Perhaps the Excelsior had once, in a past too long ago to remember, indeed excelled—but the Deaf Man doubted it. On the other hand, "excelsior" was the word used to describe the slender, curved wooden shavings used for packing and also—in the hands of an arsonist—for starting fires. So perhaps the building had been appropriately named, after all, in that it was most certainly an excellent fire trap. The word "excellent" also derived from the Latin—*excellens*, which was the *present* participle of the same word *excellere*, "to excel."

The Deaf Man loved words.

The Deaf Man also loved to excel.

He sometimes felt he would have excelled as a novelist, though why anyone would wish to pursue such a trivial occupation was far beyond his ken.

Charlie Henkins was studying the combinations when the Deaf Man came into the room.

"I was going over the combinations again," he said.

"Let me hear them," the Deaf Man said. "Outer door."

"Seven-six-one, two-three-eight."

"And the inner door?"

"Nine-two-four, three-eight-five."

"Good. And the safe itself?"

"Two-four-seven, four-six-three."

"Good. Again."

"Outer door, pad to the right, seven-six-one, two-three-eight. Inner door, pad to the right again, nine-two-four, three-eight-five. Opens into the vault itself, the cashier and her assistant at two desks, the money in the safe. Pad to the right, two-four-seven, four-six-three."

"You shoot them at once," the Deaf Man said.

" 'Cause there's alarm buttons on both desks."

"*Under* both desks, yes. Foot-activated. You say, 'Merry Christmas, ladies,' and shoot them."

"This silencer's gonna work, huh?"

"It's going to work, yes."

" 'Cause I never used a piece with a silencer on it."

"It'll work, you have nothing to worry about."

"After I pack the money in the bag . . ."

"Not only the money. Everything in the safe."

"Checks, everything, 'cause there's no time to do any sorting. I just throw everything in the bag."

"Correct."

"And then I leave by the employees' entrance."

"Correct."

"And you'll be waiting outside on the sidewalk."

"With 'Silent Night' going."

"Yeah, 'Silent Night,' " Charlie said, and smiled.

Detective Richard Genero opened the top drawer of his desk and sneaked another peek at the invitation:

YOU ARE INVITED TO A PARTY

FOR: *Detective-Lieutenant Peter Byrnes*

DATE: *January 5*

TIME: *8:00 P.M.*

PLACE: *87th Precinct Squadroom*

Scrawled on the flap of the card in the same handwriting was the message:

*Richard— I haven't been able to invite everyone, so please keep this a secret, won't you? Harriet.*

He had received the invitation two days ago. It had taken him a long while to figure out that Harriet was Harriet Byrnes, the lieutenant's wife. He had asked Hal Willis a discreet question—"Hey, who's Harriet?"—and Hal Willis had winked and said, "Pete's wife." Genero suspected that Hal Willis had been invited to the party, too, but he was sworn to secrecy and so he hadn't said another word. He wondered now what the party was for. It seemed funny to him that Mrs. Byrnes hadn't mentioned what the party was for. Also what should he call Mrs. Byrnes on the night of the party? She had signed the invitation "Harriet," hadn't she? Should he call her Harriet? Should he call the lieutenant Pete? He had never in his life called him Pete.

Genero hated it when things got complicated.

For example, why had Mrs. Byrnes called him Richard? The only person in the entire world who called him Richard was his mother. Nobody on the squad called him Richard. Nobody on the squad called him Dick, either. Nobody in the world called him Dick. On the squad they called him Genero. Always his last name. Genero. They called Carella "Steve," and they called Hawes "Cotton," and Kling "Bert," but they always called *him* "Genero." His last name. Of course, they called Meyer "Meyer," but that was because his first name and his last name were exactly the same. His mother told him that was a sign of respect, people calling him by his last name. He told his mother they didn't call him *Mr.* Genero, they just called him Genero. She insisted it was a sign of respect.

She also insisted that he should find out more about this party because maybe he was expected to bring a present. If he was expected to bring a present and he *didn't* bring a present, this would make him look bad in the lieutenant's eyes.

*"Il mondo è fatto a scale,"* his mother said. *"Chi le scende e chi le sale."*

This meant: "The world is made of stairs, and there are those who go up and those who go down."

This further meant: If Genero ever wanted to get anyplace in the police department, he'd better bring a present to the lieutenant's party if a present was expected.

*"Ognuno cerca di portare l'acqua al suo molino,"* his mother said.

Which meant: "Every man tries to bring water to his own mill."

Which further meant: It was in Genero's own interest to bring a present to the lieutenant's party if he wanted to get anywhere in the police department.

But Harriet Byrnes had asked him to keep the party a secret.

So how was he supposed to *ask* anyone if a present was expected?

It was all very complicated.

Genero sighed and looked out the window to the parking lot behind the precinct.

Early afternoon sunlight glinted off the white roofs of the patrol cars parked there.

The forecasters were promising snow for Christmas, but you wouldn't suspect it from today. There were days in this city when you wondered why anyone bothered moving to the Sun Belt. Cold, yes, the day was cold, you couldn't deny that. But the cold merely quickened your step and made you feel more alive. And the sky was so blue you felt like hugging it. And the brilliant sunshine made everything seem like summertime, despite the cold.

The big stores had all taken out full-page ads in the newspapers, announcing that they would be open till six tonight, business as usual. It was a glorious day for shopping. The benevolent sun, the crisp cold air reminding you that this was indeed the day before Christmas, the streets alive with a sense of anticipation and expectation, the welcoming warmth of the stores with their glittering displays, even the shoppers more polite and courteous than they would have been if not sharing the knowledge that this was Christmas Eve.

On the sixth floor of Gruber's uptown store, not far from the 87th Precinct station house, Santa Claus—or rather the man *pretending* to be Santa Claus—was amazed to see a line of kids still waiting to talk to him at five in the afternoon. He told all the little boys who climbed up onto his lap that they had to give him their toy orders real fast because he had to hurry on up to the North Pole to feed the reindeer and get ready for his long chilly ride tonight. The little boys were all in awe of Santa, and they reeled off their requests with the speed of tobacco auctioneers. The little girls took their good sweet time, perhaps because this would be the last shot they had at Santa till he came down that chimney tomorrow morning or perhaps because the man pretending to be Santa encouraged them to take all the time they needed.

Actually the man pretending to be Santa was named Arthur Drits, and the closest he'd ever come to the North Pole was Castleview Prison upstate, where he'd spent a good many years for First-Degree Rape, a Class-B felony defined as:

Being a male, engaging in sexual intercourse with a female:
1. By forcible compulsion; OR
2. Who is incapable of consent by reason of being physically helpless; OR
3. Who is less than eleven years old.

The personnel manager who'd hired Drits to portray Santa for Gruber's uptown store did not know that he had a prison record or that he loved children quite so much as he claimed to love them—especially little girls under the age of eleven. The personnel manager saw only a jolly-looking fellow with a little potbelly and twinkly blue eyes, and he figured he would make a good Santa. Even after Drits started working for the store, the personnel manager never noticed that Santa gave most little boys pretty short shrift while he kept even ugly little girls on his lap for an inordinately long time.

Today, at a little past five now and with the store officially closing its doors at six, Drits kept a little eight-year-old curly headed blond girl on his lap for almost five minutes, his eyes glazed as he listened rapturously to her various requests. He reminded her to leave a cup of hot chocolate for him before she went to bed tonight, and then he helped her off his lap, his big meaty right hand clenched into her plump right buttock as he lifted her to the floor, and then he turned to the next little girl in line—a darling little Hispanic girl with bright button eyes and a mouth like an angel's—and he said, ''Come, sweetheart, sit up here on Santa's lap and tell him what you want for Christmas.''

Drits wanted *her* for Christmas.

He looked at the clock hanging on the wall across the store and wished this job would never end.

This was what burglars called a lay-in job.

One guy went in the store, he hid himself someplace inside the store, stayed there till they locked up and went home. Then the lay-in man knocked out the alarm, let his partner in, and together they ripped off the joint. Only this wasn't going to be a burglary, this was going to be an armed robbery. And Charlie wasn't going to wait till the place was locked up because then he'd *never* get the fuck out of here. In every other respect, though, it was a lay-in job. Charlie here in the men's room on the sixth floor of Gruber's, waiting for the store to chase all the customers out. Then down the hall to the cashier's office, and Merry Christmas, ladies.

Not many people realized that a lot of department stores had their own vaults, same as banks. The vaults were necessary because department stores did a big cash business, and most of them stayed open later than the banks did. So what did you do with all that cash once the banks were closed? What you did, you had a vault of your own, with security just like a bank's, and you kept the cash locked up overnight till you could go deposit it. *Some* department stores had armored cars picking up the cash to take to a security vault overnight, but Lizzie Turner had told them that Gruber's didn't have any armored cars coming around for any pickups. Gruber's had its own vault with its own safe inside it.

Tomorrow was Sunday.

Under ordinary circumstances Saturday's cash receipts would be tallied in the cashier's office early Monday morning, and then a pair of Gruber's armed square-shields would take it to the bank for deposit.

But tomorrow was not only Sunday, it was also Christmas Day.

Which meant that Monday, December 26, was the *legal* holiday, and the banks would be closed then, too. If all went well, Dennis figured that nobody would even realize the store had been robbed till Tuesday morning, when the cashier's office was opened again.

Charlie was sitting on a toilet bowl with his trousers down around his ankles. He had been sitting on the toilet bowl for close to half an hour now, listening to the traffic in and out of the men's room on Gruber's sixth floor. He was not expected to make his move until six forty-five.

Lizzie had told them that the security in the cashier's office was very good, better than some banks had. Two different combinations on the two steel doors that led into the vault, another on the safe itself. No windows in the vault. Just the two desks, the various adding machines and computers and such, and the big walk-in safe on the far wall. After the store closed at six, it normally took a half hour at most for each department head on the separate floors to tally his or her cash register receipts, put them into zippered plastic bags, and carry them up to the cashier's office on the sixth floor.

Lizzie said that she and her assistant then put the plastic bags of cash in the safe, triggered the safe alarm, and triggered the alarms for both vault doors before they left the office at a little before seven each night. It was rare that any employee, including all the managers, were still in the store after seven. The employees all left by the employees' entrance on the ground floor. The security officer there watched them while they punched out at the time clock. When all employees had punched out, the security officer set the store's external alarm.

She had told them all this while they were laying out the job.

Nice girl, Lizzie. Smart, too. Quit Gruber's early in October, was laying low now till it was time to split the money. That would be tomorrow morning. Christmas

Day for the three of them. Christmas in Charlie's room at the Excelsior the minute Dennis arrived with the . . .

A loudspeaker on the wall suddenly erupted with the sound of a woman's voice, startling here in the men's room.

"Ladies and gentlemen, Gruber's will be closing in twenty minutes," the woman's voice said. "We ask you to kindly complete your shopping before six o'clock. Thank you and Merry Christmas."

Charlie looked at his watch.

He rose then, pulled up his undershorts and his trousers, belted the trousers, and reached for the suitcase he'd tucked against one side of the stall.

He checked the lock on the door again and then opened the suitcase.

A huge red banner trimmed in gold hung from a flagstaff and flapped in the wind outside Gruber's side street entrances. Greetings were stitched in gold to the banner, one beneath the other:

MERRY CHRISTMAS
FELIZ NATAL
JOYEUX NOËL
BUON NATALE

Under the banner, and closer to the curb, a man in a Salvation Army uniform stood alongside an iron kettle hanging from a tripod. A sign affixed to the tripod read:

A cassette player blared "Silent Night."

The man in the Salvation Army uniform was wearing a hearing aid in his right ear, but no one could see it because he was also wearing ear muffs.

"God bless you," he said to a man who dropped a quarter into the kettle.

"Ladies and gentlemen, Gruber's will be closing in fifteen minutes," the woman's voice said. "We ask you to kindly complete your shopping before six o'clock. Thank you and Merry Christmas."

In the sixth-floor men's room Charlie looked at his watch again. He had already fastened the pillow to his own not-insignificant potbelly and had put on the red trousers and the black boots, and now he was slipping into the red tunic. He buttoned the tunic. He tightened the wide black belt around his waist and then put on the beard and the red hat with the white fur trim. He would give the beard a final adjustment at the mirrors over the sink before he left the men's room. He reached into the suitcase again, took out the big canvas sack with MERRY CHRISTMAS lettered on it in green and red, and then picked up the gun with the silencer on it. He tucked the gun under the tunic, over the pillow and his own potbelly.

Outside the stall someone was pissing in one of the urinals.

"Ladies and gentlemen, Gruber's will be closing in five minutes," the woman's voice said. "We ask you to kindly complete your shopping before six o'clock. Gruber's will be open again on Tuesday, December twenty-seventh, at which time all items in the store will be on sale at thirty- to fifty-percent savings. Thank you and Merry Christmas."

The sidewalks outside Gruber's looked like an oriental bazaar.

Aware of the fact that the store would close at six o'clock and further aware that this was Christmas Eve and late late shoppers might be willing to plunk down a few bucks for that last last-minute gift, the street vendors were out in droves, the overflow spilling from the choicer locations at the avenue entrances to here on the side street. Standing to the right of the Salvation Army kettle was a Puerto Rican man with a wide variety of wrist watches for sale, all of them displayed on a folding case set up on a folding stand. If the Law showed and the man did not have a vendor's license, he would fold the case and the stand, like an Arab folding a tent, and disappear into the night just as swiftly. The Deaf Man assumed all the watches were stolen. Otherwise, why was the man selling them for five dollars apiece?

"Fi' dollar!" the man shouted. "Bran' new wriss washes, fi' dollar!"

On the Deaf Man's left, shouting over the strains of "Silent Night" coming from the Deaf Man's cassette player, another sidewalk entrepreneur was displaying on a moth-eaten army blanket two dozen or more scarves in various brilliant colors.

"All silk!" he shouted to the passersby. "Take your choice, three dollars apiece, four for ten dollars, all silk!"

On the corner, where side street and avenue intersected, a man sold hot dogs from a cart. Another man sold pretzels. A third man sold 100% Fresh-Squeezed Orange Juice and Italian ices.

Up the avenue the bell in the tower of the Church of the Ascension of Christ began tolling the hour two minutes too soon.

The personnel manager came into the sixth-floor Toy Department at two minutes to six. Santa was sitting alone on his throne. The personnel manager—whose name was Samuel Aronowitz—went over to him and said, "We won't be getting any more little girls and boys tonight, Santa. Come on, let's have a drink."

Santa sighed forlornly.

They walked down the hall past the bewildering array of signs pointing in every direction of the compass: MANAGER'S OFFICE. CASHIER'S OFFICE. CREDIT OFFICE. RETURNS. PERSONNEL OFFICE. TOY DEPARTMENT. SANTA CLAUS. TELEPHONE OFFICE. REST ROOMS.

As they entered the personnel office, Aronowitz heard the woman's voice over the loudspeakers again.

"Ladies and gentlemen, it is now six o'clock. If you are still in the store, we advise you to use the Fourth Street exit. We take this opportunity now to wish you all a Merry Christmas from Gruber's uptown, downtown, all around the town. Merry Christmas to all and to all a good night."

"That was in our radio ads," Aronowitz said.

"Sir?" Drits said.

"The 'uptown, downtown, all around the town' line. Very effective. Come in, come in, what would you like to drink? I have scotch and gin."

"A little scotch, please," Drits said.

* * *

In the cashier's office Molly Driscoll and Helen Ruggiero both looked at the clock at the very same moment. Molly was the cashier. She had been the cashier since the middle of October. Helen was the assistant cashier and was angry that she had not been promoted to cashier when Liz Turner left the job.

It was now a quarter past six, and all but Better Dresses, Housewares, Major Appliances, Juniors, and Luggage had already delivered their zippered bags containing receipts from cash registers all over the store, dropping them into the little steel drawer set into the wall at right angles to the vault's outer steel door. Both steel doors to the vault were closed and locked. The safe door was open. They would lock that and set the alarm on it after the last of the receipts were in.

Helen and Molly were very eager to get the hell out of here.

Molly wanted to hurry home to her husband and three kids.

Helen wanted to hurry over to her boyfriend's apartment. He had told her he'd bought some very good coke that afternoon.

"What's keeping the rest of them?" she asked.

"Mr. Drits, I want to thank you personally for the splendid job you did for Gruber's," Aronowitz said. "Your warmth, your patience, your obvious understanding of children—all added up to the best Santa we've ever had. Would you care for another drink?"

"Yes, sir, thank you," Drits said.

"It was my hope, Mr. Drits, that you would come back to work for us again next year. Frankly we have a difficult time hiring convincing Santas."

"I'd be happy to come back next year," Drits said, accepting the drink.

Provided I'm not in Castleview, he thought.

* * *

In the locked stall in the men's room Charlie looked at his watch again.

Six-thirty.

Fifteen minutes before he made his move.

He was beginning to sweat behind the fake beard.

On the sidewalk outside the store the Deaf Man looked at his watch.

Twenty-five minutes to seven.

"Four dollar!" the Puerto Rican yelled. "Bran' new washes!"

"Silk scarves, all of them silk, two dollars apiece, four for six dollars!" the other man yelled.

"Si-uh-lent night," the cassette player blared, "ho-uh-lee night . . ."

The man at the rest room sinks was singing "Silent Night" at the top of his lungs.

In the locked stall Charlie looked at his watch again.

Six forty-two.

"Allllll is calm," the man sang, "alllllll is bright . . ."

In the cashier's office Helen looked at her watch and said, "So where's Better Dresses?"

It was six forty-five.

Charlie had to make his move.

The man at the sinks was still singing.

"Round yon vir-ih-gin, mother and child . . ."

Charlie waited. The man stopped singing. Charlie heard the sound of the water tap being turned on. He looked at his watch again. He couldn't wait a moment longer.

He came out of the stall.

He was looking at Santa Claus.

Santa Claus was washing his face.

His beard rested on the sink top.

Santa turned from the sink.

Charlie was looking at Arthur Drits, who'd served time at Castleview when Charlie was also a resident up there. A short-eyes offender.

"Hey, man," Drits said, looking surprised.

Drits was surprised because he was looking at a Santa Claus just like himself. He hadn't known there were *two* Santas in the store. Charlie, forgetting he was wearing a beard, thought Drits looked surprised because he'd recognized him. Charlie ran out of the men's room before Drits could take a better look.

Molly closed the safe door and pressed the buttons that set the alarm.

Two-four-seven, four-six-three.

"Well, that's it," she said.

*"Finalmente,"* Helen said.

When Drits came out of the employees' entrance of Gruber's, he was wearing his beard again. Made him feel good, wearing the beard, all dressed up like Santa, best damn Santa the store had ever had—who was that fuckin' imposter in the men's room? What made him feel even better was the quantity of scotch he'd drunk in Aronowitz's office. Very nice scotch. Nice and warm in his little round potbelly.

There was a man selling two-dollar watches on the sidewalk.

There was a man selling scarves at a dollar apiece.

There was a Salvation Army guy standing near a big black kettle.

"Here!" the Salvation Army guy said.

Drits looked at him.

"Ho, ho, ho," Drits said.

"Where's the bag?" the Salvation Army guy whispered. Drits figured he was nuts.

He threw him a finger and walked up the street.

* * *

Molly and Helen were about to leave the cashier's office when the inner steel door opened.

They were looking at Santa Claus.

"Merry Christmas, ladies," he said, and shot them both between the eyes.

The silencer worked fine.

The Deaf Man was confused only momentarily.

Of course, he thought, the *real* Santa. Or at least the *store's* Santa.

He looked at his watch.

Five minutes to seven.

Charlie should be coming out that door any minute now.

He glanced toward the corner where the side street intersected the avenue. A uniformed cop was just turning the corner.

"You!" the cop yelled at the Puerto Rican selling the hot watches.

The security officer at the door to the employee's entrance thought he'd seen Santa leave already.

"Two of you, huh?" he said to Charlie.

Charlie was at the time clock. The canvas sack with the red and green MERRY CHRISTMAS lettered onto its side was bulging with the money he'd taken from the safe. He lifted Helen Ruggiero's card from the rack and punched her out.

It was almost seven o'clock.

"Two of us, right," he said.

"Well, have a Merry Christmas, Santa," the security officer said, chuckling at his own little joke.

"You, too, Mac," Charlie said, and stepped out onto the sidewalk, where suddenly all hell broke loose.

The cop wanted to see a vendor's license.

The Puerto Rican didn't have a vendor's license.

The cop said he was giving him a summons.

Somebody in the sidewalk crowd yelled, "Come on, you shit, it's Christmas Eve!"

The cop yelled back, *"You* want a summons, too?"

Everybody in the crowd started razzing the cop.

That was when the Puerto Rican decided this would be a good time to make a break for it.

That was when Charlie came out of the store, carrying the sack of money.

The plan was to put the sack of money down near the kettle, where it would look like a Salvation Army prop.

The plan was for Charlie to disappear into the night, lootless.

The plan was for the Deaf Man to wait five minutes before picking up the sack and walking off with it.

That was the plan.

But the Puerto Rican collided with Charlie as he was coming out of the store.

And the sack fell to the sidewalk.

And zippered plastic bags of money spilled out onto the sidewalk.

And the crowd thought Santa was distributing money for Christmas.

And the cop thought Santa was a fuckin' thief.

The crowd surged forward toward the money on the sidewalk.

The cop's pistol was already unholstered.

"Stop or I'll shoot!" he yelled at Santa.

The crowd thought he was telling them to stop picking up the money.

The crowd yelled, "Fuck you, pig!"

The Puerto Rican was halfway up the block by then.

A gun suddenly appeared in Santa's hand.

The Deaf Man winced when the cop fired at Charlie.

Charlie went ass over teacups onto the sidewalk, a bullet hole in his right shoulder.

A lady dropped a dime into the Salvation Army kettle.

"God bless you," the Deaf Man said.

"Sleep in heav-enn-lee pee-eeese," the cassette player blared, "slee-eeep in heav-enn-lee peace . . ."

Shit, the Deaf Man thought.

And then he melted away into the crowd.

## 11

NEITHER CARELLA NOR BROWN WANTED TO BE working on Christmas Day.

They had both deliberately chosen to work the four-to-midnight on Christmas Eve so that they could spend the big day itself with their families. But at approximately seven last night a man named Charlie Henkins had inconsiderately held up Gruber's department store, managing to kill two women in the process. Carella and Brown were catching when a frantic patrolman called in to say he'd just shot Santa Claus. The case was officially theirs, and that was why—at ten on Christmas morning—they were questioning Henkins in his room at Saint Jude's Hospital.

"I'm an innocent dupe," Henkins said.

He did look very innocent, Brown thought. In his white hospital tunic, his left shoulder bandaged, his blue eyes twinkling, his little potbelly round and soft under the sheet, he looked like an old Saint Nick without a beard and settling down for a long winter's nap.

"It was the other Santa Claus done it," Henkins said.

"What other Santa Claus?" Carella asked.

"Arthur Drits," Henkins said.

Carella looked at Brown.

"Let me get this straight," Carella said.

"I'm an innocent dupe," Henkins said again.

"What were you doing in that Santa Claus outfit?" Carella said.

"I was going to an orphanage to surprise the kiddies there."

"What orphanage?" Brown said. "We don't *have* any orphanages up here."

"I thought there was an orphanage up here."

"Were you taking a gun to the orphanage?"

"That gun is not mine, officers," Henkins said.

"Whose gun is it?"

"Santa's," Henkins said. "The *other* Santa."

"Let me get this straight," Carella said again. He was having a difficult time getting it straight. He knew only that Henkins had come out of Gruber's with a sackful of zippered plastic bags containing—according to the count made before the cash was delivered to the property clerk's office—eight hundred thousand, two hundred fifty-two dollars in cash plus a sizable number of personal checks. Henkins had drawn a gun—identified and tagged as a .32-caliber Smith & Wesson Regulation Police—and a silencer fitting that gun had been found in the cashier's office at Gruber's, alongside the body of one of the victims, a woman named Helen Ruggiero, who incidentally had four marijuana joints in her handbag. The police officer on duty had shouted the customary warning and then shot him. He was currently at Headquarters downtown, filling out all the papers that explained why he had drawn his service revolver in the first place and why he had fired it in the second place.

"Let me explain it," Henkins said.

Brown knew he was about to tell a whopper.

"I went in Gruber's to use the facilities," Henkins said.

"What facilities?"

"I went up to the sixth floor to take a leak."

"Then what?"

"I ran into Drits in the men's room."

"Arthur Drits."

"Arthur Drits, who I knew from long ago."

"Yeah, go ahead," Brown said.

"Drits was dressed as Santa Claus. Also he had the gun you're now saying was my gun."

"How'd *you* get the gun?"

"Drits gave it to me."

"Why?"

"He said, 'Merry Christmas,' and gave it to me."

"So you took it."

"It was a present."

"So when you came out of Gruber's you had the gun."

"Exactly."

"And you pulled the gun."

"Only to give it to the police officer, because by then I was having second thoughts about it."

"What kind of second thoughts?"

"Who knew but what that gun may have been used in a crime of some sort?"

"Who indeed?" Brown said.

"Where'd you get the sackful of money?" Carella asked.

"That was the Puerto Rican's."

"What Puerto Rican?"

"The one with all the wrist watches. He had the watches in the sack. When he bumped into me, the watches and the money fell out of the sack."

"So the gun belonged to Drits, and the sack belonged to the Puerto Rican."

"You've got it," Henkins said. "I'm an innocent dupe."

Carella looked at Brown again.

"There are barbarians in this city," Henkins said. "You should have seen all those people scrambling to pick up that money." He shook his head. "On Christmas *Eve!*"

"Let's talk about this Arthur Drits character," Brown said.

"Yes, sir," Henkins said.

"You say he was a friend of yours?"

"An acquaintance, sir," Henkins said.

Brown knew from all the "sirs" that he was onto something.

"You said you knew him from long ago."

"Yes, sir."

*"How* long ago?"

"Oh, four or five years ago."

"And you ran into him accidentally in the men's room at Gruber's."

"That is exactly what happened, sir," Henkins said. "I swear on my mother's eyes."

"Leave your mother out of this," Brown said.

"My mother happens to be dead," Henkins said.

"So are two people in Gruber's cashier's office," Brown said. "Who were killed with the gun *you* were carrying."

"Drits's gun," Henkins said.

"Who you met long ago."

"Four, five years ago."

"Where?" Brown said.

"Where what, sir?"

"Where'd you meet him?"

"Well, sir, that's difficult to remember."

"Try," Brown said.

"I really couldn't say."

Brown looked at Carella.

"You understand," Carella said, "that we're talking two counts of homicide here, don't you? *Plus . . .*"

"Drits must have killed those two people," Henkins said.

"Where'd you meet this Drits?" Carella said. "If he exists."

Henkins hesitated.

"Forget it," Brown said to Carella and then turned to Henkins. "You're under arrest, Mr. Henkins. We're charging you with two counts of homicide and one count of armed robbery. In accordance with the Supreme Court ruling in Miranda-Escobedo . . .''

"Hey, hold it just a minute," Henkins said. "I'm a fuckin' innocent *dupe* here."

"It was Drits and the Puerto Rican, right?" Carella said.

"It was Drits gave me the gun. I don't know where the Puerto Rican got all that money those animals were scrambling for."

"Where'd you meet him?" Brown said.

"On the sidewalk outside. He crashed into me on . . ."

"Not the Puerto Rican," Brown shouted, *"Drits!* Where the fuck did you meet him? Was he in on this with you? Did the two Santa Claus outfits have something to do with . . . ?"

"I told you once, I'll tell you again. I was taking a leak in the men's room when Drits . . ."

"The *first* time!" Brown shouted. "Where'd you meet him the *first* time?"

"Well. . . ."

"Make it fast," Brown said. "My Christmas is waiting."

"Castleview, okay?" Henkins said.

"You did time at Castleview?"

"A little."

"How much?"

"I grossed twenty."

"For what?"

"Well . . . I got thirsty one night."

"What does that mean?"

"I went in this liquor store."

"Where?"

"Calm's Point."

"And?"

"I asked the guy for a fifth of Gordon's."

"And?"

"He didn't want to give it to me."

"So?"

"I had to persuade him."

"How'd you persuade him? With a gun?"

"Well, I suppose you could call it a gun."

"What would *you* call it?"

"I suppose I would call it a gun."

"What did the *judge* call it?"

"Well, a gun."

"So this was an armed robbery."

"That's what they said it was."

"And you drew twenty for it."

"I only done eight."

"So now you're back at the same old stand again, huh?"

"I keep tellin' you it was *Drits's* gun. It must've been Drits who shot those two ladies. If I'da known the gun was hot, I'd never have taken it."

"Who said they were ladies?" Brown asked.

"What?"

"Who said the two dead people in the cashier's office were ladies?"

Henkins blinked.

"You want to tell us about it?" Carella said.

The room went silent. The detectives waited.

"Dennis must've shot those two ladies," Henkins said.

"Dennis who?"

"Dennis Dove. He must've been the one who went in the cashier's office and shot those two ladies. I was no-where near the place when the robbery went down. I was waiting on the ground floor. I didn't even know a robbery was happening. All I was supposed to do was wait for Dennis and take the gun and the sack . . ."

"*Wait* a minute," Carella said, "let me get this straight." He was having difficulty getting it straight again.

"Dennis asked me to do him a favor, that's all," Henkins said. His twinkling blue eyes were darting frantically. "What he asked me to do was wait downstairs and take this sack he wanted me to bring to the orphanage . . ."

"The orphanage again," Brown said.

". . . to give to the little kiddies there on Christmas Eve."

"And the gun?"

"I don't know how Drits got the gun. Maybe he was in on it, too. An ex-con, you know?" Henkins said, and shrugged.

"Is that why he was in Castleview? For armed robbery?"

"No, he digs kids."

"What do you mean?"

"Short eyes, you know?"

"A child molester?"

"Yeah." Henkins shrugged again.

"But you think he was in on this robbery with Dove, huh?"

"Musta been, don't you think?" Henkins said. "Otherwise, how'd he get the gun?"

"But you were on the ground floor."

"That's right."

"Nowhere near the cashier's office."

"That's right."

"The cashier's office is on the sixth floor," Brown said.

"So's the men's room," Carella said.

"Coincidence, pure and simple," Henkins said.

"Bullshit, pure and simple," Brown said.

"Who's Dennis Dove?" Carella asked.

"Guy I met a while back. Asked me to do him this favor on Christmas Eve."

"Is that his full name? Dennis Dove?"

"Far as I know."

"Where does he live?"

"I don't know."

"What does he look like?"

"He's a big tall blond guy," Henkins said. "Wears a hearing aid."

Both detectives looked at each other at exactly the same moment.

"A while back when?" Brown asked.

"Huh?" Henkins said.

"When you met him."

"October sometime. When Lizzie was filling us in."

"Lizzie who?" Carella asked. He had the sinking feeling that Henkins was not talking about Lizzie Borden.

"Some broad he was banging. Crazy about him. She used to work at Gruber's. Not that I knew what they were planning. I was only there because they wanted me to do them a favor, you see. Whatever else . . ."

"Lizzie who?" Carella asked again.

"Turner," Henkins said.

So there they were.

And where they were . . .

They didn't know where they were.

It seemed as though the Deaf Man had been behind the armed robbery at Gruber's. It further seemed that Elizabeth Turner had worked at Gruber's—they would check to see if she had worked in the cashier's office, a likelihood considering her past employment—and that she had been intimate with the Deaf Man. They did not know how she had met the Deaf Man. They knew for certain that Henkins was lying through his teeth about the robbery itself—the murder weapon had been in his possession, and only *his* fingerprints were on the gun—but they didn't know if he was also lying about this person named Dennis Dove, whose description fit the Deaf Man's. He could not have pulled the name Lizzie Turner out of a hat, though. And on the night of her murder a man fitting the Deaf Man's description had been seen carrying a woman fitting Elizabeth Turner's description. It seemed to make sense. Sort of.

But what did the Gruber's job have to do with the notes the Deaf Man had been sending them?

Nothing that they could see.

Two nightsticks.

Three pairs of handcuffs.

Four police hats.

Five walkie-talkies.

Six police shields.

Seven wanted flyers.

Eight black horses.

Nine patrol cars.

Ten D.D. forms.

Eleven Detective Specials.

Twelve roast pigs.

And then, at eleven on Christmas morning, while Carella was typing up the report on their interview with Henkins, and Brown was on the phone with a parole officer seeking a last-known address for Arthur Drits, a delivery boy arrived at the slatted wooden railing that separated the squadroom from the corridor outside. He was carrying a package wrapped in green paper. It was a rather bulky package, and he was having difficulty holding it in both arms.

"Is there a Detective Stephen Louis Carella here?" he asked.

"I'm Carella," Carella said.

"Di Fiore Florist," the delivery boy said.

"Come in," Carella said.

"Well . . . somebody wanna help me with the latch here?" the delivery boy said.

Carella helped him with the latch. The delivery boy

struggled the package into the squadroom, looked around for a place to put it, and set it down on Genero's vacant desk. Carella wondered if he was expected to tip the delivery boy. He dug in his pocket and handed him a quarter.

"Can you spare it?" the delivery boy said. "Merry Christmas," he added sourly and walked out.

Carella tore the green wrapping from the package.

He was looking at what he expected was supposed to be a pear tree. He didn't know if it was a *real* pear tree, but at any rate there were pears hanging on it. They weren't *real* pears, but they were clearly pears. Little wooden pears hanging all over the tree.

There was also an envelope hanging on the tree.

The envelope was addressed to Detective Stephen Louis Carella.

He tore open the envelope.

The card inside read:

On the first day of
Christmas my true love
gave to me a partridge
in a pear tree...

Carella searched the tree for a partridge.

A little package wrapped in red foil was hanging on

the tree. Carella unwrapped the package. Something decorated with feathers was inside it. It was not a partridge, but it looked like a bird of some sort, feathers glued all over it. Chicken feathers, they looked like. But it was not a chicken either, too small for a chicken. He took a closer look.

The thing was a severed human ear.

Carella dropped it at once.


On December 26, the second day of Christmas, two nightsticks arrived at the squadroom. They were wrapped in Christmas paper, and they were addressed to Carella.

The detectives looked at the nightsticks.

They did not appear to be new ones. Both of them were scarred and battered.

"Still he could've bought them," Kling said.

In this city a police officer was responsible for the purchase of every piece of equipment he wore or carried, with the exception of his shield, which came free with the job—the pin used to hold the shield to the uniform cost him fifty cents. Each officer was given a yearly allowance of three hundred and seventy dollars for his uniform. He bought his own gun—usually a Colt .38 or a Smith & Wesson of the same caliber—and his own bullets—six in the gun and twelve on his belt—and his own whistle, which these days was selling for two dollars. He also bought his own shoes. A foot patrolman wore out at least two pairs of shoes a year. A two-foot-long wooden nightstick cost the police officer two dollars and fifty cents, plus another forty cents for the leather thong, His short rubber billy cost three dollars and fifty cents with—again—another forty cents for the thong. Handcuffs were currently selling for twenty-five dollars.

Most policemen bought their gear from the Police

Equipment Bureau downtown near the Police Academy, but there were police supply stores all over the city. Kling himself was wearing a Detective Special he had bought in one of those stores. He'd had to identify himself when purchasing the pistol, but he'd bought uniform shirts and even handcuffs when he was a patrolman, and no one had even asked him his name. He was also wearing, at the moment, one of the ties Eileen Burke had bought him for Christmas. It was a very garish tie, but no one was looking at it. They were still looking at the nightsticks.

"Better run them through for latents," Meyer said.

"Won't be any on them," Brown said.

"I don't get it," Carella said. "He sends us a note with two pictures of a nightstick on it, and then he sends us two nightsticks. Do *you* get it?"

He was addressing all of them, but only Hawes answered.

"He's crazy," he said. "He doesn't *have* to make sense."

"So tomorrow we get three pairs of handcuffs, right? And the day after that . . ."

"Let's see what happens tomorrow," Meyer said.

On December 27 they caught up with Arthur Drits.

Carella and Brown talked to him in the Interrogation Office.

Drits had been inside interrogation offices before. He knew that the mirror he faced was a one-way mirror, and he suspected that someone was sitting in the adjoining office, watching his every move. Actually the adjoining office was empty.

Brown laid it flat out.

"What were you doing in Gruber's department store the night it was held up?"

"This is the first I'm hearing of any holdup," Drits said.

"You don't read the papers?" Carella said.

"Not too often," Drits said.

What he read were the advertisements for children's clothing, the ones showing little girls in short dresses.

"You watch television?" Brown asked.

"I don't have a television," Drits said.

"So you don't know Gruber's was held up on Christmas Eve, is that right?"

"I just heard it from you a minute ago."

"You know anybody named Elizabeth Turner?"

"No."

"She used to work in the cashier's office at Gruber's."

They had already confirmed this with the personnel manager. Elizabeth Turner had begun working there on August 8 and had left the job on October 7—seventeen days before her murder.

"Never heard of her," Drits said.

"How about Dennis Dove?"

"Him neither."

"Charlie Henkins?"

Drits blinked.

"Ring a bell?" Brown said.

"Yeah," Drits said.

"Met him at Castleview, didn't you?"

"Yeah."

"Where you were doing time for First-Degree Rape."

"So they said."

"See him again since you got out?"

"No."

"How about Christmas Eve? Did you see Henkins on Christmas Eve?"

"No."

"Were you in the sixth-floor men's room at Gruber's on Christmas Eve?"

"Yeah?" Drits said, looking puzzled.

"Did you see a Santa Claus in the men's room?"

"Yeah?"

"Did he look like Henkins?"

"No, he looked like Santa Claus."

"That was Henkins."

"Coulda fooled me," Drits said.

"What were you doing in the men's room at Gruber's?" Brown asked.

"Washing my face. This guy come out of the booth, the stall there, he was wearing a Santa Claus suit same as me. I nearly shit."

"*You* were wearing a Santa Claus suit, too?" Carella said.

"Well, sure."

The detectives looked at each other. They thought Charlie Henkins had been lying about Drits and the Santa Claus suit, but now . . .

"As part of the job?" Brown asked.

"Sure."

"The holdup called for *two* guys in Santa Claus suits?"

"What?" Drits said.

"What the fuck were you doing in a *Santa* Claus suit?" Brown asked.

"I worked for the *store,*" Drits said. "I was the store's *Santa* Claus."

Both detectives looked at him.

"I was a very good Santa," Drits said with dignity.

"And you never heard of anyone named Elizabeth Turner? Never met her?"

"Never."

"Or Dennis Dove?"

"Never."

"Did you hand Charlie Henkins a gun in the men's room at Gruber's?"

"I didn't hand him anything. I didn't even know he *was* Henkins till you told me. I was surprised to see another guy in a Santa Claus suit, is all. *He* looked surprised, too. He just ran out."

"What'd *you* do?"

"I dried my face, I put on my beard again, and I left the store."

"To go where?"

"Home."

"Which is where?"

"I live in a hotel on Waverly."

"Were you outside the store when Henkins got shot?"

"I didn't know Henkins *got* shot."

"Didn't see the shooting, huh?"

"No."

"What *did* you see? When you came out of the store?"

"Who remembers what I saw? People. I saw people."

"Who? What people?"

"People. Some guy selling watches, another guy selling scarves, some nutty Salvation Army guy . . ."

"What do you mean by 'nutty'?"

"Nuts, you know? He told me, 'Here.' "

"He told you what?"

"Here."

"H-e-a-r?"

"No, h-e-r-e. I *think*. Who knows with nuts?"

"Here? What'd he mean?"

"I don't know *what* he meant."

"What'd you *think* he meant?"

"I think he was nuts. He asked me where the bag was."

"What'd he look like?" Carella asked at once.

"Tall guy in a Salvation Army uniform. Nuts."

"What color was his hair?"

"I don't know. He was wearing a hat."

"Was he wearing a hearing aid?"

"He had ear muffs on."

Carella sighed. Brown sighed, too.

"All right, keep your nose clean," Brown said.

"I can go?" Drits said.

"Why?" Brown said. "Did you *do* something?"

"No, no, hey," Drits said.

"See that you *don't,* " Carella said.

That afternoon three pairs of handcuffs arrived.

They had already questioned George Di Fiore, the proprietor of Di Fiore Florists, about the man who'd ordered the pear tree, and he'd told them first of all that it wasn't a real pear tree, it was in fact a *Ficus Benjamina,* but they were all out of pear trees when the man came in asking for one. Di Fiore had also told them that the man had personally picked out the little wooden pears to fasten to the tree, and then had personally affixed the card and the little wrapped package to the tree. Di Fiore hadn't known what was in the little wrapped package, and did not consider it his business to ask. Carella wanted to ask if Di Fiore—which meant "of the flowers" in Italian—had chosen his profession because of his name. He knew an anesthesiologist named Dr. Sleepe—although he pronounced it Sleh-puh—and a chiropractor named Hands. Instead he asked what Di Fiore's pear-tree customer had looked like.

"Tall blond man wearing a hearing aid," Di Fiore told him.

So now the three pairs of handcuffs.

They all looked brand-new.

They could have been purchased, as Kling again suggested, at any police-supply store in town.

December 27, the third day of Christmas, and three pairs of handcuffs.

Tomorrow, Carella knew for certain, four police hats would arrive.

And they did.

Arrived by United Parcel delivery, all boxed and wrapped in festive Christmas paper.

The hats were definitely not new.

Their sweat bands were greasy, and their leather peaks were cracked with age. Moreover, they had police shields pinned to them. And unlike the *pictures* they'd received earlier, *these* shields had numbers on them.

There were four different numbers on the shields.

Carella called Mullaney at Personnel and asked him to identify the shields for him.

"This Coppola again?" Mullaney said.

When he came back onto the line, he told Carella that those shields, and presumably the hats to which they were pinned, belonged to four different police officers at four different precincts. He asked Carella if he wanted the patrolmen's names—one of them, actually, was a female cop, but in Mullaney's world all police officers were patrol*men*. Carella took down the names and then called each precinct. The desk sergeant on duty at each precinct told Carella that yes, indeed, such and such an officer worked out of this precinct, but he—or, in the case of the woman, she—had not reported having lost his, or her, hat. One of the sergeants asked Carella if this was a joke. Carella told him he guessed it wasn't a joke.

But if it wasn't a joke, then what the hell *was* it?

Carella grunted and picked up one of the police hats.

The man or woman who'd worn it had dandruff.

"Those are *police* walkie-talkies," Miscolo said. "Standard issue."

Miscolo was a clerk and not a detective, but it didn't take a detective to see that each of the walkie-talkies that arrived by United Parcel delivery on the fifth day of Christmas, December 29, were marked with plastic labeling tape of the sort you printed up yourself with a lettering gun. Each of the walkie-talkies had two strips

of tape on it. The first strip was identical in each case.
It read:

RETURN TO CHARGING RACK

The second strips differed. One read:

PROPERTY OF 21ST PRECINCT

Another read:

PROPERTY OF 12TH PRECINCT

And so on:

PROPERTY OF 61ST PRECINCT
PROPERTY OF MIDTOWN EAST
PROPERTY OF 83RD PRECINCT

Five different walkie-talkies from five different precincts.

"Those were stolen from five different precincts,"
Miscolo said. "This man is entering police precincts all
over town."

The six police shields that arrived on December 30, a
Friday and the sixth day of Christmas, similarly belonged
to police officers from six different precincts. None of the
officers had reported his shield missing or stolen; a cop
does not like to admit that somebody ripped off his goddamn potsie. Moreover, the six precincts from which the
shields had been stolen—Carella was sure by now that
they'd been stolen—were not any of the precincts from
which the walkie-talkies or the police hats were stolen. In

short, fifteen precincts had been entered—four police hats, five walkie-talkies, and six shields for a total of fifteen—and police equipment had been removed from them under the very eyes of the police themselves. There were twenty precincts in Isola alone. Some of the police equipment had been stolen from precincts in Calm's Point and Majesta. None had been stolen from either Bethtown or Riverhead. But someone had been very busy indeed, even assuming that neither the nightsticks nor the handcuffs were similarly stolen, which would have brought to twenty-four the number of precincts whose security had been breached.

For what purpose? Carella wondered.

Toward what end?

The seventh day of Christmas was New Year's Eve, a Saturday.

Naturally seven wanted flyers arrived in that morning's mail.

And naturally there was a power failure at three-thirty that afternoon, fifteen minutes before the eight-to-four was scheduled to be relieved. It would not have been New Year's Eve unless something happened to prevent the outgoing shift from leaving when it was supposed to. The day shift detectives, eager to get the hell out of the squadroom to start the festivities, knew only that somehow the Greater Isola Power & Light Company (formerly the Metropolitan Light & Power Company) had screwed up yet another time, and they would not be able to complete their paperwork before four o'clock. What they did not know was that Greater Isola Power & Light—known to its millions of dissatisfied customers as the Big (for Greater) Ipple (for I. P. L.)—was totally innocent of any malfeasance this time around.

Gopher Nelson had caused the power failure.

The power failure lasted exactly one minute.

Gopher caused it by throwing a switch pinpointed on the

"Composite Feeder Plate Map" the Deaf Man had provided. The map was one of four the Deaf Man had given Gopher, explaining that he'd acquired them—along with several others—years ago, when he was planning to place a bomb under the mayor's bed. Gopher wondered why the Deaf Man planned such peculiar things, but he didn't ask; the money was good.

The first map was stamped "Property of Metropolitan Light & Power Company" and was titled "60-Cycle Network Area Designations and Boundaries Upper Isola." It showed the locations of all the area substations in that section of the city. The area in which the 87th Precinct station house was located was designated as "Grover North." Into this substation ran high-voltage supply cables, also called feeders, from switching stations elsewhere on the transmission system.

The second map, similarly stamped, was titled "System Ties," and it was a detailed enlargement of the feeder system supplying any given substation. The substation on the first map had been labeled "No. 4 Fuller." By locating this on the more detailed map, Gopher and the Deaf Man were able to identify the number designation for the feeder: 85RL9.

Which brought them to the third map, titled simply "85RL9" and subtitled "Location Grover North Substation." This was a rather long, narrow diagram of the route the feeders, or supply cables, traveled below the city's streets, with numbers indicating the manholes that provided access to the cables themselves. The cable-carrying manhole closest to the 87th Precinct station house was three blocks way on Grover Avenue and Fuller Street. On the "Composite Feeder Plate Map" it was numbered "R2147-12O'ESC-CENT."

The manhole was a hundred and twenty feet east of the southern curb of Fuller in the center of the street—hence the designation "12O'ESC-CENT"—just opposite the bronze statue of John G. Fuller, the noted balloonist. The cables were five feet below the surface of the street, protected by a three-hundred-pound manhole cover. Gopher set up a Big Ipple manhole stand, raised the manhole cover with a crowbar, went down into the manhole, found the cable switch, opened it, and then closed it a minute later. The lights in the 87th Precinct station house—and indeed in all the surrounding residential houses—were out for only that amount of time. But that was all the time Gopher needed for his purposes.

It was four-fifteen when he arrived at the muster desk, wearing a G. I. P. & L. tag pinned to his coveralls. He presented his phony credentials to the desk sergeant and told him he was here to see about the power failure. The sergeant looked across the desk at this little guy with the floppy brown mustache and the blue watch cap and told him there hadn't been any *real* power failure, lights just went out for a minute or so, that was all. Gopher said, "A minute or so is a power failure to us."

"So what do you want to do?" the sergeant asked. He was thinking that a sergeant from the Eight-Four was having a big bash at his house tonight, and he was hoping it'd still be going strong when he got there. He'd be relieved at a quarter to twelve. Figure fifteen minutes to change in the locker room, another half hour to get crosstown . . .

"I gotta put a voltage recorder on the line," Gopher said.

"What's the big fuss?" the sergeant said. "We got lights, don't we?"

"For *now*," Gopher said. "You want them to go out again when you got some big ax murderer in here?"

The desk sergeant didn't even want them to go out when they had some little numbers runner in here. The desk sergeant was thinking about putting on a funny hat and blowing a horn.

"That your voltage recorder there?" he asked, peering

over the top of the desk to the wooden box at Gopher's feet. Gopher hoisted the box onto the desk. It was about the size of a small suitcase. It looked like a larger version of the sort of box one might use to carry roller skates, with metal edges and a handle and clasps to open the lid. But on the face of the box there was a rectangular dial with a yellow band, a red band, and a green band. The yellow band was marked at the end farthest left with a stamped metal tag reading "60 volts." The green band was marked at its center point with a similar tag reading "120 volts." The red band was marked at the end farthest right with a tag reading "200 volts." A needle was behind the glass covering the dial. Three knobs were under the dial.

"So what's that for?" the sergeant asked.

"It's got a tape disc and graph paper inside it," Gopher said. "It monitors the incoming voltage, lets us know we're getting any surges or fluctuations in the . . ."

"I'm sorry I asked," the sergeant said. "Go do your thing."

Gopher started up the iron-runged steps to the squadroom.

There was no graph paper or tape disc inside the wooden box.

The dial was real enough—Gopher had taken it from a genuine voltage recorder—but it was connected to nothing, and the knobs beneath it, used on a genuine recorder to calibrate the meter, had absolutely no function.

Inside the box there was a timer with a seven-day dial. The timer was normally used for programming heating, airconditioning, and ventilating equipment, as well as lights, pumps, motors, and other single-phase to three-phase loads. Seven sets of trippers, supplied with the timer, enabled its user to set a different ON/OFF program for each day of the week. The timer looked like this:

When the swing-away cover was moved to the left, the terminals looked like this:

This was December 31, a Saturday.

The timer was already programmed for next Thursday, which would be January 5.

It was set for 8:15 P.M., at which time it would turn on whatever electrical appliance its wires were connected to.

Its wires were not connected to any electrical appliance.

There was a five-pound charge of dynamite inside the box. There was a plastic bag of black powder inside the box. One of the wires from the terminal led to a ground. The other wire was loosely twisted around the first wire. At 8:15 P.M. next Thursday, when the timer triggered the ON switch, a surge of electricity would arc through the loosely twisted wires and cause a spark, which would ignite the black powder and subsequently the fuse leading to the dynamite charge. All Gopher had to do now was plug his phony voltage recorder into an ordinary 110-volt outlet and set the present time on the timer.

The rest would take care of itself.

In the squadroom upstairs the detectives were discussing the wanted flyers that had arrived in that day's mail.

"These have got to be the real article," O'Brien said.

"Could've got 'em from a post office," Fujiwara said.

"Beautiful crowd, ain't they?" Willis said. "Rape, arson, armed robbery, kidnapping . . ."

"You don't think he's pinpointing them, do you?"

"Pinpointing who?"

"The ones who did the Gruber's job with him."

"What he's doing," O'Brien said, "he's telling us he can go into any goddamn squadroom in this city and do whatever the fuck he wants inside them."

"*If* he got them from a squadroom," Fujiwara said.

"That's where he got them, all right," Willis said.

Gopher stopped at the slatted rail divider separating the squadroom from the corridor outside.

"Electric company," he said. "Got to put a voltage recorder on your line."

"Come on in," O'Brien said.

"Where's your fuse box?" Gopher asked.

"Who knows?" Willis said.

Gopher had no reason to locate the fuse box. He simply wanted an excuse to look the place over. He set the box down near one of the desks and began poking around. Plenty of outlets all over the room, but he needed someplace to plant his incendiaries.

"What's in here?" he asked, his hand on a doorknob.

"Supply closet," Fujiwara said.

A naked light bulb with a pull chain was hanging inside the closet. Gopher pulled the chain. A 40-watt bulb, amazing these guys could *see* anything in here.

"Mind if I smoke?" he asked.

"Long as you don't set fire to the joint," O'Brien said.

Gopher laughed.

He checked the closet baseboard for outlets. Usually you didn't find an outlet in a closet, but some of these old buildings, they divided a big room by throwing up walls wherever they felt like. He found a double outlet on the rear wall of the closet. Good. He could plug in his box right here, where there was plenty of flammable shit. Give it a roaring start with his incendiaries, should have a nice little blaze in minutes flat. Nice old wood all around the room. Oh, this would be a very pretty fire.

"I'll be through in a minute here," Gopher said. "You got an ashtray?"

"Just grind it out on the floor," O'Brien said.

It took Gopher a minute and a half to carry his box into the closet, set it on the floor under a shelf at the rear, and plug it in.

It took him three minutes to set the timer with the present time, which he read off the squadroom clock.

"I have to bring some other stuff up here," he said. "Some chemicals to keep the closet dry. Otherwise, the recorder won't give us a true reading. I'll stack them on the shelves, out of your way."

He went downstairs for his incendiaries.

He stacked three innocent-looking cardboard cartons in the supply closet, one on each of three shelves above the box. As he worked, he listened to the detectives.

"So why's he trying to tell us he can get into squad-rooms?" Fujiwara said. *"If* that's what he's trying to tell us."

" 'Cause he's crazy," Willis said.

Over the past several years it had become a ritual.

On New Year's Eve, before they left the house for whatever party they were going to, Carella and Teddy made love. And when they returned to the house again, in the New Year this time, they made love again.

Once a long time ago Carella had been told by a detective of Scottish ancestry that in the northern parts of Great Britain the custom of first-footing is still honored on the first day of the New Year. A dark-eyed, dark-haired person—presumably because Britain's enemies in days of yore were fair-haired and light-eyed—carries a symbolic gift, usually a piece of coal and a pinch of salt, over the doorsill of a friend's house. The gift bearer is the first person to set foot in the house in the New Year: hence, first-footing. His or her gift is a wish for health and prosperity throughout the coming year.

Carella didn't know whether he was recalling the story faithfully or even if the Scotsman had been telling the truth. He suspected, however, that one doesn't kid around when it comes to custom. He liked the story, and he wanted to believe that such a custom, in fact, existed. In a world where too many people came bearing death, it was comforting to know that in some remote little village far to the north, someone—on the very first day of the bright New Year—came bearing the gift of life: a piece of coal for the grate, a pinch of salt for the pot. In a sense, the Scotsman had said, the custom was a reaffirmation of life.

For Carella love making was a similar reaffirmation of life.

He loved this woman completely.

This woman was his life.

And holding her in his arms on New Year's Day—dark-eyed, dark-haired people both, no enemies here in this bed—he silently wished her the best that life could afford.

But New Year's Day was also the eighth day of Christmas.

And someone would come bearing tidings of death.

# 12

BEFORE THE GRUBER'S HOLDUP THE DEAF MAN
had planned to hire someone else to do the horses—just as
he had hired Gopher to do the cars and the squadroom. He
did not enjoy messiness. Even cutting off the wino's ear,
a necessity if he was to make a point to the clods of the
Eight-Seven, had been distasteful to him. The Deaf Man
liked things clean and neat. Precise. The festivities he'd
planned for the enjoyment of the detectives who worked
out of the old station house on Grover Avenue were initially conceived as a fillip to the department store job. First
let them know that he could do whatever the hell he wanted
to in this precinct, pull off the job, get away clean, and
then teach them once and for all that he would no longer
tolerate their meddling in his affairs. End the relationship.
Good-bye, boys.

He changed his mind after the Gruber's job ended in
disaster.

Again by accident.

All that work for nothing.

And now he was angry.

He did not normally enjoy excesses of emotion. A
woman in bed was not an object of love to him, but merely
something to control. In his lexicon ''to love'' meant ''to
risk.'' Elizabeth Turner had made the fatal mistake of falling in love with him and thereby risking all. She had
pleaded with him not to execute the Gruber's job, to change
his way of living, move with her to another city, forget the
past.

The whiff of danger had been all-pervasive.

Her love for him could have led her into dangerously

unexpected paths: perhaps a visit to the police to warn them of the impending job, with a tearful scene later in which she would confess her indiscretion and beg him once again, now that she had made the job impossible, to give it up.

She had never threatened him with such a course of action—she knew better than to threaten him—but he sensed in her shifting moods that she now regretted the information she had given him and, because she "loved" him, might do something foolish to "protect" him. What the Deaf Man dreaded most were the good intentions of well-meaning people, the fools of the world.

But he had not killed her in anger.

Anger was wasteful, a silly energy-consuming extravagance.

He had, in fact, killed her immediately after making love to her, whatever *that* meant. Two people "making" love. Two heavy-breathing individuals—although he hadn't been breathing quite so heavily as she—together constructing a dripping edifice known as—ta-*rah*—LOVE! The architect and the contractor in passionate collaboration, "making" love.

To make.

The verb itself as many-faceted as a diamond, the way most words in the English language were.

To make.

To create, construct, form, or shape: *I made a chair*—or a bomb.

To give a new form or use to: *I made a silk purse from a sow's ear*—or a symbolic partridge from a wino's ear.

To earn: *to make money*—which I failed to do on Christmas Eve.

To prepare and start: *to make a fire*—which I will do on Twelfth Night.

To force or compel: *I made her do my bidding*—which I thought Elizabeth Turner *was* doing until she began to have those fatal second doubts.

To cause to become: *I made her dead.*

But without anger.

The kiss of death.

When one pimply-faced teenager asks another similarly blossoming pal, "Did you *make* her last night?" is he actually asking, "Did you force her to succumb?"

The Deaf Man had not forced Elizabeth Turner to succumb.

She had offered herself to him of her own volition, and he had casually shot her afterward—she on her knees before him, head bent, expecting God knew whatever further pleasure from behind.

No anger.

But now there was anger.

The old brick armory on First Street and Saint Sebastian Avenue had been used to stable horses for longer than any of the neighborhood residents could remember. At one time in the city's history as many as a hundred horses were kept there, all part of the then-elite Mounted Patrol. The Golden Nugget Squad, as the mounties were familiarly, derisively, and enviously called by their fellow police officers, had been slowly reduced in numbers over the years—two successive mayors believing that men on horseback were too reminiscent of cossacks—and was now virtually defunct. Cops on horseback were used only for ceremonial occasions or events expected to draw huge numbers of crowds. There had, for example, been twelve mounties on duty last night on the Stem downtown, where hundreds of thousands of people watched the red ball's descent into the New Year. The horses those twelve cops were riding were all stabled in the armory up here in the 87th Precinct, together with another twelve, the two dozen being the remnants of a once-proud legion. Most of those horses were brown. Only ten of them were black.

On New Year's Day there was only one police officer on duty at the armory. Even on days that were *not* legal holidays there were three officers there at most. The stable hands—four of them—were civil service employees, but not policemen. On New Year's Day only one stable hand was at the armory. Both he and the patrolman were nursing terrific hangovers.

It was a cold rainy day—a bad harbinger for the year ahead.

The man who arrived at the armory was carrying a pizza in a white cardboard carton. He was also carrying a white paper bag. He approached the big wooden door with its iron hinges, lifted the knocker, and waited.

The patrolman on duty opened the door and looked out into the rain.

"Yeah?" he said.

"Got a pizza and some sodas for you," the man outside the door said.

He was wearing a black trench coat. He was blond and hatless. There was a hearing aid in his right ear.

"Nobody ordered no pizza," the patrolman said, and started to close the door.

"It's from the Eight-Seven," the man said.

"What?" the patrolman said.

"Okay to come in?" the man said. "It's kinda wet out here."

"Sure," the patrolman said.

The delivery man went into the armory. The patrolman closed the door behind him. It thundered shut—or so it seemed to him because of his hangover—with a ponderous roar, which caused him to wince. The armory smelled of horses and horse manure. From somewhere in its cavernous reaches one of the horses whinnied.

"They don't like rain," the patrolman said.

"Where do you want this?"

"Bring it in the office here," the patrolman said.

The office was a small cubicle that still had regimental flags on its walls. The stable hand was sitting in the office, his feet up on the desk.

"That smells good," he said.

"Little present from the boys of the Eight-Seven," the

delivery man said, putting the carton down on the desk.
"Thought you might be getting hungry all alone here on
New Year's Day." He took two Pepsis from the white
paper bag and put them down on the desk beside the
pizza carton. He reached into his pocket for a bottle
opener and uncapped both bottles. The caps came off
easily and soundlessly, with no fizzy pop of released car-
bonation.

"That's very nice of them," the patrolman said.

He did not know anybody at the Eight-Seven. He himself was a Bow-and-Arrow cop, who'd once been a
mountie. He was still officially assigned to the Mounted
Patrol, but he never rode a horse anymore, nor was he
permitted to carry a weapon—hence the sobriquet "Bow
and Arrow." The police department had taken away both
his horse and his gun three years ago, after he rode a big
black stallion into a gathering of some thousand people,
firing the gun into the crowd. He was drunk at the time.
Nobody got hurt but the horse, who bolted at the sound
of the pistol and slammed into a lamppost, breaking his
leg. The horse had to be shot. Horse lovers all over the
city protested.

"What's on it?" the stable hand asked.

He had already opened the lid of the box. The delivery
man was hanging around as if he expected a tip.

"Sausage and cheese," the delivery man said.

The patrolman and the stable hand were looking at each
other, wondering how much they should tip for something like this, guy delivering a pizza on a cold rainy
day.

"Better eat it before it gets cold," he said.

The stable man took a slice of pizza from the carton. He
bit into it.

"Good," he said, chewing.

He reached for one of the Pepsi bottles, tilted it to his
mouth, and drank.

"This is a little flat," he said.

The patrolman took a slice of pizza.

"Still nice and hot," he said. "You want a piece?" he asked the delivery man.

"No, thanks."

"You got any change?" he asked the stable hand and reached for the other Pepsi bottle.

"Yeah, just a second," the stable hand said. He took another bite of pizza, washed it down with the flat Pepsi, and then reached into his pocket.

"No, that's okay," the delivery man said. "Happy New Year."

"Sure you don't want a piece?" the stable hand said.

"Just want to warm up a little before I go out there again," the delivery man said.

"Sit down, sit down," the patrolman said, and tilted the Pepsi bottle to his mouth again.

The patrolman and the stable hand sat eating pizza and drinking Pepsi. Somewhere in the armory another horse whinnied. The delivery man kept rubbing his hands together, trying to get warm.

Ten minutes later the patrolman and the stable hand were both unconscious on the floor of the office.

The Deaf Man smiled.

The chloral hydrate had worked swiftly and efficiently.

He reached into the pocket of his trench coat for the pistol. As he walked back to the stalls, where the horses were kept, he affixed the long silencer to its barrel.

The eighth day of Christmas was a legal holiday, and nobody expected anything from the Deaf Man. No mail delivery on legal holidays. No United Parcel deliveries. No Federal, Emory, Purolator, or whatever *other* kind of express deliveries. Just peace and quiet. As befitted New Year's Day.

Car Adam One was dispatched to the armory at one-thirty that afternoon because someone in the neighborhood had called 911 to report horses screaming.

Sixteen horses were still alive when the two patrolmen got there. They were not actually screaming. Just white-eyed with terror and—one of the patrolmen described it as "keening," but he was Irish.

Eight horses were dead.

Each of them had been shot.

They were black horses.

So now it was serious.

Well, maybe the severed ear had been serious, too. Maybe the severed ear hadn't been merely the Deaf Man's way of announcing himself for certain, but was, in addition, a promise that this was going to get bloody.

Carella and Brown looked at the dead horses.

There was a great deal of blood.

"It doesn't make sense," Carella said.

He was thinking the horses hadn't done anything.

He was thinking they were beautiful, innocent animals.

Eight of them dead.

All of them black.

Brown was thinking this had been planned all the way back in October. The thought was chilling.

Both men stood looking at the dead horses for a long time.

Outside it was still raining.

The rain stopped on the second day of the New Year, the ninth day of Christmas. It was replaced by clear blue skies and arctic temperatures. Gopher did not mind the cold. Rain would have been troublesome. Explosives had to be kept dry.

Getting in was easier than Gopher had expected.

There was a uniformed cop at the entrance gate in the cyclone fence, but Gopher was wearing a plastic-encased tag on his coveralls, and the tag showed his picture in full color and over that the words ISOLA P.D. DEPARTMENT OF VEHICLES. He was also carrying an order form, printed on an *Isola P.D. Department of Vehicles* letterhead, which authorized him to check the electrical wiring of all fifteen cars issued to the 87th Precinct.

The cop at the gate glanced at his tag and said, "What's up?"

Gopher showed him the order form.

The cop at the gate said, "Did you talk to the sergeant?"

"Told me to come on back," Gopher said.

Actually he hadn't talked to *anybody*. Never ask, never regret, that was his motto. March in as if you belonged wherever you were, explain only if you're questioned. He hadn't wanted to show himself *inside* the precinct again because, even though he'd shaved the mustache he'd been wearing ever since Nam and though he was now wearing windowpane eyeglasses, he didn't want to chance anybody's recognizing him. He figured he could bluff his way through if a sergeant popped out here and asked him what the hell he was doing. Show him the papers again, say he didn't know he was supposed to check inside to service a few fuckin' cars, you'd think they'd be happy to see him here instead of giving him static. If it got tight in any way, he was ready to back out of the job in a minute. No job was worth doing time. Work out here with the puffy lip and the phony glasses, hope nobody made a connection with the guy who'd been upstairs in the squadroom on New Year's Eve. He was counting on the fact that most people—even cops—only noticed the trimmings.

"Most of the junk's on the road," the cop said. "The shift don't change till a quarter to eight."

It was now ten minutes past seven. Full daylight would not come till seven twenty-two. It would get dark this afternoon at four forty-six. The light behind the station house was what Gopher had heard called morngloam in some parts of the country.

"I'll do whichever ones I can get to now," Gopher said. "Catch the others when they come in."

"Since when did you guys start making house calls?" the cop asked. "We used to have to bring them to the garage downtown, anything went wrong."

"The holidays," Gopher said. "We're backed up downtown."

"Well, go ahead," the cop said. "Christ knows, they can use it."

It had been that easy.

The 87th Precinct territory was divided into eight sectors, and a radio motor patrol car was assigned to each sector. The patrol sergeant had a car and driver of his own, which brought the total to nine cars in use at any given time. In addition, there were six so-called standby cars. These six were often pressed into service because police cars—like police stations—took a hell of a beating in any given twenty-four-hour period, and there were a great many breakdowns on the road. A team of officers would often be driving one car at nine in the morning and a different car at eleven.

No differentiation was made between the standby cars and the ones they often replaced. In the jargon of the precinct they were *all* called "the junk." Cops would pile into the junk when their tour of duty started and would drop off the junk when the tour ended. The junk was both singular and plural. One patrol car was the junk. Six patrol cars were the junk. A hundred patrol cars would have been the junk. Whenever a car broke down, it was called "the fuckin' junk." To listen to the motorized cops of the Eight-Seven, you'd have thought they were narcotics dealers. Only one of the cars had ever had a name. This had been the favorite car in the precinct, an old workhorse that rarely broke down. The cops called her Sadie. Eventually Sadie's motor gave out, and the city decided it was cheaper to replace her than to repair her. The cops of the Eighty-seventh held a small ceremony for Sadie when she died. She still remained their favorite.

As a matter of practice all the junk in the precinct—the regularly assigned cars and the standby cars—was used on a more or less rotating basis. There were also several unmarked sedans, which the detectives drove, but these were not considered part of the junk. The junk had white door panels with the city's seal and the number of the precinct painted on them, black fenders, a black hood, and a white roof with a row of lights on it. The unmarked detectives' cars were always parked in the lot behind the station house. The junk was parked either there or in front of the station, angled into the curb.

There were seven cars parked in the lot behind the station house when Gopher got to work—the six standby cars and the sergeant's car. It took him literally three minutes to wire each of the cars. By seven twenty-two, when dawn came, he had already wired four of them. By seven-forty, when the cars on the midnight-to-eight tour began drifting in, he had finished wiring the remaining three and was waiting to do only two more. As soon as a pair of patrolmen left a car to go into the station house, Gopher threw up the hood. Between the grille and the radiator he planted a box containing a plastic bag of black powder and a five-pound charge of dynamite. He attached a ground wire to the chassis. He unplugged the connector wire he knew would be there, and loosely twisted the cleaned ends of both wires. The wires ran into the plastic bag of black powder. The dynamite fuse ran into that same plastic bag.

By seven forty-five, when the cars began pulling out for the eight-to-four tour, Gopher was packing his tools in the truck.

He wished the relief cop at the gate a Happy New Year, got into the truck and drove off.

The first explosion did not come until the four-to-midnight tour was almost a half hour old.

The patrolmen assigned to Charlie Two had checked out the car at ten minutes to four. The patrol sergeant, who was a pain in the ass when it came to the junk, came out to look over the vehicle for dents or scratches, jotting down even the slightest mark for comparison when the car was checked in again at eleven forty-five that night. The sergeant's name was Preuss, but the patrolmen called him

"Priss" behind his back. Charlie Two left the precinct at five minutes to four. At four-fifteen, after a single run at the sector, they decided to stop for some coffee. The shotgun cop got back into the car at four twenty-two, a container of coffee in each hand.

"Starting to get dark," he said.

The driver reached for the container of coffee with his right hand and the light switch with his left hand. He pulled the light switch. The plug-in connector wire Gopher had removed from the right front headlight and twisted into his ground wire was suddenly alive with current from the 12-volt battery. The loosely twisted wires lying in the plastic bag of black powder shorted and sparked, the powder flashed, the fuse flared, and the dynamite went up an instant later.

That was at 4:23 P.M.

At 4:27 P.M., nineteen minutes before sunset, the patrolmen riding Boy One saw a man running up Culver Avenue in Sector Two. Patrolmen were normally assigned to the same sector on each of their tours, on the theory that familiarity bred better crime prevention. If a patrolman spotted something that looked unusual to him—a grocery store closed when it was supposed to be open, a snatch of hookers standing on the wrong corner—he immediately checked it out. A running man was always suspicious. If you were a runner in this city, you were supposed to be wearing a track suit and running shoes. Everyone else *walked* fast, but they rarely ran. A running man in ordinary clothing was usually running *away* from something.

The patrolman riding shotgun in Boy One said, "Up ahead, Frank."

"I see him," the driver said.

The time was 4:28 P.M.

The driver eased the car over into the curbside lane. The man was still running.

"In one hell of a hurry," the shotgun cop said.

They kept watching him.

"He's just trying to catch that bus on the corner," the driver said.

"Yeah," the shotgun cop said.

The man got on the bus. The bus pulled away from the curb.

"Getting dark," the shotgun cop said. "Better put on the . . ."

The driver was already reaching for the light switch.

An instant later, Boy One exploded.

Preuss, the patrol sergeant, looked at his digital watch as he came out of the station house and started for his car, his driver immediately behind him. The time was 4:31 P.M. The watch also told him that this was Monday, January 2. Watches could tell you almost anything these days. Preuss knew somebody who had an alarm clock, when it went off, you said "Stop" to it, and it let you sleep for another four minutes.

As Preuss got into the car, he was thinking one explosion could be an accident, two explosions were a conspiracy. He had dreaded a conspiracy ever since he'd made sergeant. He knew that the cops in this city wouldn't stand a fuckin' chance if all the bad guys got together and decided to wipe them out.

The driver put the key into the ignition switch and turned it.

The engine roared into life.

And because it was rapidly becoming dark, he reached for the light switch.

By 4:38 P.M. six of the eight cars on patrol were out of service. The remaining two cars all received an urgently radioed 10-02—REPORT TO YOUR COMMAND. The Bomb-Squad was already on its way to the 87th Precinct.

Neither of them made it back safely to the station house.

Sunset was at 4:46 P.M.

By then nine cars—the eight on patrol and the sergeant's car—had gone up.

Three police officers were killed—one of them a woman—and five were hospitalized, two of them in critical condition for third-degree burns.

"He's telling us to go piss in the wind," Brown said.

It was bitterly cold outside, and frost rimed the grilled windows of the squadroom.

This was the tenth day of Christmas.

January 3 by the calendar on the wall. Five minutes after ten by the clock. Four detectives were on duty that morning. Brown, Kling, Meyer, and Carella. They were all looking at the ten blank D.D. forms that had been delivered by Federal Express earlier that morning. The forms looked innocent enough. Standard police department issue. Printed for the department by municipal contract.

"He's telling us to go write up our reports," Brown said. " 'Cause it won't help one damn bit."

"These forms are legit," Kling said. "You can't buy them anyplace, he had to have got them from a squadroom."

"Or *ten* squadrooms," Carella said.

"Write up your dumb reports, he's saying," Brown said. "File your shit on the eight black horses and the nine cars . . ."

"And he planned that way back in October?" Meyer asked. "To send us ten D.D. forms so we could write up *reports?*"

"Ten D.D. forms, right," Brown insisted. "For the ten separate . . ."

"Are we supposed to write up a D.D. report on *this* shit, too?"

"On *what* shit?" Brown asked.

"On *this* shit. The D.D. forms we got today."

"That's what you write the shit *on,* isn't it?" Brown said, looking at the other men as though Meyer had momentarily lost his wits. "You write the shit on D.D. forms."

"I meant *about* the forms."

"What?"

"Does he expect us to file a report *about* these forms?"

"Who knows what he expects?" Brown said. "The man has a twisted mind."

"So he's telling us to write a report on the pear tree, right? And the two nightsticks . . ."

"Don't go over them again, okay?" Kling said. "I'm tired of hearing all that stuff over and over again."

*"He's* tired," Brown said, rolling his eyes.

"No, *let's* go over it again," Carella said. "This is all we've got, so let's go over it."

Kling sighed.

"First the pear tree," Carella said.

"On the first day of Christmas," Brown said. "I told you all along it'd be the twelve days of Christmas."

"Give him a medal," Meyer said.

"With the ear attached to it," Carella said.

"To let us know it was him," Brown said.

"Then the two nightsticks . . ."

"Easy to come by," Kling said.

"Ditto the three pairs of handcuffs," Brown said.

"Easy stuff."

"Then all that stuff from precincts all over the city . . ."

"Four police hats, five walkie-talkies, six police shields . . ."

"The wanted flyers . . ."

"Seven of them."

"From *squadrooms,* had to be," Brown said.

"Not necessarily. Any muster room bulletin board . . ."

"Yeah, okay, so he coulda got them in a muster room someplace."

"And then it gets serious," Carella said.

"Eight black horses," Kling said. "Six blocks from here."

"And the nine cars. Our *own* cars."

The men were silent.

"Ten D.D. forms," Meyer said.

"You don't find *those* hanging on no muster room bulletin board," Brown said.

"*Those* came from a squadroom," Kling said.

"Or *ten* squadrooms," Carella repeated.

"So tomorrow we get eleven Detective Specials," Brown said.

"And on Thursday we get the big feast. Twelve roast pigs."

"And a hundred dancing girls," Meyer said.

"I *wish*," Brown said, and then looked quickly over his shoulder, as if his wife, Caroline, had suddenly materialized in the squadroom.

"Maybe he's finished," Kling said. "Maybe the nine cars were the end of it, and now he's telling us it's finished, we can go write up our reports. Like Artie says."

"What about the guns tomorrow?" Meyer asked. "*If* he sends them."

"He'll be telling us to shove our guns up our asses," Brown said.

"He's roasting the pigs, don't you get it?" Kling said.

"Huh?"

"Pigs," Kling said. "Cops."

"So?"

"So didn't you ever watch 'Celebrity Roast' on television?"

"What's that?" Meyer said.

"A roast," Kling said. "It's this testimonial dinner, all these guys get up and rake another guy over the coals. They tell jokes about him, they make him look foolish—a roast. Didn't you ever hear of a roast?"

"Those cops yesterday got roasted, all right," Meyer said.

Carella had been silent for some time now.

"I was just thinking . . ." he said.

The men turned to him.

"My grandmother once told me that in Naples . . . in other Italian cities, too, I guess . . . whenever someone important dies, his coffin is put in a big black carriage, and the carriage goes up the middle of the street . . . and it's drawn by eight black horses.''

The men thought this over.

"Was he telling us there'd be some funerals the next day?" Kling asked.

"First the eight black horses and then the dead cops? On the following day?"

"I don't know," Carella said.

The squadroom windows rattled with a fierce gust of wind.

"Well," Kling said, "maybe those cars yesterday *were* the end of it."

"Maybe," Carella said.

The invitation read:

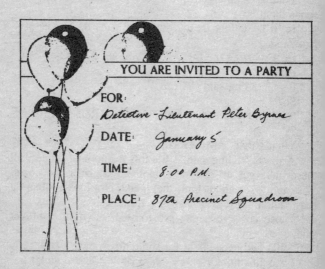

YOU ARE INVITED TO A PARTY

FOR:
Detective-Lieutenant Peter Byrnes

DATE: January 5

TIME: 8:00 P.M.

PLACE: 87th Precinct Squadroom

Scrawled on the flap of the card in the same handwriting was the message:

*Andy — I haven't been able to invite everyone, so please keep this a secret, won't you? Harriet.*

Andy Parker was touched.

He hadn't even realized the lieutenant's wife knew his name.

He wondered if he was expected to bring a present.

On January 4, the eleventh day of Christmas, eleven .38-caliber Colt Detective Specials were delivered to the squadroom. They were not new guns. Even a preliminary examination revealed that all of them had previously been fired, if only on a firing range. Each of the guns had a serial number stamped on it. A check with Pistol Permits revealed that the eleven guns were registered to eleven different detectives from precincts in various parts of the city. None of the detectives had reported a pistol missing or stolen. It is shameful for a cop to lose his gun.

"Like I told you," Brown said, "he's telling us to stick our guns up our asses."

"No," Carella said. "He's telling us he's been inside eleven different squadrooms."

"Not necessarily," Parker said. "I know blues who pack the Special."

"That ain't regulation," Brown said.

"As a backup," Parker said. "Anyway, what are *you*, a fuckin' Boy Scout?"

The fact remained that the Detective Special was the weapon of choice for most detectives in this city. All three detectives sitting there at Carella's desk were carrying a gun similar to the ones spread on its top like a small arsenal.

"Only an asshole gets his gun ripped off," Parker said, and wondered if Carella and Brown had been invited to the lieutenant's party tomorrow night. "What we oughta do, we oughta wrap them like presents, send them back to those assholes,'' he said.

And wondered again if he was expected to bring a present.

I don't even *like* the lieutenant, he thought.

## 13

THE DEAF MAN WOULD HAVE BEEN THE FIRST
to agree that most catastrophes were caused by the fools of
the world. He would not have dreamed, however, that
sometimes a fool can *prevent* a catastrophe, thereby rising
above his lowly estate to achieve the stature of a hero.

Genero's first opportunity to become a hero came at two
forty-five on the afternoon of January 5, the twelfth day of
Christmas. The city had by then taken down all its Christmas
trimmings. It looked somehow naked, but there were
probably eight million stories in it anyway. The temperature,
hovering at twelve degrees Fahrenheit—which was
twelve *above* zero here, but approximately eleven *below*
zero in Celsius-speaking countries—did much to discourage
the fanciful notion (twelve days of Christmas indeed!)
that the holiday season had lingered beyond New Year's
Day. The citizens knew only that winter was here in earnest,
and Easter was a long way away. In between there'd
be the short holiday crumbs thrown to a chilled populace:
Lincoln's Birthday, Valentine's Day, Washington's Birthday,
Saint Patrick's Day—with only Washington's
Birthday officially observed. For now, the city and the
months ahead looked extraordinarily bleak.

The cops were nervous.

Only three days ago nine police cars had been blown up.
This did not indicate an attitude of civic-mindedness on the
part of the populace.

In some quarters of the city, in fact, some citizens were
heard to remark that it served the cops right. Now they
knew what it felt like to be victimized. Maybe now they'd
do something about the goddamn *crime* in this city. Maybe

223

they'd make it safe to ride the subways again. What patrol cars had to do with subways, no one bothered clarifying. The talk was all about the shoe being on the other foot, and turnabout being fair play, and what's sauce for the goose is sauce for the gander. The people of this city, even when police cars weren't being blown up, felt ambivalent about cops. If they came home one night to find their apartment burglarized, the first thing they did was call the cops. And then complain later about how long it took for them to get there and about how they'd never recover the stolen goods anyway. In this city a vigilante could become a hero, even if he was a fool.

To the cops of the Eight-Seven, Genero was not a fool. The word was too elite for their vocabulary. Genero was a complainer and a whiner and an inefficient cop and a dope, but he was not a fool. Just a jackass. Not many of the detectives enjoyed being partnered with Genero. They felt, perhaps rightfully, that if push came to shove, Genero wasn't the candidate they'd elect to help them out of a tight spot. A cop's very life often depended upon the reaction time of his partner. How could you entrust your life to a man who couldn't spell "surveillance?" Or perhaps even "vehicle." Even the worst male chauvinist pig on the squad would have preferred being partnered with a woman rather than with Genero. Tell them that Genero was about to become a hero, and they'd have laughed in your face.

By two forty-five on the twelfth day of Christmas, Genero—because he'd done some splendid detective work at the office—was in possession of the lieutenant's home number. He did not know what he would do if the lieutenant himself answered the phone, but he would cross that bridge when he came to it. He also did not know what he would call Harriet Byrnes if she answered the phone, but he guessed he would think of something.

A woman answered the phone.

"Mrs. Byrnes?" Genero said.

"Yes?" Harriet said.

"This is Richard," he said.

He felt funny announcing himself as Richard, but that's what she'd called him in the invitation, wasn't it?

"Who?" she said.

"Richard," he said.

"Richard who?" she said.

"Genero. Detective Richard Genero," he said. "Detective/Third Grade Richard Genero."

"Yes?" she said.

"You know," he said.

"Yes?" she said.

"I work with your husband," he said. "Peter Byrnes. Detective-Lieutenant Peter Byrnes. Pete."

"Oh, yes," she said. "I'm sorry, but he isn't here just now. Can I . . . ?"

"Good," Genero said. "I mean, actually I wanted to talk to *you*, Mrs. Byrnes."

"Yes?" Harriet said.

"Am I expected to bring a present?" he said.

"What?"

"Tonight."

"What?"

"To the party."

There was a long silence on the line.

"I'm sorry," Harriet said. "What party do you . . . ?"

"You know," he said, and almost winked.

There was another long silence.

"I'm sorry," Harriet said, "but I don't know what you're talking about."

"I haven't told anybody, you don't have to worry," Genero said.

"Told anybody what?" Harriet said.

"About the party."

Harriet thought one of her husband's detectives had flipped. That sometimes happened during the holidays. Cops had a habit of eating their own guns during the holidays. Some cops even ate their own guns on Halloween. But the holidays had come and gone, hadn't they?

"What did you say your name was?" she asked.

"Genero," he said. "You know. Richard."

"Is there some problem, Detective Genero?" she said.

"Only about whether to bring a present."

"Well, I'll have to ask Pete . . ."

"No, don't do that!" he said at once.

"What?"

"It's supposed to be a surprise, isn't it?"

"What?"

"I thought . . . the invitation makes it sound like a surprise party."

"Well, does it mention a present?" Harriet asked, and wondered why she was entering into this man's delusional system.

"What?" Genero said.

"I said . . ."

"Well, no, that's why I'm calling." He suddenly thought he might have the wrong number. "Is this Harriet Byrnes?" he asked.

"Yes, this is Harriet Byrnes."

"Lieutenant Byrnes's wife?"

"Yes, I'm Lieutenant Byrnes's wife."

"So should I bring a present?"

"Detective Genero," Harriet said, "I'm sorry, but I can't advise you on that."

"You can't?" Genero said.

"Maybe this is something you ought to discuss with someone who can really help you," she said. "If you're deeply troubled about some sort of present . . ."

"Who?" Genero said.

"You," Harriet said. "Aren't you the one who's troubled about . . . ?"

"I mean, who should I *discuss* it with?"

"I think you should call the Psychological Service," she said.

"How do you spell that?" Genero asked.

"Just call the Psychological Service at Headquarters," she said. "Tell them you're extremely worried about this present, and tell them you'd like to make an appointment

to see someone. Once you've talked to them, you'll be able
to judge for yourself whether . . ."

"Oh, I get it," Genero said. "Okay, don't worry.
Mum's the word."

"Meanwhile, I'll tell Pete you . . ."

"No, no, don't blow the surprise, Mrs. Byrnes, that's
okay. Thanks a lot, I'll probably see you later, huh? Thanks
again," he said, and hung up.

Harriet looked at the telephone receiver.

She found it difficult to believe she had just had this
conversation.

She wondered if she should call Pete and tell him that
one of his detectives had gone bananas. And then she wondered if perhaps someone really *was* throwing a surprise
party for her husband. She sighed heavily. Sometimes police work got very, very trying.

Genero could have become a hero when he spoke to
Harriet Byrnes. He could have realized then that she hadn't
sent him an invitation at all and that there wasn't going to
be any surprise party for the lieutenant. But Genero was a
dope, and he didn't realize anything at all, and he *still*
didn't know whether he should bring a present or not.

What he figured was that Mrs. Byrnes had told him to
use his own judgment.

The thing of it was he didn't have any judgment on the
matter. Suppose he *didn't* bring a present, but a present
was expected, he'd look like a jackass. Or suppose he *did*
bring a present, but he was the only one there with a present, he'd still look like a jackass. The one thing Genero
didn't want was to look like a jackass. He sat there in his
room in his mother's apartment—he still lived with his
mother, which was nice—and wondered what he should do.

If only he knew which of the detectives had been invited.

But he didn't.

If only he knew which of the detectives he could trust.

He figured he could trust Carella, maybe. But he admired Carella, and he didn't want Carella to think he was

a jackass, asking whether he should bring a present or not, assuming Carella had even been invited to the party, which maybe he hadn't.

Another detective he admired, perhaps even more than he admired Carella, was Andy Parker.

He called the squadroom and asked to talk to Parker.

Santoro, who was catching, said Parker had the four-to-midnight tonight.

Genero wondered if he should ask Santoro about the party. Instead, he asked for Parker's home number. Parker answered the phone on the third ring.

"Yeah?" he said.

That was one of the things Genero admired about Parker. His gruff style.

"Andy?" he said.

"Who's this?" Parker said.

"Genero."

"What do you want?" Parker said. "I ain't due in till four."

"You're gonna be there tonight, huh?" Genero said.

"What?" Parker said.

"In the squadroom."

"I got the duty, I'll be there," Parker said.

"With or without?" Genero asked slyly.

"What?" Parker said.

"You know," Genero said, and suddenly wondered if he *did* know. "Never mind, forget it," he said, and hung up.

Fuckin' jackass, Parker thought.

In the squadroom supply closet the timer inside the wooden box read 3:15 P.M.

At midnight the timer had moved into the pie-shaped segment marked "Thursday." There were seven such segments on the timer, one for each day of the week. These segments were subdivided into fifteen-minute sectors.

Now, soundlessly, the timer moved into the 3:15-to-3:30 sector.

* * *

A giant step on the way to Genero's becoming a hero was his decision to buy the lieutenant a present. He figured he would make it something impersonal. He bought him a pair of pajamas. He also figured he would hide the present under his coat until he saw whether the other guys had bought presents or not. That way, he would be covered either way. If the other guys hadn't bought presents, he would take the pajamas home and wear them himself; he had bought them in his own size, even though Byrnes was taller and heftier than he was.

He wondered whether the other guys would be bringing presents to the party.

He wondered how many other guys had been invited.

There were sixteen detectives assigned to the 87th Squad. Of those sixteen, two were on vacation. Of the remaining fourteen, four had pulled the four-to-midnight shift on that fifth day of January and would have been at the squadroom even if they hadn't received an invitation to the party. Unlike the blues, who worked five fixed eight-hour shifts and then swung for the next fifty-six hours, the detectives made out their own duty schedules. Usually—because vacation schedules and court appearances depleted the roster—only four of them were on duty in any given shift. The four detectives who arrived at the squadroom at fifteen minutes before the hour that afternoon were Parker, Willis, O'Brien, and Fujiwara. Each of them had received an invitation to the lieutenant's party. None of them had discussed it with anyone else. Cops were very good at keeping secrets; in a sense secrets were a major part of the line of work they were in.

In the supply closet the timer moved into Thursday's 3:45-to-4:00 P.M. sector.

It began snowing at six-thirty.
The forecasters were still promising only light flurries.

The people of this city knew that when the forecasters promised light flurries, they could expect a blizzard.

All of the other detectives who'd been invited to the party figured they'd better leave for the squadroom earlier than they'd planned.

The other invited detectives were:

Steve Carella.

Bert Kling.

Alexiandre Delgado.

Cotton Hawes.

Richard Genero.

Arthur Brown.

Meyer Meyer.

And the guest of honor himself, Peter Byrnes.

Byrnes thought Carella was the guest of honor. That was because his invitation had said it was a party for Steve Carella. The handwritten scrawl on the flap of his invitation had been signed "Teddy." He had been tempted to call Teddy and ask if a present was expected. But he hated talking to that bitchy housekeeper of theirs. Instead, he had bought Carella a pair of cuff links and had hidden them in the top drawer of his desk.

As he dressed that night, he wondered why Teddy hadn't cleared this with him first. A party in the *squadroom*? A squadroom was a place of business. Or had she gone downtown over his head, talked with a deputy inspector or something, asked if it would be okay to give a small party in the squadroom for her husband's . . .

Her husband's *what*?

Was it Steve's birthday?

Byrnes didn't think so.

He was vaguely troubled about the party in the squadroom. He hoped to hell no departmental rank walked in, and he hoped Teddy hadn't planned to serve anything alcoholic. Only once could he remember a party in the squadroom, and that was when Captain Overman retired, more years ago than Byrnes could count. No booze. Just sandwiches and punch, though Byrnes later suspected one of the patrol sergeants had laced the punch with vodka. Still it wasn't like Teddy not to have checked with him first. He was again tempted to call her, ask if she'd got some sort of clearance. Teddy knew how the goddamn department worked, she'd been a cop's wife for a long time now.

Harriet watched him as he knotted his tie.

"Who's this party for?" she asked cautiously. She figured the surprise was premised on his thinking the party was for someone else.

"Steve," he said.

"You didn't tell me about it," she said.

"I wasn't supposed to tell anyone," Byrnes said.

"I'm not anyone, I'm your wife," Harriet said.

"Still it's supposed to be a surprise."

She wondered suddenly if the party really *was* for Carella. On the phone the detective who'd called—whatever his name was—had only said, "It's supposed to be a surprise, isn't it?" He hadn't said it was a surprise for *Pete*.

"Did you buy a present?" she asked.

"Yeah, a pair of cuff links."

"Gennario wanted to know if he should bring a present."

"Who?"

"Gennario. One of your detectives."

"Genero?"

"Yes, Genero, right. He called here, wanted to know if he should bring a present."

"What'd you tell him?"

"I said I didn't know."

"He's a jackass," Byrnes said.

The clock on the dresser read six forty-five.

"What time will you be back?" Annie Rawles asked.

"I don't know actually," Hawes said.

Annie was wearing one of his Christmas gifts. He had given her seven pairs of silk panties, one for each day of the week. The panties were in different colors. Blue for

Monday. Green for Tuesday. Lavender for Wednesday. Purple for Thursday. Red for Friday. Black for Saturday. White for Sunday. She had asked him why he'd chosen those particular colors for those particular days. He said they had to be blue for Monday because of Blue Monday, and then he'd simply worked his way through the color spectrum until he got to the weekend. Friday was the beginning of the weekend, and the appropriate kickoff color seemed to be red. Saturday was all slinky and sexy, hence black. Sunday was as pure as the driven snow—white. Elementary, my dear Watson.

This was Thursday, and she was wearing the purple panties.

She was also wearing a lavender garter belt, a lavender bra, one purple nylon stocking and one black, and a gold chain and pendant, which she never took off. Thirty-four years old with brown eyes and black wedge-cut hair, long slender legs, and small perfectly formed breasts, she stood in high-heeled purple satin slippers, her hands on her narrow hips, and looked more like a Bob Fosse dancer than a Detective/First Grade earning $37,935 a year. She also looked like a woman scorned. Hawes was looking at the clock on the dresser. It read six forty-eight.

"Well, what kind of a party is it?" she asked.

"For the lieutenant," he said.

"And it's in the *squadroom?*"

"Yeah."

"Do you always have parties up there at the old Eight-Seven?"

"First one I can think of," he said.

Annie looked at him.

"Are you telling me the truth?" she said.

"What do you mean?"

"Is there *really* a party tonight . . ."

"Of course there . . ."

". . . in the *squadroom*, of all places . . ."

"That's where . . ."

". . . or is there something you'd like to tell me?"

"Like what?"

"Like why you're rushing out of here . . ."

"Who's rushing?"

". . . when I'm all decked out like a whore?"

"A whore? You look gorgeous!"

"Why didn't you tell me about this party earlier?"

"The truth is I forgot about it. I got the invitation a few days before Christmas."

"I'll bet."

"Would you like to *see* it?"

"Yes, I would like to see it," Annie said. "Please," she added. She felt dumb in the sexy underwear. All dressed up for a party of her own, and nobody coming.

Hawes took the invitation from his jacket pocket.

Annie looked at it.

"Why all the secrecy?" she asked.

"I have no idea."

"A small party, huh?" she said.

"It looks that way, doesn't it?"

"How many people?"

"I don't know. I didn't discuss it with anyone. Harriet specifically . . ."

"Well, if it's in the *squadroom* and she's telling you to keep it a secret, then I guess it *has* to be a small party."

"Yeah."

"The reason I'm asking all these questions . . ."

"Mm?"

". . . is not because I'm a mastermind detective trying to figure out why anyone in her right mind would throw a party in a grubby squadroom, but only because I'm standing here half-naked wondering how long the damn party will *last.*"

"Why? Do you have other plans?"

"I'm thinking of making some," Annie said. "So the hooker outfit won't be a total waste."

He went to her. He took her in his arms.

"I don't have to leave here till seven-thirty," he said.

"Great. That gives us what? Half an hour?"

"Hookers can do it in ten minutes," he said.

"Oh, but I'm not a *real* hooker, sir," she said, and clasped her hands together and rolled her eyes.

"I'll break away as soon as I can," Hawes said.

"That may be too late," Annie said. "There's a captain at the Seven-Two who's been making eyes at me."

"What's his name? I'll go shoot him."

"Big talker," Annie said. "Gonna shoot a captain, can't even take off a lady's purple silk panties."

Genero got to the squadroom earlier than any of the others.

This was not because he was normally a punctual person but because he didn't want to keep his coat on and look like a jackass. The pajamas he'd bought the lieutenant were hidden under his coat. If he took off the coat, everybody would see that he'd brought a present, and if none of the other guys had presents, he would look like a jackass. On the other hand, if he kept his coat on in the heated squadroom, everybody would still think he was a jackass. So what he did, he got to the squadroom at a little before seven-thirty, and he went directly to the supply closet without taking off his coat, and he put the present on top of a wooden box that had some kind of meter on its face.

That was the second time he came close to becoming a hero.

The timer inside the box silently moved into the 7:30-to-7:45 P.M. sector.

"Hey, guys," Genero said, taking off his coat and hanging it on the rack. "How's it going?"

None of the four-to-midnight detectives answered him.

Parker was wondering if the lieutenant's wife had been dumb enough to invite this jackass to her party.

Eileen Burke was crying.

Kling looked at the bedside clock, thinking he had to get out of here soon because of the snow. It was snowing like the arctic tundra out there, and the clock read seven thirty-two. Knowing this city, traffic would be stalled for miles—and the squadroom was all the way uptown.

But Eileen was crying.

"Come on, honey," he said.

She was wearing what she'd worn to work that morning. Gray suit, black shoes with French heels, a white blouse. She had stopped wearing earrings ever since the rape. She had always considered earrings her lucky charm. Her luck had run out on the night of the cutting and the rape, and she had stopped wearing them.

They were in her apartment. He had rushed there the moment she called.

"You don't understand," she said.

"I do," he said.

"I was *scared,*" she said. "I turned it down because I was *scared.*"

"You had every right to be scared," he said.

"I'm a *cop!*" she said.

"They shouldn't have asked you in the first place. A gang of . . ."

"That only makes it worse," she said. "A gang, Bert. A goddamn *gang* that's running around raping women!"

"They can't expect you to handle a gang," he said. "Setting up a decoy for a gang is like . . ."

"There'll be backups," she said. "Four of them."

"A lot of good they'll do if you're jumped by a dozen guys. Who the hell requested this anyway?"

"Captain Jordan."

"Where?"

"The Seventh."

"I'll go see him, I'll talk to him person . . ."

"No, you *won't!*" Eileen said. "It's bad enough as it is! Chickening out in front of four hairbags who . . ."

"What four? Are you talking about the backups?"

"From the Seventh Squad. I don't remember their names. All I remember is their eyes. What was in their eyes."

"Let one of *them* go out in drag," Kling said angrily.
"Let *him* face a gang of . . ."

"Their eyes said, 'She's scared.' "

"You *should* have been scared."

"No," she said.

"Yes."

"No. I'm a cop. Any other decoy cop wouldn't have batted an eyelash. You got a gang out there? Piece of cake. When?"

"That's not true, and you know it."

"It's true."

"Any woman who'd agree to go out there alone against a dozen men . . ."

"Eight."

"What?"

"It's only eight."

"Terrific. Eight guys dragging a woman into the bushes . . ."

"They're working the subways."

"Better yet. You'll end up on the fucking tracks with another scar on your . . ."

He stopped all at once.

"I'm sorry," he said.

She was silent for a long time.

Then she said, "That's the point, isn't it? I'm afraid I'll get hurt again."

"You don't have to prove anything," he said.

"I'll call Jordan," she said, sighing. "I'll tell him I've thought it over, and . . ."

"No."

"Bert . . ."

"*No,* damn it!" he said, and took her in his arms. "Eileen," he said, "I love you. If anything ever happened to you . . ."

"Who told you to start up with a cop?" she said.

"You did the right thing. I'd have turned it down, too."

"You wouldn't have."

"I would've."

They were both silent.

"I love you, too," she said.

He held her close.

"I don't want anything to happen to either of us," she said. "Ever."

"Nothing will happen to us," he said. "Ever."

"But I'm going to call Jordan . . ."

"Eileen, please . . ."

". . . tell him I want a bigger backup team. All over the platform. Men *and* women. Wall to wall cover."

"You don't have to."

"I want to."

"You *don't* want to."

"I don't want to, right. But I *have* to," she said. "Or I never will again."

She looked at the clock.

"You're going to be late," she said.

"Will you be all right?"

"Yes," she said. "Go. Come back soon."

He kissed her gently and went to the door.

"Be careful," she said.

The clock on the dresser read a quarter to eight.

In the park across the street from the station house the Deaf Man watched them trickling in. Big men, most of them. You could almost always tell a detective by his size. All of them bundled up against the cold. A very cold night. Well, they'd be warm enough soon enough.

He looked at his watch.

Ten minutes to eight.

In exactly twenty-five minutes . . . Armageddon.

He began pacing again.

The snow blew furiously around him.

He hoped none of them would be late.

By five minutes to eight on the squadroom clock, all but three of the invited detectives had arrived. Since none of the detectives knew who had been invited, none of them knew who was missing. But since they knew that anyone there *had* been invited, they felt free to talk about the party.

"What's it for?" Brown asked. "You got any idea?"

"Did you bring a present?" Genero asked.

"No," Hawes said. "Were we supposed to bring presents?"

"Anybody know what it's *for?*" Brown said.

"It said eight o'clock, didn't it?" Delgado asked. "The invitation?"

A man in the detention cage said, "What the hell *is* this?" He had been arrested by Parker not ten minutes earlier. "I'm locked up in a fuckin' cage here, like a fuckin' animal here, and you guys are havin' a *party?*"

"Shut up," Parker said.

"Where's my lawyer?" the man said.

"On the way," Parker said. "Shut up."

Even the four detectives who had the duty were all dressed up. Suits and ties, polished shoes. Parker was upset that he'd got blood on his shirt while arresting the man in the detention cage. The man in the detention cage had slit his wife's throat with a straight razor.

"My wife's dead, and you guys are havin' a *party,*" he said.

"You're the one killed her," Parker said.

"Never mind who killed her, is it right to have a party when a woman is dead? Anyway, I *didn't* kill her."

"No, that razor just jumped off the sink all by itself," Parker said.

"That wasn't even my razor."

"Save it for when your lawyer gets here," Parker said. "You got blood all over my fuckin' shirt."

He walked to the sink near the supply closet, tore a paper towel loose, opened the cold water faucet, and began dabbing at the blood stains.

Inside the box in the supply closet the timer moved into the 8:00-to-8:15 sector.

Carella was just walking into the squadroom.

Genero noticed at once that he was carrying a present.

"Where's Harriet?" Carella asked.

In the park across the way the Deaf Man looked at his watch again. He had just seen Carella going into the station house. Carella, he *knew*. Carella, he *recognized*. In exactly fourteen minutes, though, Carella—and all the others—would be unrecognizable. The moment . . .

There!

Another one.

Blond and hatless, his head ducked against the flying snow.

The Deaf Man smiled.

Alfred Hitchcock, a director whose work the Deaf Man admired greatly—except for *The Birds*, that silly exercise in science fiction—had once described for an interviewer the difference between shock and suspense. The Master had used a parable to explain.

There is a boardroom meeting. Twenty men are sitting around a table, discussing high finance. The audience doesn't know that a bomb has been planted in the room. The chairman of the board is in mid-sentence when the bomb goes off.

That is shock.

The same boardroom meeting. The same twenty men sitting around a table, discussing high finance. But this time the audience *knows* there is a bomb in that room, and they know that it is set to go off—as an example—at 8:15 P.M. The men keep discussing high finance. The camera keeps cutting away to the clock as it throws minutes into the room.

8:08.

8:12.

8:14.

*That* is suspense.

The detectives in the squadroom across the street did not know that a timer was programmed to set off an explosion and a subsequent fire at 8:15 sharp. They were in for one hell of a shock.

The Deaf Man, however—in this instance, the audience—*did* know, and the suspense for him was almost unbearable.

He looked at his watch again.

8:03.

It was taking forever.

The confusion started the moment Lieutenant Byrnes walked in.

"Where's Teddy?" he said.

"Where's the sandwiches?" Delgado said.

"Where's Harriet?" Carella said.

The detectives all looked at each other.

"You jerks got the wrong night," the man in the detention cage said.

Brown looked at the clock.

8:05.

The invitation had specified eight o'clock.

"Where's my lawyer?" the man in the detention cage said.

All Genero knew was that Carella had brought a present.

He began moving at once toward the supply closet.

Nine minutes, the Deaf Man thought.

He had specifically asked them to arrive at eight because he wanted to be sure they were all assembled by eight-fifteen.

Another man was entering the police station across the street.

The Deaf Man had lost count.

Were all twelve pigs already present and accounted for? Waiting for the big barbecue?

Which by his watch should happen in eight minutes now.

"I'm Harry Lefkowitz," the man at the slatted rail divider said. "Is that my client I see in the cage there?"

"If your client is Roger Jackson, then that's your client," Parker said.

Lefkowitz came into the squadroom. Genero was opening the door to the supply closet. The clock on the wall read 8:08.

"I hope you read him his rights," Lefkowitz said, and went to the cage.

"They're havin' a fuckin' party up here," Jackson said. "My wife's dead, and they're havin' . . ."

"Shut up," Lefkowitz said.

In the supply closet Genero pulled the chain hanging from the naked light bulb. For a moment he forgot where he'd put the lieutenant's present. Oh, yeah, the box there against the back wall, under the lowest shelf.

"Okay, Steve," Byrnes said, "what's this all about?"

"Me?" Carella said.

"Teddy's invitation said . . ."

"Teddy's?"

"Harriet's," Brown said.

"What?" Byrnes said.

Genero knelt down and reached for the present. The wrapped pajamas fell off the top of the wooden box and behind it. "Shit," Genero said under his breath and then quickly looked over his shoulder to check if the lieutenant had heard him using profanity in the squadroom.

"What's the story, Loot?" Willis said.

"Where's the sandwiches?" Delgado said.

"What's going on here?" Byrnes said.

Genero lifted the wooden box by its handle, planning to move it aside so he could get at the lieutenant's present. Something was snagging. The box wouldn't move more than six inches from the wall. He gave a tug. He gave another tug, stronger this time, almost falling over backward when the short cord attached to the box pulled out of the wall socket behind it. Flailing for balance, he banged his elbow against one of the shelves on his right. "Shit!" he yelled, and lost his grip on the box's handle. The box fell on his foot—the same foot he'd shot himself in a long time ago.

"Ow!" he yelled.

The detectives all turned at the sound of his voice.

"*Damn* it!" Genero yelled, and kicked at the box, hurting his foot again. "Ow!" he yelled again.

Carella came to the supply closet.

He looked at the box.

"What've you got there?" he asked.

Genero had just become a hero.


Nothing happened at eight-fifteen.

The Deaf Man looked at his watch again.

Nothing happened at eight-sixteen.

And nothing happened at eight-twenty.

By eight thirty-five the Deaf Man began to suspect that nothing *would* happen.

By eight-forty, when the Bomb Squad truck pulled in across the street, he was *certain* nothing would happen.

The Bomb Squad team rushed into the building.

The Deaf Man kept watching.


They found the cartons of incendiaries in forty seconds flat.

That was after the detectives showed them the open wooden box with the timer and the dynamite inside it. It was Carella who'd unlatched the box. But it was Genero, the hero, who'd found it and yanked it out of the wall socket.

"Lucky thing you pulled this loose when you did," one of the Bomb Squad detectives said to Genero.

"I try to keep my eyes open," Genero said.

"You guys woulda been cinders," the second Bomb Squad detective said. "I never seen so many different kinds of incendiaries in one place in my entire life. Look at all this shit, willya? A dozen fire bottles, six cakes of paraffin sawdust, a whole box full of flake aluminum thermite, eight bottles of mineral oil, five bottles of kerosene—you ever see anything like this, Lou?''

''This timer here was set for eight-fifteen,'' the second detective said to Genero. ''You unplugged it just in time. Very nice little timer here.''

''I recognized it right off,'' Genero said. ''Who gets to keep it?''

''What?'' Byrnes said.

''I found it, do I get to keep it?''

''What?'' Willis said.

''It might work like a VCR,'' Genero said. ''To tape television shows.''

''This city has endangered the safety and well-being of my client,'' Lefkowitz said.

Kling was thinking maybe something *could* happen to him or Eileen. Maybe it *wouldn't* be forever.

Hawes was thinking Annie had come within an ace of wearing the *black* silk panties. To his funeral.

Carella was thinking that maybe the Deaf Man had played it fair after all. On the first day of Christmas he'd announced his intentions clearly and unequivocally; they'd be hearing from him on the eleven days to follow. On the second to the sixth days he'd sent them all that police paraphernalia to let them know he was planning something for *cops*. On the seventh day the wanted flyers arrived, a segue from the uniformed force to the plainclothes cops in that the posters could be found in a muster room as well as in a squadroom. On the eighth day he'd let them know he was dead serious, but he'd also told them he was moving into the Eight-Seven itself; the armory was right there on First and Saint Sebastian. On the ninth day he'd started zeroing in. Those nine cars were 87th Precinct cars, no question about it. And on the tenth and eleventh days he'd let them know he was coming into the squadroom itself—ten D.D. forms, which only detectives used, and eleven Colt Detective Specials, a detective's pistol of choice. The twelve roast pigs—by Carella's count, there were twelve detectives in the squadroom right this minute, and they'd just come pretty damn close to being incinerated. He never wanted to come this close again.

"There's a bottle of scotch in the bottom drawer of my desk," Byrnes said. "Go get it, Genero." He turned to Carella. "Also, I bought you a pair of cuff links."

"I bought you a shirt," Carella said.

"I bought you a pair of pajamas, Pete," Genero said, and hurried into the lieutenant's office.

"What'd he call me?" Byrnes asked.

"Do you men plan to drink *alcohol* in this squadroom?" Lefkowitz asked.

The Bomb Squad detectives came out of the station house at a few minutes before nine.

The Deaf Man watched them as they drove off.

Oddly he was neither angry nor sad.

As he walked way into the falling snow, his only thought was *Next time*.

# POLICE THRILLERS by
# "THE ACKNOWLEDGED MASTER"
### *Newsweek*

# ED McBAIN

| | |
|---|---|
| CALYPSO | 70591-5/$3.50 US/$4.50 Can |
| DOLL | 70082-4/$4.50 US/$5.50 Can |
| THE MUGGER | 70081-6/$3.50 US/$4.50 Can |
| HE WHO HESITATES | 70084-0/$4.50 US/$5.50 Can |
| KILLER'S CHOICE | 70083-2/$3.50 US/$4.50 Can |
| BREAD | 70368-8/$4.50 US/$5.50 Can |
| 80 MILLION EYES | 70367-X/$4.50 US/$5.50 Can |
| HAIL TO THE CHIEF | 70370-X/$4.50 US/$5.50 Can |
| LONG TIME NO SEE | 70369-6/$4.50 US/$5.50 Can |

# Don't Miss These Other
# Exciting Novels

| | |
|---|---|
| DOORS | 70371-8/$3.50 US/$4.50 Can |
| WHERE THERE'S SMOKE | 70372-6/$3.50 US/$4.50 Can |
| GUNS | 70373-4/$3.50 US/$4.50 Can |
| GANGS! | 70757-8/$3.50 US/$4.25 Can |
| THE SENTRIES | 70489-7/$3.50 US/$4.50 Can |